Leave No Trace

ALICIA WILDER

To me. For daring to climb.

Part One

It's All Uphill From Here

Can Zack Ryder Do It All?

By Hollywood Weekly

After making a name for himself leaping through fires in the White House, jumping out of spiraling helicopters, and other monumental scenes in the "White House Rising" franchise, Hollywood heartthrob Zack Ryder is looking to hide his four-alarm charisma behind the screen with his directorial debut "Zeitgeist."

The movie, which boasts an impressively star-studded cast that seems composed exclusively of Ryder's former co-stars, premieres at the Telluride Film Festival this September. This year's festival will be a first for Ryder, known for flashing his high-watt smile on the big screen rather than in smaller, indie-budget flicks.

Early buzz says the movie will fit in well with expectations for a quieter, more contemplative film. "The movie shows Zack's vision of fame," said one industry exec who asked to remain anonymous in order to speak freely. "It's like stepping into his brain."

Ryder calls the movie a "personal journey."

"I wanted to step behind the camera in order to take a different approach to this business," he said in a press release. "It's easy to miss the million tiny choices that go into making a tentpole blockbuster. Directing is my chance to appreciate the behind-the-scenes magic and learn to make some of those choices myself."

It remains to be seen what critics will think of Ryder's choices, and whether his fans will come out to support a Zack Ryder picture that doesn't showcase the star's face.

one

VALENTINE

I'M READING naked in the lobster pool when I hear his name again.

"...Zack Ryder."

Ugh. The feel of the water in the hot spring contrasted with the cool air on my shoulders, the sound of the chickadees enjoying the aspens that are starting to turn yellow nearby, even the mild smell of the sulfur underground is ruined by the reminder *he* exists.

"It says his new movie is screening at the festival this weekend, so he'll definitely be here," the woman interrupting my peace continues. The interruptor is sitting nearby in the hot spring, in a nook formed by smooth rocks. Her substantial bare breasts are spreading against the ledge. She's holding a glossy magazine that looks wilted from the steam as she speaks to another woman wearing a tiny pink bikini with only the toes of her feet stuck in the water.

The second woman scoops up a cup of hot water in her hands and trickles it over her goose-flesh legs. She looks skeptical while she does this, like the water might be too much. "Do you think we'll see him, just walking around? Like a normal person?"

The other woman scoffs, waving the magazine around so it dips slightly into the water, wilting even further. "No way the biggest movie star in the world is walking around without a security detail or *something*."

I roll my eyes and try to go back to my book. It's an old paperback that's been dipped in the spring water many times already —it has my name, Valentine Arnaud, handwritten on the inside cover in fading ink—but I'm resting it on the rock rim running around the pool in an attempt to keep it readable. This hot spring is usually my happy place. I come here regularly to get naked, as God intended, and read.

But the women are still talking. Still saying *that* name.

"It's not like Zack would be mobbed. Not *here*."

"If I saw him, I'd want to mob him. If you know what I mean."

They both laugh, gleefully ignoring the fact that rich movie stars like Zack Ryder are ruining the valley and everything else about the world where they live. They push the property values up and the locals out, and ruin the environment with their private planes.

Too annoyed to read any more, I put my book face down to hold it open and slither deeper into the hot water so it covers my shoulders. I've already been in here nearly 10 minutes and shouldn't stay in the extra-hot pool for too much longer, but the air is chilly and the water feels so good. I like to imagine my skin detoxing and circulation improving every minute I'm in here. It's what I imagine a spa day would be like.

"Are you going to see his new movie?" I can still hear them talking, unfortunately. I keep moving farther away but their voices trail me and the pool is small, only the length of a person from rocky side to side.

"Of course. I can't wait to see him running around shirtless again. I love that series."

"No, the new one...the one at the festival."

"Oh. Probably not. I hate those indie ones, you know? So serious. And he's not even in it."

Impossible not to picture his face as they discuss him. Tall, white, with dark brown hair. Typical good-looking elements. But then a jaw that puts some rocks in this area to shame, even wearing a tidy beard like he did in his last movie. A broad smile that takes over movie posters. A body—with wide shoulders and a narrow waist—that earned him Sexiest Man Alive titles. And the way his butt flexes when he runs in those action movies...

"God, it smells. How do you tolerate the smell?" Bikini girl is complaining, pulling her feet out of the spring and standing up.

"You get used to it," says the friend, which is what everyone says when introducing people to a natural hot spring. I barely smell the sulfur anymore. It's probably imbued in my pores after the years of soaking I've done, starting in childhood. My parents refused to buy me a swimsuit, even when I begged to be like the other kids, instead urging me to "embrace your body" and "live without shame."

There were some rough teenage years when, thankfully, Mom relented. And that first visit by myself after choosing to go natural, walking out into the fenced area and dropping my robe, was terrifying. I couldn't help worrying about people discussing how I trim my pubic hair. But now, I can't imagine putting cloth between my skin and this natural experience. I like my body — it's strong from all the outdoor activities — and I like walking around with nothing between it and nature.

Thankfully, the two women gather their things and leave me in peace. The hot spring, at 8 a.m. on a Tuesday, is mostly empty.

But my vibe is broken, like a polluted pool.

I haul myself out, shivering in the cool mountain air as the heat evaporates off my skin. My favorite towel is waiting on a chair nearby—a gift from my mom every year, so I have the luxury of a fresh, fluffy towel every time I have a chance to visit the springs—and I envelope myself in it, like a lavender hug. I slip my flip-flops on and go inside to shower, walking past the variety of other hot spring pools, ranging in temperature and size. Most of them are empty, steaming quietly into the chilly mountain air.

Before leaving, I make myself a cup of cocoa in the communal kitchen, waving at Daisy, who is reading a book behind the front desk. She's wearing a giant Sherpa hoodie this morning, and I stop to ask her which flea market she found it at.

We get to talking about the books we're reading—Daisy picked up a thriller from the community shelf, and I'm re-reading my favorite western about a cowgirl—so my cocoa is cold by the time I step outside, which is unfortunate because it's chilly despite the fact it's September. That's what nearly 8,000 feet above sea level in Colorado gets you. But the sky is blue as far as I can see, and the ground beneath my feet is nearly vibrating with potential. It's adventuring weather.

Too bad I have to work in a few hours.

Blucifer, my trusty four-wheel-drive blue Subaru and one of my only true possessions, is waiting patiently where I left her. She's covered in a light frost and residue from dirty roads kicking up over her tires. I always say this shows she's an adventure car rather than that her owner doesn't have the discipline—or the will to request my parents' driveway and exterior faucet—to give her a bath once a week.

Maybe this week. I wouldn't mind crashing a night at my parents' either, given how cold the nights have been.

I tap on the dash of Blucifer. *Not that I don't appreciate you*, I add, speaking in my head because my car is telepathic.

Sure, some people probably think it's weird that I have this intense connection to my car. But to me, Blucifer is so much more than a car. She's home. She's there for me, not judging, 24/7. Blucifer is magic: A roof over my head, wheels to get me everywhere, storage for all my shit, and enough heat to keep me from dying of hypothermia.

Still...my parents have Wi-Fi.

They've really come around to modern conveniences since they made enough money to retire. I'd be happy for them, except they sold the bit of land they'd owned since the '60s to Zack Ryder, who immediately built a mansion on it where he only lives one weekend out of the year for the film festival. Maybe two, if he decides to fly in for a ski holiday.

Rich assholes who push up the property values and contribute nothing to the community should be banned.

Blucifer is starting to warm up inside now, so I ask her where we should go. I'm free until 3 p.m., when my shift starts at The Bivy.

"OK, OK," I agree with the car that we should go visit Mom and Dad. It's been a week since I was there. My mom hasn't texted yet asking if I'm dead in a ditch, but that's probably only because she's lost her phone again.

Mom's interference is limited by her organizational skills. If I lived with my parents full-time, I'd get a lot more exposure to the former. Another reason I sleep in my car as often as possible—by choice as well as necessity.

The route is so familiar, Blucifer can basically make the drive by herself, so I point the SUV toward home and keep an eye out for any new potholes or rock slides.

My parents live in a tiny house near Telluride that they could now sell for a million dollars if they wanted, property values have shot up so much. Instead, they fill it with my mom's wood-working crafts and my dad's used book finds.

The garage door is open when Blucifer and I arrive, which means my mom is working. No one deserves the ire of Valkyrie "Val" Arnaud when she's interrupted at her crafts, so I go inside to find Dad, hauling my laundry with me.

"Hi," I call into the kitchen on my way to the basement washing machine. "I'll be right back!"

"I'll warm a cinnamon roll for you!" My dad is the best.

Given that I wear the same clothes over and over, I don't have much laundry. I can usually survive a week or two without a washing machine, but only because I wear a lot of wool and don't mind rinsing a few things out in the sinks at work and hanging them on Blucifer to dry overnight in the mountain air. In my pile, it's mostly underwear, which I change religiously every day, even when it's so cold taking off my pants feels like punishment for something. I've learned I'll regret it otherwise.

I'm back upstairs in less than five minutes, with a warm, gooey breakfast roll waiting for me. Dad is getting so into his baking he's started supplying one of the coffee shops downtown to get a few pastries out of the house.

"Hi, Dad," I say, giving him a kiss on the cheek that leaves a little frosting. I brush it off his whiskers, and then off the flannel shirt he's wearing.

"How is my favorite daughter?" asks the man with only one child, continuing to frost another tray of rolls without looking up.

"Living the dream, Dad." It's true: I have freedom, health, youth, and even some beauty. So I'll never make enough money to buy a house in the valley I was born in. Who wants to be held down? Living out of my car in a beautiful location is hashtag goals for some millennials.

My free-spirited parents are making it work, though. I move

a stack of books off a dining table chair so I can sit down and look at the intricate woodwork project on the table. It seems to be a doll's jewelry box.

"How's that video thing coming along?" Dad asks.

"It's OK." I shrug, thinking about the short video platform that takes up a chunk of my free time. It's a free platform for my activism, for trying to educate people who couldn't care less about existing peacefully with nature. Maybe I'll reach a few of them. "I keep making them. A few thousand people watch them. Sometimes I get likes or comments. Mostly mean ones. Screaming into the void, probably."

"That is your fate, your burden, and your privilege," Mom announces, catching the tail end of my response as she enters the kitchen through the garage door. She takes off her gloves and tosses them on the side table already piled high with mail and miscellaneous things. "When your father and I had that sexathon in June 22 years ago so that we could have a little Pisces baby, we knew you'd be a dreamer."

"Mom, I'm an Aries." I'd arrived a week late and messed up my parents' plans by a day. My mom had been torn between refusing the "intrusive medicine" of inducing and getting the Zodiac sign she wanted her child to have.

"In name only!" This is always Mom's response. I'm surprised my mom didn't just fudge my birthday on the family calendar to get her own way. Dad probably wouldn't let her.

Mom leans down and gives me an abrasive hug that nearly crushes my bones—a.k.a. the Valkyrie hug she's known for. "How is my strong, independent daughter?"

One of her usual affirmations, because she doesn't want me to only worry about being pretty or successful. "I went to the springs this morning. Work the late shift tonight. The usual."

"How have the tourists been?" Mom reaches for a cinnamon

roll, only to get swatted away by Dad. He points at the sink, and Mom obediently washes her hands.

"We're in the lull between ski season and the film festival, so it's been slow. It's kind of nice it's so quiet, but it means terrible tips." It's shoulder season. Warm enough that I can sleep outdoors, as I love to do, but there's not enough snow yet for city people to fly in for skiing.

"More time for your art," Mom says staunchly. She closes her eyes as she lets a piece of the cinnamon roll dissolve in her mouth. "Mmm. Rick, this is your best batch yet."

"You said that last time," Dad replies.

"And I'll keep saying it." She leans in to him and kisses him on the mouth—a warm, gooey kiss I look away from, even though I should be used to it. My parents are in love. It's sweet. And yet another thing I don't have, never have, and maybe never will if I stay in this tiny town where I've known everyone my whole life.

"I'm not sure I'd call it art," I sigh, picking up the thread of conversation. "It's more educational." My last video was about the proper way to dispose of poop in the wilderness. Hint: It's not in a hole in the ground that can leak into the water supply. That one got zero comments, probably because the average person doesn't want to think about pooping. Try living in your car without a nearby toilet; strategies become important.

"You're expressing yourself by creating unique material that you're sharing for the world's judgment. You're an artist." With finality, Mom eats the last bite of her cinnamon roll, picks her gloves back up, and disappears back into the garage.

"I agree with your mother on this, you know," Dad says, holding up a frosting-covered knife. "Stick with it. There will always be trolls. There were trolls in my day that said mean things to my face. Now they're behind their screens. Don't let them get you down."

"I know, Dad." I smile. "Thanks."

Their encouragement in mind, I scroll through my video feed sitting on the back porch while I wait for my laundry to finish. Most of the short clips served to me are about outdoor activities, since that's what I post and interact with. It's a lot of influencers hiking in tight leggings that show off their butt, or cringey crashes on adrenaline-fueled adventures.

But algorithms being what they are, eventually a viral post from Zack freaking Ryder pops up to accost my eyes. He filmed it here in Telluride, casting his camera out over the astonishing beauty of the pristine nature view from his back porch. Then a close-up on his own astonishingly beautiful, movie-star face. Those wide, expressive eyes filled with excitement. Then back to a chipmunk sitting on his wooden railing.

Then. *And then*. He feeds the chipmunk a piece of bread from his sandwich.

My own eyes widen. I look at the number of likes ticking up on the right side of the video. The thousands of people watching Zack Ryder teaching wildlife to associate people with food.

Oh no. No, no, no. Rich assholes are going to asshole, but he can't bring this dangerous ignorance into my world and not expect me to take a stand.

He probably doesn't properly store his garbage, either. Instead of following Leave No Trace principles—the framework for minimum impact on nature—he's making the wilderness collateral damage.

I look around to find the nearest wildlife, plenty of it available in my parents' backyard, set up a shot, and hold down the record button.

two

ZACK

YOGA ISN'T SUPPOSED to hurt, right?

That's what I always *thought*, but it *does*.

Damn these stupid action movies turning me into a rusty old man before I'm even 30 years old. Last year, I tore my ACL during a stunt—not even the real stunt, the lead-up to the point my stunt man took over—and I'm still not the same.

"Zack, straighten out your back leg as much as you can," my coach encourages. She's standing with her back to the view, so that I can enjoy my backyard vista. My house-length balcony overlooks the valley in such a way that it's like no other humans are around. There are some kind of trees turning gold next to the railing and I saw a deer the other day. The house in LA is on a hill that overlooks the city lights, and the contrast to all this endless nature takes my breath away every time I'm here.

Although something else is taking my breath away right now.

"This...is as straight...as it gets," I manage, trying to will my knee to cooperate by glaring at it. I'm dripping sweat. Warrior pose didn't used to be this hard.

"That's what he said," my assistant, Drew, or as they prefer to be called, Zack's "body man," is sitting in the wooden booth-style table tucked up against the glass wall looking into the kitchen. They don't glance up from their tablet.

"Why don't you join me?" I demand. "Solidarity and all."

"Thanks but I already went for a six mile run before work this morning." Drew still doesn't look up. They're probably reading the comments on my social media pages, which they call their gratitude practice because "I'm thankful I'm not you."

I roll my eyes. Early-morning runs are so last year, back when I was pre-injury, pushing my body to its limits training for my latest giant White House-set blockbuster where I play the vice president. It comes out this summer. The director claimed that the infamous stunt looked great in post.

It's my failsafe if my directorial debut bombs, as my agent so politely puts it. It'll keep me on magazine covers and stop me from falling too deep into a slump. As if I'm not already worried people will hate my movie and take back the money I've raised to make another. I'm a good director. Maybe. At least from time to time, making the movie that will screen for the first time next weekend at the film festival, I had moments where I felt like my creativity was flowing, I was on the same page as my actors, and I hadn't forgotten any of the three million administrative details that are, as it turned out, part of the director's job to manage.

It's just that—as my agent, publicist, and Drew have explained—people want to see me in front of the camera, not behind it. Preferably running into a burning (historical) building, driving a sports car really fast, or kissing the starlet of the moment.

"Let's start to cool down," Kimberly says and sits down cross-legged. I follow her to the floor. This mat doesn't seem particularly clean even though it's mandatory in my household that everything be disinfected between uses. I look around for a distraction before I spiral over the germs that might be melding with my sweat like a warm soup right now.

"Wait," I say. "Did you run outside? How?" The trail out back goes straight up. It'd be like six miles of stairs.

My assistant finally looks up. "Lord, no, I used the treadmill downstairs. Do I actually want to die? There are probably bears. We all know I'm a snack."

I snort. Bears are something you see in a zoo. "There aren't bears. The town is right down the hill."

"Pay attention to your breath," Kimberly suggests. "Count to three as you draw in, hold for three, then gently blow out for another count of three."

"Uh oh," Drew says.

I lose count of my breath as I look at them. They take their blinking blue Bluetooth earpiece out and stand up, holding the tablet out. It's never good when Drew takes off the Bluetooth.

I unfold and stand. I go to the table and use antibacterial gel on my hands before I take the tablet.

Kimberly, a pro at dealing with celebrities who barely listen, keeps her eyes closed and stays in the moment. "Breathe into your limbs. Reach into every part of your body, find those knots of tension, and relax them one by one."

A video is open on the tablet, a pretty young woman with high cheekbones and a long, dark braid over one shoulder gesturing widely on the frozen screen. I hit play. "This is Telluride," she says. "A mountain community where celebrities, mostly Hollywood stars, have built giant, over-priced mansions that sit above the town."

Images of real estate listings—$39.5 million, $10.75 million—flash on the screen, with the woman superimposed over them as she keeps talking. "These stars buy a piece of land but never learn how to live here. They fly in and out on their private jets at the airport no native can afford to book a flight into. They bring in their own staff, rather than offering jobs to locals. They rarely come into town to buy anything from our shops. And."

She pauses, and the screen shifts to a picture of my own house. "Zack Ryder," she says, her voice dripping with disdain. "Posts something like this."

Half the screen fills with the video of the chipmunk I saw on my back porch yesterday. I look at Drew, who had approved the post although I'd worried we should keep all marketing focused on my directorial debut. It "humanizes you," they'd said. Drew shakes their head.

On one half of the screen, the woman keeps up a running criticism of what I'm doing on the other. "Around here, we know how important it is to keep wildlife wild. We don't give chipmunks food and we lock up our trash to avoid drawing bears." She gestures behind her at a square metal trash bin with a lock on it. "Because when you teach a wild animal that people equals food, you put that animal in danger."

Now the woman walks down the main street in town, the small shops and breathtaking view the area is known for behind her. "This is all part of being a good citizen of a mountain community," she concludes. "Something Zack Ryder clearly never learned."

I pause the video before it starts playing on a loop and look at Drew, whose face is white. "I told you there were bears!" they say.

I frown, then try to consciously smooth out my forehead like my aesthetician has taught me. "Not the point, Drew."

The video has a lot of likes and replies. I start to hit the button to open the comments and Drew snatches the tablet back.

"My whole job is saving you from the comments," they say, clutching the tablet to their chest like I have a death wish.

"OK but this is just an online thing, right?" I can handle some people on a social media app hating on me. No big deal. I rub antibacterial gel into my hands again after handling the tablet.

"One of the tabloids picked it up," Drew says reluctantly. "Says the locals are criticizing you in your mountain paradise."

"OK," I sigh. I take a deep breath before continuing, "Diane?"

Drew cringes. Diane is my crisis publicist. My normal publicist is tough as nails; Diane is tough as titanium. "I don't think it's quite *that* bad," Drew says.

I'm relieved. "Great, then we ignore it for now. Let the team handle it. They've probably already seen the clip anyway. It'll go away."

"And no more feeding chipmunks. On video, anyway," Drew adds.

I scowl, turning back to my morning torture. "Damn chipmunk. Wanted his five minutes of fame."

***

It did not go away.

The video jumped from one short video platform to another. The on-air entertainment shows picked it up. And then it became a joke during late-night TV and a sketch on SNL. It was a mock crime show segment: "Zack Ryder: Chipmunk Killer. Hollywood's biggest star; wildlife's biggest nightmare."

On Sunday, Diane called. "You didn't think," she says calmly, "you might need a little help from me?"

I've been too busy working on the launch of my movie to pay much attention. Drew said a few things about the situation "spiraling out of control" that bothered me, but there were so many details, so many decisions, so much to worry about *already—*

would my movie flop, even on the festival circuit? Was it too weird? Not weird enough? Would people laugh at me after they left the first screening?—I hadn't dedicated much of my already sleepless time to it.

Drew has stopped talking about the chipmunk fiasco and started suggesting things like Ambien and melatonin. And under-eye concealer.

"It's not that bad, is it?" I ask. "It was just a chipmunk."

I hear Diane take a deep breath.

I know when I've made a misstep. "I haven't *said* that to anyone! But come on, it's not like I killed the chipmunk live on air or something. It's fine. It's living a very happy life in the forest or...wherever."

"Have you *spoken* to the chipmunk? Can we get the chipmunk to make a statement to that effect?" Her voice is dripping with sarcasm: Diane's particular version of it where she's so dry it circles back around and makes you wonder if maybe she means it. "Then let's operate from the assumption that the chipmunk is waiting for an offer to trash talk you all over *Hollywood Weekly*."

Drew is sitting across the room, Bluetooth and tablet in place, and raises their eyebrows as I look at them helplessly. "Is it that bad?" I mouth. Drew nods once, firmly. *Shit*.

"Look, Diane...I really want to focus on my movie. The debut is next Saturday and that's the whole reason I'm here. It's...it's got to go perfectly. And nothing's ready..."

She cuts me off. "And the chipmunk is a distraction."

"Well, yes." I'm surprised at the empathy.

"No one is going to pay attention to your movie while they're thinking about Chipmunk Killer and hashtag CancelZackRyder," she goes on.

"That's a *thing*?" I have never said or done anything controversial enough to be canceled in my life. I don't stand up for causes or weigh in on issues. My team calls me the "perfect blank slate" for audiences to project their fantasies onto. That's my brand.

"Put me in charge," she demands. "Your regular team can't handle this. It's gotten too big."

She's sufficiently scared me with talk of being canceled, so I hand her the reins and promise to let my team know they can step back from Crisis Chipmunk. When I hang up, I decide I can put the whole issue out of my mind and go back to final edits and emailing my most high-profile friends to convince them to fly in for the screening on Saturday. Focus on real, concrete tasks, not rumors out in the cloud. I'm an *action* star, after all.

Tuesday, Diane shows up at my door.

"We've got a problem," she says, sweeping in with her giant Coach bag and two assistants trailing her. They both park at the massive dining room table that I've never used and start unpacking laptop bags. "The girl who made the video has been approached by numerous outlets and finally said yes to an interview. We have to get to her first."

"And what...knock her off?" Bemused, I watch one of the assistants pull a cucumber and knife out of her giant handbag and start slicing it. The other one pulls a water purifier out of hers and heads for the sink. "Why not take care of the chipmunk, too, while you're at it?"

Diane sweeps a small decorative...something...onto the floor when she puts down her bag. "You're not funny, Zachary. Do you want me to save your career or not?"

"Oh come on, my career can survive this...right?" This is what people like Diane prey on: The fear that it can all go away. I know that, but I'm not immune.

I pick up the wooden figurine. It is, of course, a chipmunk. Have I always had this? Drew wouldn't buy something like this as a joke, right?

"That's why I'm here," she replies. "To make sure it doesn't become a career-ending event."

I stand there rubbing my thumb over the smooth wood of the chipmunk's tail and feeling my plans to completely focus on the movie drain away. But maybe, if I throw Diane out and ignore this whole mess, I can still achieve my goals? I made a *list*. I never make lists.

"And," she adds. "If you let me do my thing, we should be able to take care of this before the premiere and keep it from overshadowing your directorial debut."

Those are the magic words and she knows it. "OK," I say. "I put myself in your hands, Diane. Whatever you need me to do."

She smiles and I know with absolute clarity I'm going to hate the next week of my life.

three

VALENTINE

BLUCIFER LOOKS SMALL AND HELPLESS, hanging off the back end of the tow truck.

I want to ask Dave, my mechanic, if I've been a bad mom. Is it my fault my baby is crippled? I refrain. It's not Dave's job to be my therapist.

Dad drove out to pick me up from the public land where I was dispersed camping. I'm not sure if he followed Dave or vice versa. They both called half a dozen times trying to find me, and I barely have any service out here, so I walked two miles toward the highway along a dirt road to get a better signal and try to flag them down. Ultimately, they both showed up at the same time. Between the three of us, we got all my worldly possessions transferred between my car and Dad's.

Dad has a hand on my shoulder, holding me up as we watch Blucifer being handled like any other old car. I'm having flashbacks of driving along with the windows open and the perfect song playing, of using the hatchback as a shield against rain while I sat on the back bumper with hot coffee between my hands, and all the times we found the perfect camping spot along a creek. I have so much to lose.

"Do you think she'll be OK?" I whisper. My sweet car just wouldn't start this morning, even when I hooked up my portable jump starter.

"They work wonders at that garage," Dad replies. "What your mom does with wood, they do with cars."

Car art won't be cheap. I know it, and I also know my parents won't offer to pay. They've already offered to let me stay with them as long as I need to, a generous enough assumption. But my parents are funny about cash gifts. They use their money to feed their art and their oven and their library but never hold it in their hands if they can help it. Their adviser at the bank handles the rest of their bills.

I would never ask, anyway. Blucifer is my responsibility. My only responsibility, by design. Without my car, who am I? Just a homeless girl with a dream. But no. I've got this.

Still, I feel so alone, even standing here with Dad, as my car gets towed away.

"Come on, honey," he says, guiding me to his car. "It's chilly out here."

I couldn't charge my phone and I'd been conserving battery to stay in touch with Dave and Dad, so it's at a bright red 8 percent power. When I plug it into the cigarette lighter in Dad's 1996-model car, about 300 notifications ping all at once as it comes off power-saving mode.

WTF is wrong with you? Zack Ryder is a national treasure...

Would love to speak with you on-air about your thoughts on Zack Ryder...

Get a real job.

Ugh. That video attracted the wrong kind of attention. It was supposed to be educational. Now I have 10,000 new followers who expect me to feed them exclusively Zack Ryder content.

I've been trying to figure out how to turn this into a win since Sunday, when my friend Mollie came in while I was at work and brought it up. She said three people sent her the video over the weekend, including some of her old friends in Denver. "You're famous!"

"I'm viral," I'd said drily. "It's not the same thing."

I had answered an unknown number calling my phone once before I learned my lesson, and asked the TV producer on the line if I could give a demonstration of proper bearproofing on air. The producer, a very young woman who turned all her sentences into questions, said she'd get back to me—"Maybe, like, in a few hours?"—and never did.

I didn't want to go on TV and talk about Zack Ryder. I'd prefer to pretend the movie star didn't exist.

But I'd love to teach more people about keeping wildlife wild, something that could actually make a difference in the world.

One of the newest messages catches my eye: *How do you feel about Zack Ryder playing a Coloradan in his upcoming film?*

Sitting in the passenger seat of my dad's car as I watch my loyal companion get towed up the dusty road ahead of us, I write back before I think: *Terrible. Shouldn't happen.*

The person on the other end of the conversation—probably another young woman straight out of school—responds immediately. I can see them typing in-app. *Would love to have you on to explain why. We're particularly interested in discussing stereotypes and misinformation.*

I'm also interested in discussing stereotypes and misinformation. But I need money right now, not fame.

The faceless person on the other side of her phone continues: *We'd come to you in Telluride over film festival weekend. You can show us how the locals live compared to the movie star on the hill. We'd cover all expenses.*

Tough to turn down a vague offer like that. I'm not cheap, but I can be bought.

OK, I am cheap. Last week, I worked an extra hour in exchange for a free milkshake and extra tips.

And if some of my other expenses are covered, I can save up to get Blucifer back on the road. I can't be without her for long. Blucifer is my literal *home*.

Still, the niggling hesitation over linking myself to Zack freaking Ryder makes me send back my email address and ask for more information before I commit to anything.

My phone dies before I can do anything but message the group chat for The Bivy servers asking to pick up shifts. *Can't make it in today. Can someone pick up?* The charging connection in my dad's car doesn't work that great and my phone is an old model.

I've got to make some money somehow. I've got to take care of Blucifer. The way my car has taken care of me for so long.

four

ZACK

"THIS FEELS LIKE A BAD IDEA."

I'm sitting in a giant SUV on the street outside a small house with a crowded lawn near Telluride. There's a giant wooden bear holding a sign that says "You're beary welcome," a bench, and a bunch of bird feeders on a tall pole with shepherd's hooks. It all looks handmade.

On my lap, my computer is open to my email, which is full of "final notes"—key edits that should have been done weeks ago —and schedules from three different teams working with me on my movie debut. I'm supposed to be at a festival Q&A and my friend Ronnie's screening at the same time somehow.

I have so much to do. And instead, I'm sitting here working on a hotspot because Chipmunk Girl isn't home.

"Well then it's a good thing my strategy isn't based on feel-ings," Diane says sweetly in reply.

"Diane. This is ridiculous. Who knows whether this woman will be happy to see me on her front porch. She might beat me over the head with, like, a squirrel."

"Zachary, very few people would react that way to your face."

I pause for a moment to think of anyone who would. Nobody dislikes me that much, do they? I haven't done anything worth hating.

"The average internet troll," Diane continues, "might post angrily about you and your wildlife manners, for example, but confronted in person would sink into a puddle of their own drool. Helpless to the thrall of your celebrity. That's what I'm counting on."

I grimace. It's not the first time I've been told I walk around in a golden glow of privilege. If I'm being honest, the only reason I doubt the effect this time is because everything with this movie feels like it's going wrong. Lately, it's like I've slightly missed my mark on stage and can't quite find my line. Poor little movie star, worrying his golden glow is a little less bright. I reach for the bottle of antibacterial gel I keep in the bottom nook of the door and clean my hands. "Do we even know when she'll be home?"

Diane glances at one of her mute assistants, huddled in the corner of the car by the driver. "Apparently she was hard to track down. This is the address on her driver's license. Her parents own the house."

It bothers me to be locked in a car with this many people at a time. I considered asking Diane, or at least her minions, to wear masks, but didn't want to look like an asshole who thought "the help" was unclean. I've dealt with these worries ever since Covid-19 happened and made it clear there'd be nothing I could do — not enough money in the world to throw at the problem, no smile big enough to paper over the issue — if I were to contract some horrible virus.

It's just that I can't get sick right now. It's not like I can send a proxy to the film debut in my place. I hit the button to roll down a window.

"Let's avoid drawing a crowd before she gets here," Diane

warns me as I stick my famous face out the window and inhale like I've been underwater. The air here is different from LA. I always forget to notice until moments like this, and then I can't get enough of it. The trees along this street are colors I've never seen before.

"People in the mountains watch movies, too, you know," Diane adds.

I look up and down the quiet street. I've never even talked to a local here. The town is so picturesque, so movie-set-like, I forget real people actually live here. And when I'm here for the film festival, the town is so crowded with people I normally see in LA or New York that the setting feels even less real. Like Cannes, a place people fly into to show off an outfit they would never wear anywhere else. Do real people actually live in Cannes? Or wear regular clothes there?

"What happens if someone takes a video and it gets around that I came begging at this woman's doorstep?" I ask. "Sounds pretty pathetic to me. Like it's made for a late-night talk show host's monologue."

"We can spin that," Diane says. She settles back in the seat and puts her giant sunglasses on. She might be settling in for a nap.

It's weird having to delegate so many decisions about my own time, career, and reputation. The best piece of advice I ever got—when my career was taking off, after the release of Attack on the White House, my first White House-set action movie—was to do that. "Hire people after you've learned to trust their decisions," a very famous actor told me at a post-Oscars party. "And then let them make those decisions for you."

"What if I don't know how to evaluate their decisions?" I'd asked, like a newborn baby opening my eyes to the scary world of celebrity. Most of the time, I barely know what I'm agreeing to do. I once fell asleep reading one of my own contracts.

"You don't have to know what they do," the actor told me. "Find something you can evaluate them on. It can be anything. I hired a lawyer last week because I liked the way he followed my mom's recipe for banana bread."

I'd hired Diane because she let me look at her insane, color-coded, spiral-bound planner once, and an item on her daily checklist was "30 min with Floof." Floof was her cat. Diane said it was important to build in time for play.

I remind myself of this whenever her decisions freak me out. Like right now.

I get a few more emails in—every one spiraling me deeper toward certainty this movie is going to be a disaster. The best-case scenario I can hope for is everyone ignoring my directorial debut and letting me get back to my "real job," acting. Eventually, a beaten-up Subaru, the car everyone around here seems to own, pulls into the driveway we're watching.

Diane pushes me out of the car bodily. "Don't underestimate your power, Zachary," she directs me as we walk across the street. She says it in a normal voice, not a whisper, so anyone listening can hear that I need an ego-boost.

An older man with a wiry build and lace-up hiking boots is getting out of the driver's side. I focus on the woman getting out of the other. She has a lot of dark hair that is in a tangled-looking bun low on her neck. I see that she's wearing hiking boots when she walks around the back of the car in the driveway, and a puffy vest over a flannel shirt. Despite all that, her walk and the way she holds her head says graceful. Her face is beautiful but distinctive, someone who would be perfectly cast in one role but not a million. She also looks unhappy, and when she raises her downcast eyes and sees me approaching, her expression doesn't change. *So much for the golden glow.*

"Hi, I'm Zack Ryder," I say, like an idiot. I stop just on the sidewalk, facing the two of them and Diane slightly behind me.

Everyone waiting for me to say something useful. I realize I can't remember, if Diane ever told me, the Chipmunk Woman's name.

I hate this part of being a celebrity. Making small talk with strangers when literally the only thing we have in common is *me*. And that knowledge is usually mismatched, between who people think I am and how I know myself. I reply to at least two fanmail notes every week, but that's different; that's writing. I actually like writing. Then, I can think about what to say before anyone else sees it.

I want to cross my arms, but resist the impulse. No closed-off body language because I'm uncomfortable. I try to channel my own, most-famous role as a man welcome at any party. This is my *brand*. This is what I do. I can be charming, charismatic and nonoffensive.

Don't say um. "We"—*stupid, don't say "we," it's exclusionary—*"saw your video and found it educational"—*and mean and irritating—*"and I wondered if you'd be up for discussing it further?" I sound like a mafia boss. *"Discussing it" could mean "let's go inside where I can kill you quietly."*

She doesn't look impressed. She is wearing zero makeup—I can't remember the last time I saw a woman's real eyelashes—and her hair looks like it air dried, loose strands clinging to her neck. It's difficult not to study her like a case study in normal life. Then she folds her arms, and I try not to take it too personally. "Where are the cameras?"

I don't look around, because I'm afraid I might see one somewhere. "There are no cameras." I hope.

Diane, whose arms are also folded *damnit*, nudges me with one finger. I know what it means and pop a high-wattage smile. A smile that appears on the cover of a prominent magazine next month. But not this month, because my own tiny movie doesn't merit a cover feature.

The woman's expression doesn't crack. Her eyes don't even

flicker. I glance at the man, hopeful. He's got one hand shielding his uncovered eyes as he looks back at me, standing with the sun at my back.

I take the $500 sunglasses hanging off the front of my shirt and offer them to him. He laughs—more of a chuckle, really—and waves off the offer.

The woman steps forward and snatches the outstretched sunglasses. She examines them, clearly recognizing the brand. Then she hands them back to me. "Selling these would cover my car repairs." Her voice is matter-of-fact. Her blue eyes are hard. There's a hint of crow's feet there, but nothing Botox couldn't counteract if she started immediately.

I turn the glasses over in my hands. That has to be an exaggeration. These sunglasses were gifted to me by the brand. "Well...take them," I suggest.

"What do you want in exchange?"

I finally look at Diane, unable to avoid it anymore. I've delegated my own negotiations as long as I could because I'm terrible at them. Diane is wearing her sunglasses, and I can't see her expression, but I suspect she's disappointed in me. I'm flubbing this.

"Are you a lawyer?" the woman asks Diane.

Diane doesn't react for a beat. Then she says, "I'm a fixer."

"Like in that TV show?"

"Exactly," Diane says briskly. "Now, we both have a problem here. You have generated a cycle of bad press for Mr. Ryder which clearly has not benefited you, either, if you are tempted by a pair of used sunglasses."

The Chipmunk Woman finally reacts, her mouth dropping open. "I wasn't going to take them."

Diane ignores this. "What, exactly, was it you hoped to accomplish with that video you made about Mr. Ryder?"

The other woman frowns. She's making the crow's feet

worse. I pinch my fingers together to avoid touching my forehead to check my own 11's. "It's important to catch the lines early," my aesthetician always tells me. "Prevention is like a coupon code for your future skin."

"It was meant to be educational," says the woman who clearly doesn't have a regular aesthetician. I wonder if she even has sunscreen on. I can see her pores and her skin tone, behind those lovely features, is uneven. The color is high on her cheeks, indicating annoyance or sun damage. Maybe both: it's very high. "Zack Ryder has an enormous audience and he was teaching them ignorance. As usual." She looks directly at me again, her voice dripping with disdain. *Wow.* No one has talked to me that way off-camera for years.

Diane hesitates. I look at her. She looks back at me, and lowers her sunglasses enough that I can see her eyes. She's asking me something. It looks a lot like, *do you want to walk away?* But that can't be it.

She raises her sunglasses again. "Despite your combative tone, my client is willing to work with you," she says. I'm not so sure that's what I meant to convey, but Diane forges on. "Here's what I suggest: The two of you will collaborate on three to five *educational* videos. Zack's team gets veto power on everything from lighting to theme. The videos can be posted to your personal feed and reposted to his at his discretion. You will do absolutely no press without prior approval from the team during the time of the contract which will last no more than one month. And we will pay all approved expenses involved in the project."

I'm torn between relief at how quickly Diane rattled off a solution and terror that I'm being committed to another month-long *project* right now. My shoulders don't know whether to lift or bow. I do a sort of shuffle instead and turn it into clapping my hands like a toy monkey. "Sounds great," I say, too enthusiastically.

The other woman puts her hands on her hips, ignoring me and staring Diane down. "I get creative control of topics."

"You have creative control unless, as I said, Zack or his team vetoes something. You understand we're looking out for his best interest and aren't certain you will do the same, Ms. Arnaud."

At least I know her last name. I eye the woman again. There is something mysterious about her, with that *I-don't-care-that-I'm-beautiful* attitude. She looks like she hasn't showered today, a real mystery to someone who can only ever smell like the cologne I'm contractually obligated to wear.

"When can we do the first video?" she asks, all business.

"We should be able to have a contract drawn up within the next 24 hours," Diane replies. "Remember, if you do *any press at all*, it will be considered a breach of contract. And if you do press before the contract is signed, I will *personally* consider it a breach of faith and void the contract."

"Does that include responding to user comments on the videos?"

I look back and forth between the two women whose brains obviously move faster than mine. The only thing I've ever done that someone didn't work out for me was this forthcoming movie that I worked on for basically my whole life—and that will probably be a flop.

"No comments for the month of the contract," Diane says.

"Give me comments about the outdoors and wildlife, and I won't comment on anything related to...him."

As the "him" in reference, I make a face. I catch the older man smiling in response. He's still holding up a hand to shade his eyes. I offer him the sunglasses again, and this time, he takes them and puts them on without either of the women noticing. The sunglasses transform him into a gray-haired Tom Cruise.

"Done, but we will be auditing your responses."

The younger woman looks at the man beside her. She looks

like she's trying to have a silent conversation with him but can't read his eyes behind the glasses. Hands still on her hips, she then turns and studies Diane. Then she looks at me. I try to appear like I understand the calculus she's doing in her head.

"My car's in the shop," she finally says. "I'll need it to do the shoots. Can you cover that?"

I turn my head to Diane, trying to hide how badly I want to roll my eyes. My world is full of people squeezing anything they can out of me. Even Diane is charging extra for her assistants to sit in the car behind us. Now I'm picking up the operating expenses for a rando to critique my worldview.

Diane doesn't return my gaze, even though I'm burning a hole into her forehead.

"Within reason," Diane responds. "We'll need to see the bill."

OK, fine. My accountant knows my finances better than I do. *Let Sydney tell them no.*

The other woman is slowly nodding. "OK."

I feel like I'm slipping downhill. "I can only devote a few hours to this," I interject, suddenly finding my voice.

"Zack's team will also handle his schedule," Diane says smoothly. "He's a busy man. While working on these videos, he will be all-in, of course. As he is with everything."

She smiles at me without teeth. My *brand*. It's a silent reminder. I nod. "Of course. Eager to get started on the...learning how to feed chipmunks."

"Why *not* to feed chipmunks!" the other woman snaps.

"Right." I peer at the older man again, the only friendly face in the bunch. "See, I'm learning already." The other man smiles. I smile back, cranking it up to eleven. I hook my fingers in my belt loops and allow my body to slouch. I'm comfortable in this situation. Or if I'm not, I can fake it.

The Chipmunk Woman rolls her eyes. I hate her a little bit.

"Would you all like a cinnamon roll before you head out?"

the man wearing my sunglasses asks. "You're welcome to discuss any other details sitting down on our back porch. It's a little more comfortable than the driveway."

This vision of hospitality is tempting, but Diane says, "We can't."

"Thank you," I add, because I don't want to lose my one ally.

"I'll get you some to go," the man replies and pivots on one booted heel to go inside before we can stop him.

"Dad, they don't want…" Chipmunk Lady sighs as her dad disappears into the house. She eyes Diane and me. "He's going to give you the icing on the side."

We both glance at Diane. She is typing on her phone, ignoring us.

"Very considerate," I mumble. I'm not going to eat a pastry, icing or not. I can't risk the calories or the potential germs from something homemade.

"I'm giving the go-ahead on that contract," Diane says without looking up. "You'll be contacted by Mindy. She'll set up a schedule and run everything by me that might be controversial." She darkens her phone and lowers it, like putting down her weapon. "If all goes well, you'll never see me again."

It sounds like a threat.

"I'm sure it will be fine." My new nemesis stares me down.

"Fine," I agree. I renew the movie star smile, and she can only stare at it a few seconds before she blinks and looks away. Too bright for her unaccustomed eyes. Good.

She has no idea who she's dealing with. I can smile nonstop for hours when I have to. I've *trained* for it.

The dad comes trotting out the front door holding a canvas bag that reads "Shop local." He hands it to me. Inside are rolls wrapped in some kind of eco-friendly reusable wrap and a small plastic bowl filled with, yep, frosting.

"Thank you," I say. "This is…unexpected." I have no idea who is going to eat this. Drew is vegan, Diane never eats, and everyone else I know is on a diet.

Maybe I can feed it to the chipmunks.

The dad looks pleased. His daughter's expression is so skeptical, I wonder if she can read my mind.

I start backing away, ready to end this face-off.

"We'll be in touch," Diane says.

I climb in the car and hand one of Diane's wafer-thin assistants the canvas tote. She gets a whiff of the sugar inside and her face scrunches up. The other one looks at me like I just threatened them with a knife, but they both remain mute.

"Oh, give it back," I sigh. I snatch the bag back and put it on the leather seat beside me. As the SUV pulls away from the curb, I watch out the window.

My nemesis has her hands on her hips, glaring back at me as we drive away. Her dad, behind her, puts a hand on her shoulder and says something that looks like, "It'll be OK, honey." He's still wearing my sunglasses.

As we round the corner to leave the dead-end street, I see the young woman's shoulders slump as she turns back to the house.

VALENTINE

"IT'S NOT like I'm selling my soul, exactly."

"'Exactly' is where the devil gets you," Mom says. This is a saying passed down from my grandmother that has always driven me crazy. Mostly because I hear it in my head when I'm having these kinds of debates with myself.

Hunched protectively over my mason jar of breakfast, I forge on, "Arguably, I'm taking advantage of him. He's the moneybags celebrity who will pay me to make content—something I usually make for free."

"He seemed like a very nice young man," Dad says. He'd placed his new sunglasses in a prime spot: The small shelf over the sink where Mom was meant to put her rings (but didn't, as she never did dishes). He keeps saying he'll return them when he gets a chance, but I have doubts. When is Zack Ryder likely to come back to their house?

"That kind of power and *nice* don't go together," Mom says darkly.

The debate wasn't the same without Blucifer. Ordinarily, I

33

would be having this conversation in my car, playing both the angel and the devil on my own shoulders. I'm not convinced by my own logic, either.

But I *have* to rescue my car. I can't handle many more mornings of sitting in this tiny kitchen, eating overnight oats, while my parents tell me everything I already know. It feels like being transported back in time to childhood, making me doubt whether I've ever made an independent, adult decision.

The contract arrived first thing that morning by courier. My dad knew the courier and they'd had a lively conversation about what was in the fat envelope—Dad knew, of course, but the courier didn't believe it—before I'd wandered into the kitchen with tangled hair and too little sleep and opened it.

The terms were generous, Dad pointed out.

And controlling, Mom added.

"They made the concessions I asked for," I say now. "It doesn't matter if he's nice or not. I stood up for myself. I'm getting what I want out of this: saving Blucifer from car jail."

"At what cost?" Mom shakes her head. "I hope you don't look back at this moment in your life and realize it's when you gave up your principles."

I throw up my hands, my spoon fortunately empty. "What principles? I'm just making a few videos. Like I would anyway."

"The principle of living a healthy, independent life!" Mom's voice rings through the kitchen. She's standing while Dad and I are sitting at the kitchen table, and she raises her hands, swinging them around over our heads. "Following your own truth without being obligated to compromise, a little here, a little there, until you don't recognize yourself anymore."

I cringe. This is not only why I've never signed a creative contract, it's why I've never had a job with benefits. I can't get her hippie voice—and her warnings about the "tyranny of an alarm clock" or the "ethics of retirement plans"—out of my head long enough to try, much less sign on the dotted line.

I barely slept last night. Am I linking myself to Zack Ryder for the foreseeable future? Will anyone take away from my videos the lessons I want to teach, or only see a movie star getting his hands dirty? Zack didn't seem *nice*; he seemed horrible. Standing there without a care, with that wide grin and sculpted jawline, his shirt rolled up past his elbows like a dream I once had. More like a nightmare.

In real life, I don't know if I'm using him to launch my brand or letting him take my brand over. The contract bars me from creating any other content while working with him. It demands that I submit my "scripts" in advance. It includes lines like, "CONSULTANT shall not make any disparaging comments in a public forum (including, but not limited to, social media, live events, and TV) about THE TALENT."

I wonder if she can even talk directly to The Talent at all, or if the entire process will be mediated. I have ideas, sure—maybe even the kind that can get people's attention—but they require authenticity. They're not *scripted*.

I work more in bullet points.

But maybe my doubts *are* my mother's voice in my head. Yesterday, I'd agreed to this because it seemed like a guaranteed way to get Blucifer back and make the type of content I believe could make a difference. I don't want Mom to be right. *This is MY thing*.

Realistically, I don't have much to lose. I have no property besides Blucifer; no one outside of Telluride knows who I am; my job is only as certain as the shift schedule. At some point, the *principles* my mom kept ranting about started to seem like they were holding me back. Not owning anything might be freedom, but it could feel a lot like poverty.

"Mom, the contract says I can back out at any point and stop making content with him if it isn't working," I interrupt. The Talent has the same right, of course. "I'm guessing I'll get one video out of this and then it'll be done. And I'll make them pay for Blucifer first. It'll be fine."

Mom shakes her head, her entire willowy frame moving with it. "Every time you look at that car now, you'll know it was bought with dirty money."

"Mom! Don't take it out on Blucifer!" I get up and put my oatmeal jar in the sink. I scoop up the thick contract on my way out of the kitchen, exiting before I can add something resentful about how my parents could have paid to fix my trusty companion and then this wouldn't be necessary.

They could have paid for me to go to college, too, but they didn't think that was necessary, either. I may be uneducated and broke, but I'm an adult forging my own way in the world now, and I get to make this decision. Alone.

I'm going to sign the contract. I owe it to Blucifer, and maybe, a little bit, to myself. It's not like good options are beating down my nonexistent door.

six

ZACK

IT'S the worst kind of interview day: a "phoner" day. Not only do I have to talk through an endless list of interviewers on the phone, each of them asking at least three of the exact same questions, but my team had to "lower the bar" to fill out my schedule.

I'll be talking to bloggers—eccentric people who have clung to their audience since the '90s or will use my name to build subscriptions—influencers hoping to squeeze something controversial out of me, and niche movie-industry writers who only care about what brand equipment I used behind the scenes.

These are the people who care that I directed a movie. *Terrific.*

Mindy, my handler for the day, assures me there are "big names" coming to the premiere who want me on camera for their interviews. I'll have another day of in-person interviews closer to the event.

Most of her day will be spent politely reminding people not to ask about my big-budget films and to stay focused on my indie debut.

Drew offered me an edible this morning. It was sealed, single-serving style, in a brand-new container because he knows I can't handle untraceable origins.

"From the dispensary on the edge of town," he said.

"You've been to town?" I've gained a new curiosity about the little village since driving through it the other day. It reminded me of home, of the days when I drove myself around and knew how to get everywhere without a map. But with more mountains than Ohio.

"Of course. I'm not going to get recognized. It's such a sleepy little town I bet even you could wander around if you wanted to."

I doubt it. Most of my "wanders" around people have been traumatic. It's my luck to be an introvert who got famous.

I turned down the edible. The only thing worse than being nervous is being too high to be careful.

Mindy doesn't bother coming in person to handle my calls. She's on the conference line, a steady voice connecting me throughout the morning. She gives me a quick briefing on every interview before it starts: "Blogger with 100K followers on social media" or "Influential with rich mommies." I wish I knew whether she gets her info from something scientific or just a college intern clicking around online.

Mid-morning, I have an interview with the local newspaper. Mindy sighs down the line before she connects me. "They probably have about 1,000 readers and normally put traffic accidents and bear sightings on the front page, but we had to give them something, so we scheduled them today," she says.

"So I'm the bear sighting?" It's better placement than any of the other outlets today.

"If you're lucky," she says, and I'm not sure if she's being sarcastic or not. Maybe it depends on whether an actual bear walks into town today, bumping me off the front page. Who knows? It's been made very clear to me that I know nothing about bears or wildlife in general. I plan to avoid the whole subject.

"Hi, Mark, I have Zack Ryder on the line for you," Mindy transitions smoothly. "You have 15 minutes. Please remember we're only talking about Zack's movie *Zeitgeist* today."

That damn title. I'd been talked into it by someone who didn't warn me it would end up in headlines like "Zack Ryder Fails to Find the 'Zeitgeist'."

"Hello," I say warmly into the headset I'm wearing, lips moving automatically while I'm cursing my marketing team inside my head. "Mark? This is Zack."

"Hello, thanks for taking time," says the voice on the other end. It's not as young or nervous as the other voices I've heard so far today. He still asks the usual questions, though: *What made you want to direct a movie? Did you learn anything from the experience?*

I answer by route, giving the same responses I've given everybody: *I've worked with some great directors who inspired me. I learned I still have a lot to learn.*

"Why debut at the Telluride Film Festival?" Mark continues.

It's the least scary but legit festival, is the real answer. But what I say is, "Colorado plays a key role in my movie and I wanted to honor that by bringing the film here."

"That's interesting, because I understand you're getting some criticism online for your portrayal of Colorado," Mark replies. "Is that fair to say?"

I pause, waiting to see if Mindy interrupts to save me. She doesn't. I swallow to loosen the knot in my stomach. "Criticism is part of the creative process, unfortunately." I cough, because I shouldn't have said "unfortunately." I *welcome* criticism. Supposedly. I keep going, hoping to use up the rest of the 15 minutes. "Any time you put your work out there, you're going to hear that it didn't work for someone or you got something wrong. I'm new to directing and I'm learning every day." *Keep talking about learning. People like humble movie stars.*

My media trainers would be proud of me for that answer. Relatable, quotable. Solid B plus.

"We have a local creator here in Telluride who claims you didn't bother learning about life in Colorado before filming a movie about it or buying a house in the valley. Is that true?"

God, this guy is relentless. It's not the first interview where I've wanted to start screaming, *leave me alone, leave me alone, leave me alone, I'm a* person *damnit!* But as usual, I force a big, movie star smile onto my face—because it "shows in your voice"—and says, "I'm actually in the process of learning from the individual you're talking about. She's agreed to show me around the valley."

"Really." Mark's voice has sharpened. *Shit.* I know that voice. That's the voice of a reporter who knows he's got a scoop.

"Yes." *Don't ask me her name, don't ask me her name.* I still don't remember it. "I'm very willing to learn."

"We have time for one more question," Mindy breaks in. *Finally.* I grit my teeth and wonder where Mindy's been during the last five agonizing minutes. Probably painting her nails or something and barely paying attention to my meltdown.

"How much time do you expect to spend in Colorado now that you've bought a house here?" The newspaper man asks.

This feels like a trap. "Well, I'm here for nearly three weeks this time. And I'm an investor in the ski resort so I'm told I need to come back for ski season." I laugh. Mark doesn't.

What would the mountain girl say? Something harsh about only rich people hanging out at the ski resort, probably. But what can I say? I *am* a rich person and I don't know what else there is to do around Telluride. I haven't even been into town since I've been here. *Definitely don't say that.*

I gulp but Mindy smoothly ends the call with, "Thank you for your time, Mark! I sent you the bios and press notes with images you can use. Let me know if you need anything else."

I know it's not her fault that didn't go well. I revealed too much, got off script, and now my stomach is upset. And I have another call after a 15-minute break.

Should I tell Diane? Mark probably knows the mountain girl personally and will reach out to her. But she signed the contract, and that means she can't do any press. It'll be fine.

Why does nobody want to talk about my damn movie?

It's the first opportunity I've created for myself—not one someone else brought to me—since...maybe ever? I was discovered. I did one season of auditions before I landed in a blockbuster movie that made my career take off at age 19. Ever since, my challenges have been about navigating fame and picking opportunities, not finding work.

I pushed to make this movie. My agent worried it meant turning down other roles, and my marketing team worried it didn't fit my brand. The press was skeptical. My talent signed on because it was an ensemble, and I promised every one of them I'd keep their commitment to a week or less. It hadn't been easy, but I did it. And now all that work might mean nothing. Nobody wants to see what I've made. Everybody thinks they already know what it is.

Because everybody thinks they already know what *I* am.

The problem is, sometimes I wonder if everybody else is right. I am only what my handlers tell me to be. And I made this movie on my own, without their input. What if whatever I had left to put into it is...nothing?

seven

VALENTINE

BLUCIFER IS SITTING in the parking lot, looking shiny and newly repaired, and all I have to do is walk into the garage and get the keys.

My feet are glued to the asphalt. The minute I take those keys —as much as I want to—I'm officially linking myself to Zack Ryder. It feels even more real in this moment than signing the contract. I might as well be working for him, despite the "CONSULTANT is not an employee or agent of THE TALENT" language.

I put my hand on Blucifer's rear bumper. It's already done. Ryder's people wired the money straight to the garage. *I did what I had to do for you, baby.* At least now I can get out of my parents' house and back into the world, into the trees turning fall colors and the sound of moose bugling. Maybe then, I won't feel quite so much like a child who needs guiding and protecting.

"Heard you were headed over here." Mark Wadson, the editor-in-chief of the local newspaper, comes up to me, his ever-present leather messenger bag pulling him to one side as he walks. He's wearing a sweater vest and scuffed loafers. As a guest speaker in one of my high school classes—he'd just moved here from "the city," although I don't remember which one, and taken over the paper as his retirement project—he once said it was "important for your clothes to stay out of the way of your work."

He reaches into his bag and pulls out a recorder and a notepad with a pen tucked into the spiral coil holding it together. I eye them warily.

"Are you trying to *interview* me, Mr. Wadson?"

"We're both adults now, Valentine. Mark is fine." He fiddles with the recorder, like he can't figure out how to turn it on even though I've seen him whip that thing out in 90% of his conversations around town. He writes an "Overheard in the Valley" column that's very popular with locals interested in gossip. Which is all of them.

I look around. The garage is on the outskirts of town, and I don't see Mr. Wadson's car. Did he walk here? I did, but my parents live only a few streets away.

He finally turns the recorder on. "I'm recording an on-the-record conversation with Valentine Arnaud," he says into it, then aims it at me, balancing it in the same hand holding his notepad, ready with the pen in the other. "I hear you're working with Zack Ryder."

I'm not that surprised he knows more than he should. My parents probably tipped him off to where I am right now. They weren't covered by the contract, after all—a big loophole Ryder's whole team apparently missed.

"I don't have anything to say about that, Mark," I say, forcing myself to use his first name. Hopefully, it will throw him off, but it's unlikely. I remember a two-week span where every time I ran into him in town, he was talking about tracking down the same story about thefts at the ski resort. He doesn't let go when he has a news tip or a hole to fill on the front page.

Our weekly newspaper is one page of news, two pages of gossip, and one page of ads. There's always a hole to fill on the front page.

"Is that confirmation, then?"

"It is not. It's a..." What's the phrase in movies? "No comment."

"That's not what he said."

My eyebrows jump. "He?" He can't be talking about Zack Ryder. His team wanted this all to stay confidential...didn't they?

"Zack Ryder," Mark says, sure enough. "I interviewed him yesterday. He said you were going to show him around the valley."

I blink at him a few times, then look at the recorder, and shrug. I signed a contract. According to my mother, I might as well have signed it in blood. "I don't have anything to add."

"Hmmm." Mark turns off the recorder. "How about off the record?"

I don't really know what that means, but Mark is friends with my dad, so I turn to him and say, "I guess I'd just say...pay attention to my social media."

Mark's entire face scrunches up. "The video feed?" He says "video" like it's brand new technology.

"Yeah." I hesitate, then reach for his notepad. "May I?" I write down my username. "That's me."

He looks at the paper for a long moment. "OK. I'll have my new intern take a look. Thanks, Valentine." Then he tucks the recorder and notepad back into his bag as he asks, "How are you doing? Given any thought to college?"

I wince. "No...not really." Lies. Of course, I've given it thought, then dismissed it as out of reach. I can't afford a liberal arts education. My high school grades weren't good enough for scholarships, and I hate the idea of trade school. I don't want to be an engineer or a secretary. I don't want to live my life in an office. "I'm working. You know. Gives me time to hike a lot. Not a bad life."

"Hmmm," Mark says again. "Well, you know, if you're interested in writing, I bet I could throw you some work at the paper. Might lead to more opportunities. It's a powerful thing, having your name in print."

I smile. "I appreciate the offer, but I'm more about...visual work." The paper doesn't even have a website, much less social media.

"Well, I have a small budget for photography." Mark hikes his clearly heavy bag up on his shoulder.

Not quite what I meant, but I just nod and smile. "I'll let you know."

"Thanks for the tip. I'll keep it on background," he adds as he turns away. "You're a good kid, Valentine."

"See you around, Mr.—Mark."

Once he's set off down the street, I turn back to the garage and take a deep breath. I'm fooling myself if I think I'm not already linked to Zack Ryder; that conversation is proof enough. I might as well take advantage of it.

"Be right back," I tell Blucifer, and walk into the garage.

* * *

We're on a scouting mission that's also a Blucifer-is-free celebratory exploration. I let Blucifer off-road a little on public land, looking for a good backdrop for the upcoming video shoot. I want breathtaking vistas that will make people feel small, even on a phone screen. Or stomach-dropping heights. Or snow, as a surprise.

Something with mountains *and* water would obviously be the most visually interesting, so I could do a basic hike like go up to Bridal Veil Falls, but I like to do things more off-the-beaten-path.

"Am I being too ambitious?" I ask Blucifer as we climb out of a gulley, the car's engine roaring and tires spinning. She can handle it, but who knows what Zack Ryder drives. He probably airlifted in a Corvette or something else totally impractical with only two-wheel-drive.

Blucifer rises up over the ridge, and I hit the brakes because the sun is starting to set. I get out and stand for a moment in the cooling air to watch before I take a picture. This is one of the many reasons I've never left the valley. Around every corner, over every hill, there's a gorgeous moment waiting.

Ignore the fact that I can't leave the valley. I have no way to support myself anywhere else, and no "street" skills because I'm used to living away from them. But I love the valley. It's more than fine being stuck here. *It is.*

I could take Zack Ryder to the perimeter trail around Ouray or to Blue Lakes, one of the most beautiful spots in the state. But I can already imagine his complaints—carrying a bag and hiking for miles. The movie star has probably never worked out outside of a gym. The hike would be wasted on him.

But it's hard to come up with a way to showcase the wilderness without immersing in it.

Blucifer and I decide to camp right here for the night. It's public land, so camping is free. I set up my favorite folding chair with the magical butt-warmer in it—no fire, not with this drought—and my Butane-burning stove to heat up leftover soup. I'll eat and then make sure anything I have with me that smells like food is locked safely in my bear canister away from the car. It's a nice enough night to sleep outside the car, so I get out the tent and sleeping bag and find a mostly-flat spot. The stars in the sky are magical, so many of them stretching as far as I can see or until the mountains block them out.

As it gets darker and Blucifer's engine stops ticking, I drink in the quiet. No air filters running down the hall, no house settling around me.

No sugar floating in the air from my dad making pastries for the morning, either. Living with my parents wasn't *all* bad.

And sure, sometimes it gets a bit lonely out here all by myself. Especially when something breaks or something cool happens, like spotting an elk or a bear. Maybe if I could afford a tripod, I'd notice less that I have no companion for the little moments.

But tonight, the air smells like freedom.

Of course, I know tomorrow I have to meet Zack Ryder and his entourage to film a video and basically be his bitch. But that's tomorrow.

Tonight, I have Blucifer back and can go anywhere I want to go. And the place I most want to be is here, under the wide-open sky, bundled up in my favorite fleece pants and hoodie, sipping soup in silence.

I take a deep breath of open air and breathe out the anxiety.

This is the one certainty in my life: After a good night's sleep out in the open, I'll be more creative. By tomorrow, I'll have better ideas for handling Zack Ryder.

ZACK

MOUNTAIN GIRL CLAIMS I don't have good enough "ground clearance" in my SUV, so she's demanding we meet her at the bottom of some hill that only her car can handle. And then we're all supposed to hike down into some valley with a waterfall for the video shoot.

I reluctantly blocked off three precious hours for this damn excursion. Then when Mindy relayed the information that I needed to be back by noon, we got pushback from girl-who-has-all-the-time-in-the-world that it wasn't realistic timing.

Mindy actually flew out in person to "handle" things. She, Drew, and a photographer are all coming on the trek, getting up way too early to drive nearly an hour out to the trailhead where we're supposed to meet. Drew dozes in the car, but I read over my media clips, a service Mindy reluctantly granted me access to while warning me it's a bad idea to read my own press.

"I don't want to read my press," I insist. "I want to read the press for my movie. Don't worry, I get that it's not an extension of me."

Lies.

Anyway, the media clips all start with some variation of the question "can Zack Ryder succeed as a director?" so there's no getting away from the fact the press for my movie is all about me. One headline even comes out and says it: "Zack Ryder Battles for Legitimacy This Weekend."

It's Monday. The film festival starts Saturday. I have five days to build some better momentum, and I'm wasting time out in the freaking woods. I only have an internet connection for half the drive. By the time we start rolling down a gravel road, I'm sweating. What if somebody needs me while I have no service? What if the festival committee changes my screening time and I'm not there to argue?

I can't even work in the car—the roads twist and turn so much here. I finally give up and stare out the window at the trees and yellow flowers lining the road.

Mindy, sitting across from me and Drew in the back seat, seems to pick up on my state of mind. "This is going to be great!" she says. "We'll get some pictures of you out in nature that we can use to promote the movie."

She means my summer blockbuster, not the indie film I'm currently sweating over. I scowl and put my sunglasses on, two layers of dark glass separating me from the trailhead as we park next to the only other car at the end of this road—a bright blue four-door SUV.

I grab my ballcap and put it on to hide under as I climb out of the car, the others clambering out the other side.

The bane of my current existence gets out of the SUV, wearing leggings and a fleece jacket and holding a cell phone. She doesn't even meet my eyes but leaves the driver's side door open as she pans from my head to my feet. I've been filmed enough that I don't bother to mug for the camera, just let her do her thing. I suppose this is part of the whole experience: the meet and greet. These are probably going to be the most boring videos ever. Movie Star In The Wild. Who cares?

Finally, she pokes at her phone, then drops it to her side. She looks at me.

"No," she says. Then she gets back into her car and closes the door.

"No?" I look at Drew. They shrug, shading their eyes from the sun because they refuse to wear a hat with a brim. Not their "vibe," they say.

Mindy gets my look next, and it's more effective on her. She snaps into action, running up to the car and knocking on the window politely.

The window rolls down. Mindy exchanges a few words with the woman, and then the car starts up and she drives away.

Mindy walks back to Drew and me. Her face is grave. "She says you can't wear that."

"Wear what?" Drew and I look at each other. We're both wearing cotton t-shirts and last year's jeans.

Mindy drops her eyes to my feet. I look down at my flip flops. "What?" I say. "They're eco-friendly and have arch support."

"She said you're not taking this seriously."

I roll my entire head around on my neck. "Oh my god, this is ridiculous. Come on! I have better things to do!" I stomp back to the car, nearly trip when I get a rock under my sole, and catch myself by hopping on one foot.

I pause and turn back to face Drew's raised eyebrow. Maybe these shoes were not the best choice. Forest floors are slightly different from LA pavement.

"OK fine," I say, throwing up my arms. "But maybe *somebody* should have prepped me for this."

"I'm sorry!" Mindy says automatically. "I'll research what we need when we get back!"

"I think he meant me," Drew reassures her, as unfazed by my

rants as ever. "Maybe if somebody would go into town, we could get equipment that fits at a proper store."

I shoot them one more glare before I get back into the car. "Can we get back to internet service please? Now?"

I can't believe I got up early for this. I rolled out of bed and didn't even change my underwear before hopping in the car. I wasn't being *paid* to be here.

We head back toward civilization, and Mindy's phone rings before mine even seems to have a connection again.

"Hello, Diane?" Her voice is meek when she answers. I can hear Diane's strident tones blaring out of the phone at her ear. "Yes," Mindy says. "Yes. I understand."

Drew and I exchange a look.

Mindy hangs up and keeps looking at the floor of the car while she reports, "Diane says we have to try again. As soon as possible. She said your reputation is 'about to take a swing for the worse' if we don't save it with some goodwill."

I open my mouth.

"She also said if you don't care, you should remember the success of your debut rests entirely on goodwill toward you and your projects." Her voice gets so soft by the end of the sentence, I have to guess at the last word. But I've heard Diane say this before, so I have clues.

"Fine," I snap. "Call...the Mountain Girl. Ask her when we can do this again."

In LA, Zack Ryder would never bother to repeat a failed engagement. I once showed up at a birthday party where the guest of honor never appeared and haven't spoken to that person since. But Colorado Zack, Director Zack, does things differently.

Fine. I can do this. I've made millions of people fall in love with me. I can charm one simple girl from the mountains if I put my mind to it.

I open a browser window and start researching what people need for hiking.

nine

VALENTINE

THE AVERAGE PERSON—WHO doesn't have a slope-side home like Oprah or Tom Cruise—accesses Mountain Village by gondola from Telluride. It's a manufactured resort town nearly 1,000 feet above the real town. Because I prefer to have Blucifer nearby at all times, I take the long way around and drive to work. It's a nice drive, eight miles though winding roads that force me to watch for deer at every curve. I don't mind being conscientious of shared space.

I hate Mountain Village. The core looks like a front town, like a Hallmark movie could be filming around the corner from the Bavarian chocolate shop or down the quaintly-lit street. The village, a so-called company town for workers at the ski resort in the past, was designed for tourists and wealthy landowners who don't want to bother with the real town full of real people down the mountain.

But it's where I got a job.

During the busy season, my tips are bananas. I mostly save them, to use in the lean times. Except that *occasionally* I need money for food or my annual splurge on a hot springs membership. That's $300, a huge chunk for me to shell out at one time.

I'm being especially friendly tonight as a result, considering I might need to pay back the funds for fixing Blucifer soon. The movie star contract was a disaster, like Mom predicted. Now I have to rely on tips to get me out of it.

The bar will be packed during the film festival this weekend, but tonight's a quiet one until Zack Ryder walks in. A ripple passes through the bar when one person recognizes him, whispers to the person next to them, and awareness quietly but surely races through the small venue.

As seems to be his norm, he's traveling with an entourage. Two, this time. One of them I also saw this morning on the failed excursion where Ryder showed up like he was going to the beach. The other is enormous, an obvious bodyguard.

I peer over the counter to check footwear, and at least the movie star is wearing fat sneakers. Presumably a nod to the cool night and the walk from his mansion. The big houses are all tucked into the "natural landscape"—as the brochures put it—dispersed around the village, their homes impossible to tour by Hollywood bus, which I assume is why all the celebrities like buying here.

They—the rich people who live in the hills—wander into The Bivy sometimes, wearing their big hats or dark glasses, surrounded by a crew and friendly up to a point. I've never seen Zack Ryder in here. He has a reputation for being antisocial in town.

The group sits down at a high top, dropping brown paper shopping bags to the floor. Ryder, naturally, isn't carrying anything. He probably doesn't even carry his own phone or chapstick. It might ruin the line of his outfit. Or weigh him down from harassing innocent wildlife that crosses his path.

Although, so far, in real life I've only seen him dress like a college student in t-shirts and slouchy pants. I wouldn't be surprised if he showed up in sweats next.

Unfortunately, Ryder's group is in my section.

I take a deep breath and fill three water glasses to hide behind when I walk over.

"Hi, welcome to The Bivy," I say robotically, interrupting some conversation that centers around Ryder.

He looks up at me, his eyes catching briefly on my chest before hopscotching to my face. I can't even hold that quick look against him. The Bivy, like most of the bars and restaurants up here, is a little too invested in the "European village" atmosphere and makes its wait staff wear cute little backpacks with strappy suspenders that intentionally push my breasts up under my chin.

"Oh, it's you," he says. One of the entourage nudges him and, in the span of a blink, his face transforms into a welcome smile. He looks like a movie poster come to life. "Hello!"

Frozen in place by that smile, I say nothing. I don't notice my hands getting tired from holding the four plastic glasses balanced against each other, under pressure without a tray. His white teeth are like a vortex pulling me into his fake greeting, but I can't seem to resist. I hate him, but his charisma is like a freeze-ray. *Is this celebrity power?* I have to fight my way back to the surface for fresh air. It's fake. His niceness is a front he puts on to lure innocent locals to their deaths. His incredible charisma is a trap.

I put the waters down on the table, the noise of the bar coming back to me in a rush. I concentrate on passing out napkins and offering paper straws. "Can I get you anything else to drink?"

"Do you have beer?" he asks.

I avoid looking directly at him, for fear of being sucked in again. Do we have beer. "This is Colorado," I say in what I think is a neutral tone.

I can see his confusion out of the corner of my eye.

"Of course we have beer," I sigh. "Do you want a lager, a stout, a sour, an amber, a dark amber, a wheat, an IPA, a hazy IPA..."

He holds up a hand. "Whatever you think. Dealer's choice." He flashes that bright smile again, but I'm smarter this time. I'm not looking directly at him.

"Anyone else?" I ask the table. The other two order lagers. The bodyguard must not worry about drinking on the clock. None of my business.

I bring Zack Ryder a novelty pink milkshake sour with glitter in it.

"The brewery is just down the street," I say as he looks at it warily, turning it so it shines in the dim light in the bar. The others are grinning into their lagers. "Can I get you all anything to eat? We have a nachos special."

The dark-haired one from this morning, who looks even more like a frat bro than Ryder, has his arms crossed, leaning back in his chair, eying me like I'm a treat. "How about an intro, Zack?"

Zack Ryder shoots over a glare that somehow doesn't create any lines on his perfect face. "Sure," he says. "This is Drew," he says, nodding toward the man who spoke, "and Fred."

Drew extends a hand across the table. "He/them," they say, and I shake it automatically.

"And this is..." Drew prompts, eying their movie star employer.

Ryder looks at me. There's a long pause. My eyebrows start going up as I get it. *Of course.* "You don't even know my name."

Again, his face doesn't wrinkle, but I can see the cringe behind his eyes.

"It was in the contract. Didn't you read it?"

He opens his mouth, then closes it again. "No," he finally says.

Ridiculous. But I'm not surprised. "Of course," I say, speaking my thoughts out loud. "Mr. Movie Star wouldn't bother to refer to me, a lowly peasant from town, by name."

Drew grins. The other man keeps drinking his beer. Zack Ryder shifts in his chair. "That's ironic, considering you can't seem to use my name, either."

I refuse to find this pathetic attempt at debate cute. I roll my eyes. "Everyone knows your name."

He glances around the table, like someone is going to save him from this conversation. Drew raises his eyebrows back. The other man sits there with a blank face, like a giant weenie.

Then Zack Ryder turns his fake grin back on me. I try to resist, but it's so powerful I almost drop the notepad in my hand. He holds out his hand. "Hi, I'm Zack."

His smile could light this whole bar. I hate that I wonder what it would look like if he actually meant it.

I'm tempted to refuse to give him my name. But fine, I'll be the bigger person. But no way am I taking his hand. "Valentine," I say. "It's Valentine. Yes, like the date. No, it doesn't make me sweet. I'll bring you those nachos to start. On the house."

I turn my back on them. What an idiot, thinking this contract mattered as much to Mr. Big Shot Movie Star as it does to me.

Stabbing the POS screen with one stiff finger as I put in the order, my eyes are all blurry. I try to hold onto the anger, but I can't stop the embarrassment from filtering in around the edges. I really am a simple peasant from a small town who's never had to deal with a real legal contract before—or with people with legitimately better things to do than sweat over a few cents in the fine print.

I want to go curl up in Blucifer's back seat for a while, put my favorite fleece blanket over my head, and forget about stupid details like the fact I can't back out of this deal because I already took money for it.

"Fuck," I say quietly.

"Something wrong, Valentine?" The shift manager pauses at my shoulder.

I clear my throat. "Can you comp these nachos? For the celebrity table."

The manager hesitates, probably because the celebrity should be able to pay for his own nachos, but takes a look at my downcast face and nods. "Everything OK?"

I'm torn between the voices in my head—that sound like both parents—saying never run away from a problem *and* don't be a liar.

"I'm not feeling well," I say.

"Need me to cover your tables? You only have a couple left. Gwen should be able to take them." He glances over his shoulder at the celebrity table. "She'll probably be thrilled."

I really do feel terrible now. "Yeah," I say. "Thanks."

"No problem. Go ahead and clock out and I'll take care of it."

So I leave The Bivy with my tail between my legs. I manage to avoid looking directly at Zack Ryder again as I sneak out the back under cover of darkness.

But I know I can't avoid it forever.

ten

ZACK

The clothes make the character when it comes to playing a role, and today is no different. I'm playing Serious Hiker, and I've got all the gear. I have to—I practically bought out the little outdoor gear store in town.

The night after running into her at that restaurant, I toss and turn in bed, dreaming about showing up and seeing Valentine unable to do anything but give me a grudgingly respectful nod.

She's taken over my thoughts for the last 24 hours, giving me some relief from worries about the movie premiere. So what if she hates me so much she wouldn't even serve my table? I'm going to win her over, the girl with the unusual name. She's no match for my "four-alarm charisma," as *Hollywood Weekly* put it.

I've got both charisma *and* waterproof, Vibram boots now. I didn't ignore the details, either. I read online that a gusseted tongue and ankle support are important. It takes me nearly five minutes to put them on.

Drew teases me for dressing up. "You're the one who was flirting with her," I retort.

"Bisexual means equal opportunity," Drew retorts. "But I'm picking up some sensitivity in this area."

"Not sensitive," I grumble. "You just chased her away last time." Valentine disappeared before we even got our nachos. I'd been formulating some great responses to her next volley of insults. Hopefully, I'll get another chance today.

I have to get up early again this morning, but I'm actually excited to head out into the woods again. This time, I'm ready to prove a point. Mountain Girl—Valentine—picked a different trail for our second attempt. It has us—me, Drew, Mindy, and a photographer—driving an hour to a completely different world from Telluride: a flat, dry part of Colorado with no trees where my brand-new fleece jacket feels like overkill the minute I step out of the car.

"What the hell are you wearing?" Valentine says as soon as she sees me. She's already standing by her blue SUV when we arrive. "Did you buy out REI?"

I look at her face, which is decidedly not silent and respectful. She's wearing leggings and a tank top that shows off the muscles in her arms and, well, I'm not looking, but it's hard not to notice the curve of her breasts. Her arms are crossed, and she's glaring at me. Again.

"Are those carbon fiber?" She's staring at my hiking poles. I watched a video on how to hold them correctly late last night when I couldn't sleep. "How much did that cost? You must be wearing $1,000 right now."

That's probably a conservative estimate, but I didn't actually look at the receipt.

I sigh. Her reasoning is as arbitrary as The Academy handing out Oscars. "I'm not wearing shorts and flip-flops?" My tear-resistant pants even have snaps that let me turn them into shorts on the fly. The internet said Colorado weather is unpredictable and versatility is important.

"OK..." She walks over and takes the hiking poles away from me, handing them to Drew, who's grinning like this is entertainment. "You don't need these." She puts her hands on my chest and shoves my vest off my shoulders. "You don't need..." Her voice hitches at the same moment I notice her breasts are practically touching me. "This." She steps back, two paces away so I can't smell her anymore. She smells like something familiar—something I associate with my sister Laura's six-month-old son. Baby wipes?

She clears her throat. "And what's in that giant backpack? You need a hat and water and some snacks. This is a day hike."

"I have those," I say defensively. I also have a first-aid kit, emergency blanket, and collapsible shovel, but I don't mention that. There were a lot of warnings online about being prepared for anything, and I like to be prepared for anything—even when I don't leave my house.

I shoot a look at Drew, who better not mention my extensive preparations, either. Drew's lips purse, but they say nothing.

Unfortunately, Valentine doesn't take my word for it. She walks around behind me, unzips my backpack, and starts pulling things out of it. "A compass? Do you even know how to use this?"

"I don't want to get lost," I protest instead of answering. I assume I'd be able to guess my direction based on the location of the sun. I know it sets in the west, at least.

"We'll be fine. We're not going very far, and I have my watch," she says, holding up her arm, which does have a very substantial, manly-looking sports watch on it. Why didn't I buy one of those? I try not to notice how toned her arm is as her muscles flex.

"Is this a GPS locator beacon? Damn." Still standing behind me, Valentine holds the orange device up over my shoulder and stares at it like it's an artifact. "I'm not taking you into the backwoods, you know. This is a very popular trail."

"Zack is precious cargo," Drew says. "Can you imagine if he disappeared out here? It'd be like Forrest Fenn's treasure all over again."

I glare at my assistant, who clearly has too much job security.

"Don't give me any ideas," Valentine grumbles behind me.

"Is this all necessary?" Mindy asks. She's standing nearby holding a giant thermos cup with a straw and biting her nails. Her leggings bulge with two cell phones in the side pockets. "We're going to run short on time."

"Do you want him to look stupid in the video?" Valentine asks, silencing all of us. "Anyway, I signed onto this thing to make something educational, and that starts now."

She pulls out her phone and pans it over me in my gear. I let it happen for a minute, then ask Mindy, "Are we signing off on the narration for this?"

I'm imagining a before-and-after video. "What Not to Wear" or "Who Wore It Better," maybe.

"Yes," Mindy says, stepping forward. "You aren't allowed to post anything without prior approval."

Valentine rolls her eyes. "I know. I need a lot of material to work with in editing."

Boy, does that resonate. I probably did at least one take too many on every shot for my movie but still felt like I had to cut corners in post. Sometimes I spent an hour scavenging for even one extra second of film to add.

"It's fine," I tell Mindy, who looks to me for a cue on how far to escalate this confrontation. "Let her have her process."

Diane will handle it later. I trust Diane. I barely know Mindy.

"Gee, thanks," Valentine says drily. She tucks her phone back into the side pocket of her leggings. "OK, I guess we're as ready as we're going to be."

I'm not sure what to expect. The only hiking I've ever done was once behind the Hollywood sign. And that jungle movie where it was all climbing over rocks or cutting through thick palm fronds. It was mostly green screen. There was a giant gorilla added in post.

But this is just... walking? We walk for a long time in silence. It's kind of pretty, I guess, but the view from my house's back door is pretty, too, and I don't have to go anywhere to see it.

There are fewer trees here than at home, and it's hard to tell the season. It's more desert than back near town, with a gravel-and-dirt trail that starts to climb after we've been walking 15 minutes or so.

A few minutes in, I start to feel it. My butt is burning, and I can hear myself breathing. Has my injury left me this out of shape? *I've been doing yoga!* My group stops to drink water and breathe every few steps.

"I guess you're not acclimatized, then," Valentine says, watching us. We're all too out of breath to respond. She has her phone in one hand, the other on her hip, and appears to be breathing normally. People get used to this? I wish I'd bought one of those pocket-size bottles of oxygen they had by check-out at the hiking store. It'd seemed so silly at the time. Paying money for air? Joke's on me.

"Don't worry, we're only going a little farther up," she continues.

"Right," I manage. I've never wanted to take a nap so badly in my life. But I straighten up and keep putting one foot in front of the other, following the woman who is documenting everything. Drew, Mindy, and the photographer trail after me, Drew mumbling about hazard pay.

The trail starts zig-zagging back and forth as it goes up, forcing us to trudge farther to make progress. But I can see the top and what looks like flat trail again if we can make it up there. "Are we stopping up there?" I call to Valentine, who's at the front.

She looks back at me, holding her phone up as she records, and says "yes."

I can make it so much faster if I walk straight toward her, so I decide to cut the next bend in the trail, taking a big step between this dirt path and the next. See, I just need to push harder. If I can spend four to six hours a day in the gym for the duration of a three-month shoot, I can do this.

"Stop!" Valentine shouts. "Stay on the trail!"

I freeze with one foot in the air.

"The trail's there for a reason," she snaps. "It protects the mountain from erosion."

"But this is faster," I protest.

"Oh, I'm sorry the Earth is inconveniencing you by wanting to exist," she mocks me, which seems entirely unnecessary. "If you cut the switchbacks, the whole slope will start to fall."

I look back to Drew and Mindy for support. They both look too tired and sweaty, despite the cool air, to react. They're taking advantage of the pause to catch their breath.

"Okaaay," I say, pulling my foot back from, apparently, dooming us all. I have some soothing candles at home with longer fuses than this woman.

Maybe a nice epsom salt soak when we get back tonight? My feet are starting to hurt, even though the guy at the store assured me the break-in period would be "minimal."

"It's about the journey, not the destination," Valentine says then, making my imagination work even harder to put me anywhere but here. "Try to enjoy it."

We keep climbing. I resent every extra turn I'm forced to take, winding around and around the direct path up. But I finally make it to where Valentine is waiting, taking in a view of the valley that is, honestly, kind of astonishing. I didn't think we were this far up. We're standing between much higher peaks, looking through a break in the mountains, but the town of

Telluride is spread out beneath us. From here, the whole area is washed with fall colors, red and gold like something out of a painting.

"Wow," I say. "You underrated the destination." Is this why people hike? I glance at Drew and Mindy to see if they're having the same reaction. Mindy is hunching over, holding her stomach like she has a stitch in her side. Drew is sitting on the ground, head drooping. The photographer, at least, is setting up a picture.

I look at Valentine, who is smiling at the view like she owns it. I kind of get it. It feels like we found this spot and earned this vista. It's ours now, an even exchange for how hard it was to get here.

She suddenly seems to notice I'm watching her and meets my eyes. It's the first time we've made eye contact, or at least the first time it hits me this hard, like the mountain next to us is caving in on me. *Jesus. Talk about erosion.* I remind myself how much she hates me and, clearly, wishes me harm.

She's dropped her phone hand, as though she's forgotten to keep filming, but raises it again and aims it at me. "What do you think?" she asks.

I look past the phone at her face. She's not looking directly at me; her gaze is stubbornly focused on the view. OK, I can play this game. I'm a professional. I follow her gaze. "It's gorgeous," I say. "Worth the trip."

I walk over to the other side of the plateau we're on and look down the way we came up. She follows me with the camera. "And it was quite the trip," I add, looking at the camera and turning on the famous grin.

I ham it up, extending my arms to encompass everything around us. "It's like we walked to a different world. Can't wait to see what else is up here."

I walk toward the far side of the clearing, confident she'll follow. "Don't walk there," she calls after me, voice urgent. I stop short and look around, expecting there to be a drop-off I'm about to walk over.

There isn't. It's … cracked dirt, like the ground is thirsty. A few green things are sprouting where I was going to step.

I turn back to her, annoyed she ruined my shot. I was in the moment there. "What?" The ground crunches a little as I plant my feet and cross my arms.

"Oh my god," she says, glaring at me. "What the hell is wrong with you? That's live dirt. It's biocrust."

Now it sounds like she's making things up to mess with me.

"Get off of it!" she shouts. I jump and move toward her, looking back like the ground is going to follow me. I haven't been yelled at like that since the toxic set last summer where I got injured. At least then I was being paid $20 million.

"Jesus," I say. "Calm down. You don't have to scream at me."

"You're telling me to *calm down*?" Valentine's voice is quieter, but somehow scarier.

She's still filming me. Mindy, holding her side, is walking toward us. It feels like I've stepped in something far worse than live dirt.

Maybe I used a poor choice of words. My sister would murder me. But I don't need to be scolded like a child. My ears are hot. "I get you're obsessed with nature and all, but maybe take a look around at real life once in a while," I tell Valentine, ignoring Mindy stopping between us and extending her arms like a traffic cop.

Valentine ignores her, as well. She squares up to me, but at least she drops her phone so this isn't all being captured. "What would you know about real life? Do you ever even walk outside without your entourage and someone to direct you?"

Low blow, because, well, I often don't. Mindy says, "Guys, let's take a breath. This is getting out of hand."

"Don't be so high and mighty," I snap at Valentine. "You're as much a hypocrite as the next person. If you care so much about the environment, why aren't you driving an electric car?"

Her eyes widen. "What the fuck," she says. "Are you serious right now?"

Drew starts coughing and keeps going. Everyone pauses and looks over at them, clutching their water bottle and spitting on the ground. "Oh my god," they wheeze. "I feel like I'm dying."

"This is ridiculous," I say. I have the uneasy feeling I'm in the wrong, but I'm not sure why. Dirt is dirt and electric cars are affordable now! Right? "I don't have to put up with this. We're leaving. Come on."

I grab Drew's backpack from the ground and march back toward the trail we came up. I feel my assistant following me.

"Um," says Mindy, her voice drifting behind me as I descend as fast as I can. "OK, well. We'll be in touch."

I fume all the way back to the car. It's hard to tell whether it's easier to breathe because we're going back down or because I got away from that overwhelming woman and her constant superiority complex.

I hope I never have to see Valentine Arnaud again.

Part Two

No Trail Markers For This

Zack Ryder Battles for Legitimacy This Weekend

By Celebrity Tattle

Movie star Zack Ryder, who drew millions into air conditioned movie theaters during the summer months as star of "White House Rising," is gambling on warming people up over the winter with a directorial debut that features zero screen time for Hollywood's Sexiest Man Alive. The new movie, "Zeitgeist," which no one has seen yet, is already a poor bet to make back its $3 million budget.

The masses want Ryder's empty-headed popcorn flicks, not what posters for the forthcoming yawn-fest describe as a "surreal exploration of fame from one of the leading men of cinema." Yet an entire cast and crew signed onto Ryder's vanity project in hopes of converting sales of tickets to watch a shirtless celebrity running down the National Mall into sales for an academic analysis of a superstar's brain. Hint: His brain isn't what draws people to Ryder's blockbusters.

But a chilly welcome for his movie isn't the only thing Ryder is dealing with this fall. Not only is the Hollywood megastar struggling to convince people to watch his new movie, rumor has it he's struggling to fit in with the locals in the mountain town of Telluride, Colorado, where the star has a second home and plans to debut his new movie. A short film criticizing Ryder for feeding wildlife went viral over the weekend and was attributed to a local woman who dislikes Ryder's presence in the community.

A story in the local paper claimed Ryder is "learning from" the local woman who made the video, quoting the movie star as saying, "She's agreed to show me around the valley." Is that a hint of desperation in the mountain air or just the flop sweat of studio executives watching their moneymaker's reputation go down the drain? Maybe the locals can give Ryder tips on making movies.

eleven

VALENTINE

I HAVE to break the contract.

But I have no idea how. There's a clause in it that says it can be broken by either party in writing, but then there's a lot of other legal jargon that has me worried.

I heard from Mom, who heard from Linda at the tool library, that Tyler is in town to see his parents over Labor Day. Tyler is my ex-boyfriend, but he's also a law student now. Or possibly an actual lawyer at this point; we haven't really kept in touch since he left, and I have no idea how long law school takes.

Probably because I have "no ambition," as Tyler accused me when we broke up.

It's a difficult text to send, but not as difficult as facing Zack Ryder again. Tyler agrees immediately to meet me at the coffee shop where my dad's pastries are served.

"Man, I missed these," he says Wednesday morning, digging into a scone with jam that runs down the outside of both hands as he bites into it. "Nobody bakes like your dad. People in Ann Arbor are more into sandwiches than pastries, I guess."

I make a face. "I can't imagine."

He smirks, and I wonder if he's remembering the other words he threw at me before he left: *You've never been anywhere. Your worldview is so small.*

Sitting in this small café, knowing the people who walk by the windows to the street and the people who work behind the counter will report that high school lovers Valentine and Tyler met this morning, it's hard to disagree about my world being small.

By later today, my parents will be demanding what I'm up to with "that boy." My parents never liked Tyler; it's part of why I dated him. My brief, small rebellion in life. Tyler thought he could persuade me to be even more rebellious, but my feet were planted firmly in Telluride. Leaving the town felt too big, too different for me to contemplate seriously at that time.

And now? Now it feels like I shut down too many options before I realized I'd run out of them.

But before Tyler can ask too many questions about what I've been "up to" since he left, I dive right in: "So, this contract. Thanks for taking a look at it. I should have talked to someone before I signed it, I guess, but..."

"You definitely should have," he agrees.

I smile tightly and continue, "I felt like I had limited choices at the time, and lawyers are expensive."

"Ha," he says. "Plus, in fairness, I'm not sure Mr. Rogers up the street is worth the money."

"Mr. Rogers"—whose real name is Roger Smith but Tyler always made fun of his sweater jackets and homey speech— retired from some big law firm five years ago, came home to Telluride, and got bored, so he opened his own private practice. He's at least 70 years old.

"I wasn't sure if he'd ever heard of social media," I admit, although I feel bad going along with Tyler's mockery. Every time he makes fun of someone who chose to live here, I know he's really making fun of me. I probably could have asked Mollie. She's a paralegal but she would have more legal knowledge than me.

"Have you heard of digital sharecropping? That's basically what social media is," he says, wiping his hands and reaching across the table for the paperwork. "You're providing content for a platform owned by somebody else."

He's wearing a t-shirt with his college name on it, and his arms have gotten sort of flabby since I saw him last, which I choose to focus on rather than respond to him scolding me for my choices. Tyler's always been like this: sure he knows a little bit more than everybody around him. Going to law school has clearly fortified the sentiment.

He's doing me a favor, I repeat to myself. I glance up to see Dorothy, behind the counter, watching us with a smile. By the time we leave, rumors will be spreading around town that we're back together, like one of those Hallmark movies where the boy returns from the big city to his hometown sweetheart. Except it's not Christmas and I'm not interested. Some options I was right to shut down when I did.

He appears to be reading the contract, but Tyler asks, like he's reading my mind, "How's dating life around here, anyway?"

"Oh, you know," I reply. "Same old." I take an enormous bite of my chocolate chip muffin.

"Townies who work at the ski resort and drink too much to forget?" he asks, eyes still on the paper he's holding. "Tourists who fly through looking for a one-night-stand with a local?"

He's not wrong, but I don't want to give him the satisfaction of agreeing. "There's an exception to every stereotype," I offer, finishing my muffin. I can think of two couples right off the top of my head who met like that and it seems to be working out.

Anyway, I refuse to ask about the dating life in Michigan, or wherever. *I don't care.*

As he continues to read, I watch people outside on the street through the big windows at the front of the shop, playing a game with myself that I can tell the difference between tourists and townsfolk. Tyler dresses more like an outsider now, with his brand-name shirt and clean shoes. I might not have made all the right choices in my life, but I know for sure I don't want to be him: a local who grew out of the remarkable town where he was born. At least I will always have Telluride, even if I have to cling to it with the last drop in my gas tank.

"Well," he sighs and puts the contract face-down on the table next to his plate. "I'm sorry to say you got yourself into a bit of a mess."

Sure, he's sorry. "I can't get out of it?" I ask.

"Oh, you can." He picks up his scone and immediately has jammy hands again. As he waves it around, a little dribble lands on the contract. I reach across to wipe it off. "You'd just have to pay back the money they already gave you."

I take a sip of my tea to ease my tight throat. "I already used it. It's in Blucifer."

He laughs. "You still have that old car?"

This is the second time in two days a man has insulted Blucifer, and I'm sick of it. "She's more reliable than anyone else I know," I snap.

He holds up his hands, a crumpled napkin in one of them. "Hey, don't shoot the messenger."

I sigh. *Fair.* I'm frustrated and have a quick temper. The person I really want to take it out on is Zack Ryder. The zap of electricity he sent through me when we were arguing at that overlook is still running through my veins. *I should drive an EV?* With low ground clearance and no chargers to be found in the area? The color had been high in his face when he said it, and his eyes were alive like a real person's rather than a flattened poster. What a jerk.

"He probably had about a dozen lawyers work on this contract, taking advantage of you for not knowing what you were doing," Tyler continues, the words casually backhanding me to my face. "He doesn't care about the money, really. But if you break the contract, they might come after you just to earn their retainer."

Terrific. I could end up rich person roadkill. Collateral damage from the celebrity impact.

"If I were you," Tyler continues, because I'm clearly interested in unsolicited advice, "I'd do my time. Do the bare minimum and cut your losses. This is clearly a better deal for him than you, anyway."

I hesitate before I ask, because it means validating his thoughts. "Why do you say that?"

"For you, the fame will last 15 minutes, but he'll always be the movie star who bothered to hang out with a nobody in the wilderness." Tyler shrugs. His watch buzzes, and he looks at the notification. "Hey, I gotta jet. Thanks for the coffee. It was great to see you. It's always funny coming back to town and seeing how little has changed."

"Mmm." I stand with him and give him a reluctant hug.

"Good luck with the contract. Don't hesitate to reach out if you need more help."

I nod and watch him go. I can't remember if Tyler was always this arrogant or if law school brought it out of him. I choose to think the asshole levels were lower when he was a sophomore commuting to college in Montrose.

Dorothy walks over with a fresh pot of tea. "Sometimes things don't work out for a reason, dear," she says. "I thought you might need this."

"Thanks," I say, slumping back into my chair. "Could I get

one of those mini scones, too?"

Dorothy clasps my shoulder for a moment in solidarity and brings me two.

I scroll through my notifications, which are full of comments I can't reply to—most of them from angry fans, but a few asking legitimate questions I'm dying to answer. I've posted several videos since the one about Zack Ryder, but all of my interaction is on that one video. The few comments on the newer posts are all asking when I'll do another video about him. Plus a few comments like, "Do you ever see him in town?" and "I bet Zack could take on a bear, have you seen those arms?"

Last night, I'd parked in my parents' driveway—where I got a Wi-Fi signal—and spent several dark hours editing together videos from the footage I got of Zack on our two ill-fated trips. I'd felt satisfied by how foolish he looked in the final cut, but the taste of my own vindictiveness was sour. I'd saved the videos rather than posting them.

Wouldn't it be more satisfying to take someone like that, someone completely ignorant of his own ignorance, and teach him how to go into the wilderness safely and leave no trace?

"Can't teach someone who doesn't want to learn," my mom would say.

I could try it Tyler's way and edit together a more neutral video from the footage I already have. It would showcase the beauty of the trail and Zack Ryder's smile. Maybe I could even capture the way he lit up when he saw the view at the end of the trail. I could make him look good, and maybe his team would accept that as enough to fulfill the contract. I could literally phone it in.

But Tyler's wrong about me. I have ambitions. They're just not about going fancy places or making a lot of money.

I want to teach people the world is about *more* than getting degrees and making money. That if they step outside, they can have a life-changing experience and that deserves respect. That trees have names and chipmunks have lives and the ecosystem is balanced so delicately.

And I can't just accept I messed with a force of nature I don't understand and back away. Because what's the lesson in that?

No. I'm going to make a difference, even if it means I have to be nicer to *him*.

twelve

ZACK

I'M BURIED under a weighted blanket on my leather sectional sofa trying to drown out the screaming in my head.

It sounds a little like *omigod the movie isn't going to be ready they're going to have to show an early cut or cancel the premiere entirely and everyone's going to think I think it's a good movie even though it isn't done, it's not what I wanted, everything's a mess and I have no time management skills why did I think I could do this?*

"It's totally normal to have last-minute problems," Drew says, their voice muffled from outside the blanket.

"How would you know?" I retort, which is unfair, because a) Drew is only trying to help and b) Drew is the middle child of a famous director.

"The movie isn't *done*. It's supposed to be *done* and uploaded by *tonight!* They already gave us an extension!" It's getting hot under the blanket and shouting doesn't help, but I'm not ready to come out.

"It's done," Drew says soothingly. "It's just a technical issue with the conversion. They'll figure it out. You have capable people on your team."

This is true. The one thing I'm confident in is my ability to hire good people. I've never once been embezzled, and no one's ever leaked anything about me.

Of course, there's always a first time.

"Maybe you need to get your mind off things," Drew says. "Go for a walk?"

I briefly flash back to that view of the town on the hike and how peaceful it felt up there, away from everything, including my fears of failure. Maybe I could hire a guide? Someone less acerbic than the Mountain Girl.

"It'd be better for you to be out of the house, anyway," Drew adds. "We've got the rest of the housekeeping staff arriving this afternoon ahead of your crew."

Under the blanket, I open my eyes and stare at the pattern of light on the fabric in front of my face. My production crew arrives Friday, and they're staying at the house. I don't feel great about flying in housekeeping staff from LA, but I also wouldn't feel great about dumping all that training on Drew if I hired locals. My press team is staying in town somewhere, so at least they're supporting the local economy.

What would Valentine say? I wish I didn't wonder. But it would probably be something about how selfish I am.

"Are we buying supplies from town?" I ask, hopefully.

"They're bringing most of what we need with them. We'll be covered," Drew says, reassuringly. But I groan. We really did parachute into this place and ignore the resources on the ground. I'd always thought it was good to be self-sufficient. To not make demands on the town. But maybe I've been wrong.

I throw the blanket off my head and can feel my hair stand up around my face from the static. "I know what to do! I'll go into town and buy some of those rolls. The sticky ones. For the crew to eat for breakfast."

Drew stares at me, face impassive. "I'm sure the staff can handle making cinnamon rolls."

"But this way we're supporting the locals. You know, spreading the money around instead of hoarding it up on this hill." I start the process of unfurling from the heavy blanket. My therapist recommended it for anxiety, and it does help until I want to get out of it, and then it induces more anxiety because I feel trapped.

"That girl really got in your head," Drew says. I ignore him. "I can send someone to town," they add.

"You wanted me to go out!" I finally slither out of the blanket onto the floor, pick myself up, and straighten my pajamas.

It's 3 o'clock in the afternoon. I know because I've been checking my email and messages every five minutes to see if my team has uploaded the movie to the film festival portal yet. It's fine. It's not the end of the world if the movie doesn't premiere this weekend, right?

Well, it is, but breathing down my crew's necks isn't going to help.

"Do you want me to go with you? Or take Fred," Drew suggests. Fred is a bodyguard. His main function is being huge and attracting attention.

"No, I'm just going to wear a hat. You told me no one would mob me in town."

"They won't," Drew says uncertainly. "Just let Fred follow you. He doesn't have to be your bouncer. Listen," they say seriously. "This isn't some sort of...kamikaze mission?"

"What?" I pause as I'm sniffing my underarm. Should I shower before I go out?

"Or a cry for help?"

"I'm just going outside!" *Am I that bad?*

"Around people," Drew points out. When I just blink at them, they add, "You've gotten pretty...introverted lately. That's all."

That might be a nice way of pointing out I hate crowds and germs. I'm not sure when that happened, really. When I first got famous, I used to say "yes" to every party. And every woman who wanted to "party" at home.

Then I decided I wanted to work on my own project and discovered nobody wanted to talk about that. It wasn't that the invitations dried up; they just suddenly seemed filled with people who didn't care about what I cared about and weren't interested in listening. That Hollywood sheen wore off and left me—just a kid from Ohio—wondering what was real.

I wave all that away. "I'm fine. I just need some fresh air. Fred can follow me but stay back."

"OK, but let him drive you," Drew insists. "He can park on the outskirts of town, and you can walk in, Andy Griffith-style."

So that's what we do. Well, minus the sheriff outfit.

I have a moment of doubt after I put on my shoes—close-toed, of course, because I listen—but Fred and Drew are watching, so I force myself out the door into the world. I wear a ball cap and sunglasses and a jacket to cover up my overly-sculpted arms, although it's been awhile since I've been in the gym, so maybe my muscles don't scream "I have a personal trainer" anymore.

I'm doing maintenance work in my home gym. It doesn't cost me $300 an hour, but I'm not exactly seeing gains, either.

Does Valentine have an opinion about men with gym muscles, too?

Probably. I bet she only accepts muscles on a man who chops wood and, like, hauls sleds or whatever. A picture of Valentine, her dark hair spread out on a bed and her eyes bright with something besides anger, flashes in front of my eyes. I have to close them to blink away that vision.

These thoughts—disturbing thoughts, obviously—carry me

all the way to town. I hop out of the dark-tinted SUV after Fred parks it on a side street, check that my ball cap mostly covers my highlighted hair, and head toward the sound of live music.

There's a group of three people playing on a street corner near downtown. A ukulele is one instrument. Somebody standing on the street and clearly not with the band is holding a triangle. A group has gathered around, which makes me nervous because groups can turn on a dime, so I don't linger but appreciate the Bluegrass soundtrack as I walk on into town.

I like knowing Fred is behind me if I need him. But I don't. No one gives me a second glance as I walk down the street, passing random little shops that sell leather goods and wide-brimmed hats and shirts that say "I got high in Telluride: 8,750'."

I pause in front of one store with a mirrored window and check my disguise. It seems obvious, if you're looking, that I am who I am. *But who am I, really?* Maybe the people around here don't watch a lot of movies or read magazines with airbrushed faces on the cover. And does my fame really exist outside of that?

This is why I don't go outside: The looming existential crisis.

I move on.

At the coffee shop—the name of which Drew wrote down for me—I hesitate. I glance back at Fred, who shifts his weight like he's ready to come running if I so much as lift a hand. I shake my head. I can handle a little enclosed space. It doesn't even look that busy. I wave at Fred to stay outside and step in.

The bell over the door rings, and people glance up at me, but not for long. I feel a moment of flight-or-fight response before I realize it's fine. Everyone's busy with their own conversations, a book, or a laptop. There's a group of men wearing puffy vests in the corner, even though it's nearly 80 degrees outside.

I take a breath of air filled with coffee and sugar and let it out again. I really need to get out more.

As I think this, I'm reminded of a few times I walked into a venue in LA and got a very different reaction. I'm like a magnet to a certain kind of person, and they tend to travel in flocks. And live in California.

But right now, I'm fine. I just need to remember not to touch my face after grabbing the door handle.

I look around. *Now what?* The door bangs into me from behind, the bell rattling angrily. A tall stack of pastry boxes in someone else's hands starts to slide, and I catch the top one before it goes too far.

"Good catch!" The familiar sight of my own sunglasses greets me on the other side of the pile. "Well, hello there! Help me carry these to the back, will you?"

I take another box off the top and follow Valentine's dad further into the coffee shop. "I bet you were hoping for another one of those cinnamon rolls!" he calls over his shoulder.

I have no idea what happened to the roll they gave us last week. Diane's assistants probably crossed themselves as they tossed it in the trash before eating more raw spinach.

Now, I regret it. What's a few calories compared to genuinely thanking someone for a gift they spent time on?

Mom and Laura would be ashamed of me. I really did move to LA and become an asshole.

"Well, too bad," Valentine's dad continues, setting the stack of boxes on the counter inside the kitchen and turning back to take the two from me. "Today is apple fritter day."

"Wow," I say. "Do you have a specialty, or do you make everything?"

He lifts the sunglasses to the top of his head and winks at me. "My specialty is lemon loaf. That's on Sundays, but you can stop by the house again sometime and get a sneak peek."

He opens one of the boxes, giving me a good look at the glossy pastries. "Go ahead."

I want to be the kind of person who wouldn't hesitate to dig in. But I'm not. "Let me wash my hands first?" I ask feebly.

The other man smiles. *God, why am I so bad at remembering people's names?*

"Of course!" He closes the box and points over my shoulder. "Bathroom's right behind you. Don't run away, now. I'm going to grab us a table."

I can't remember the last time I sat down face-to-face with another man without it being a contract negotiation. I grew up without a dad. Is this the kind of thing dads regularly do? Chats over homemade pastries?

When I return, hands washed, Valentine's dad is chatting with the men in vests in the corner. He points me to a table nearby and says to one of the men, "Good luck with the new tour, Tom."

I slide into a seat with an apple fritter and a cup of coffee in front of me. He joins me across the table.

"So, how are you doing?" he asks. "Did you come to take your sunglasses back?"

I laugh a little. "No, no, they look better on you, Mr.... Arnaud." At least I remember that much.

He smiles. "Rick is fine. And I think we both know that's not true, but I'll take the compliment."

"Is Rick a French name?" I can't help myself. I'm curious.

Rick smiles wider. "No. Arnaud is my wife's name. I took hers when we got married."

"Oh," I say. And because I don't want to look unenlightened, I add, "Ryder is my mother's name, too." Of course, in my case, my father didn't stick around long enough to give me his name.

Rick nods without further reaction, taking a bite of his apple fritter. "Mmm, if I do say so myself." He washes it down with a sip of coffee.

I pick up my pastry. It's warm, and I can smell the apples and sugar. Am I really going to eat this? I am. Somewhere, my dietician must be screaming. I lift it to my mouth and take a small bite. It melts on my tongue.

"Wow," I say. I put it back down and mimic Rick, taking a sip of coffee to wash it down. "That's really good."

Rick smiles proudly. "Started making those when I retired. It's my little project now. It's important to work on something you love, don't you think? Keeps the mind busy and the heart at peace."

I mull over that phrase. *Keeps the mind busy and the heart at peace.* Maybe that's why I turned down a multimillion-dollar contract to work on my own movie last year. But I'm not sure my heart is really at peace with it. "That sounds nice," I say, hoping he doesn't ask me to elaborate.

"That's something I worry about with Valentine," Rick continues. "She has something she loves—the outdoorsmanship, excuse me, outdoorswomanship—but hasn't quite figured out how to turn that into her life's work." He shakes his head. "She means well, you know. Has her mom's temper."

I can't help smiling at that. "Yes, I seem to trigger it regularly."

Rick winks. "Welcome to my life. Val and I—Valentine's mother, Valkyrie—had a few years where some days I wasn't sure if we loved each other or hated each other. Things have settled down, somewhat, in our old age."

I'm not sure if I can ask, given Rick is basically a complete stranger, but decide to go ahead. Rick seems like the kind of guy who wouldn't mind. "What kept you together?" I add, hoping not to offend, "Aside from the delicious pastries."

He laughs. "The pastries came later. Shared values kept us together. And the sex, of course. It's important to make time for that. I'll be right back." He stands up, leaving me blinking too much in embarrassment. I've said more risqué lines than that in multiple PG-13 movies, but it feels different in real life—especially when I don't know what's going to come out of the other man's mouth.

"Hi." A young woman slides into Rick's vacated seat across from me. "Zack Ryder, right?"

I instinctively grab my sunglasses resting on the table beside my coffee. Too late for a disguise. "And you are?"

"I work at the town paper. I think you've talked to my boss, Mark Wadson?" She leans toward me, ready to catch me if I bolt. She looks like she's still in college, maybe, and has that expression like every fan who's ever stood outside an entrance screaming when I get out of my car. My whole body tenses.

I keep my face friendly out of habit. "I have. He made an appointment, which is more appropriate."

"Sorry!" she says quickly, but doesn't pause. "I just wanted to ask if you're dating Valentine Arnaud?"

Don't react. "I'm not," I say firmly, with as little emotion in my voice as possible. "And I don't know where you got that information." Do I need to call Fred? I glance around the coffee shop. No one's looking at us.

"It's just, her videos. And you told Mark you're hanging out with her now."

I don't respond. She opens her mouth to keep going, and my chest clenches. Just when I was starting to trust this town. I've got to get out of here. But somehow without playing the rich Hollywood asshole.

"That's my seat." Rick is suddenly standing over her. "Not to be unfriendly, miss, but I'm not sure you were invited to join us."

"Oh!" She looks up at him. "I'm from the paper? Jenn Hollis?" She glances at me like I'm going to save her.

"Hm," Rick says. "Sorry we haven't met yet. I'll be sure to talk to Mark about it. I'm Rick. Now, we were having a private conversation."

She slides out of the chair and stands there, hovering. "Um…"

"Mark has my press person's information, if you want to request an interview," I say. With Rick standing there like a disapproving parent, the situation doesn't seem like it's going to blow up in my face. I can address it calmly.

"Right, OK."

Rick stares at her until she slinks away. There are no empty tables nearby, so she heads toward the counter.

"Seems a little overeager," Rick says, sitting back down. "Don't hold it against her. I think she's from the city."

I smile. "Thank you. Perhaps I'd better get going. But this was nice!" I realize I only took one bite of the pastry and take another. Wow, I forgot how good sugar tastes.

Rick studies me. "Let me get you a to-go cup," he says, waving at the woman behind the counter. The young reporter is still standing up there, hovering near the pick-up sign and watching us. "Do you need help getting out?"

"No, I've got someone outside waiting for me." But I appreciate the offer. What would I do if I hadn't brought Fred? I should be able to handle one young woman, but I'm not sure I can. The way I wanted to leave a Zack-shaped hole in the wall and tear down the street to safety…well, there may be something wrong with me.

"Why don't you have him bring the car around?" Rick suggests. "I'll distract our young friend."

I agree, relieved to have someone else solve this problem for me. We go into the back, and I call Fred while Rick packages up some apple fritters for me to take back to the staff.

Rick pats me on the back before I make a run for it. "Don't be a stranger. I wrote my cell phone inside the box if you ever need it."

That's the first time I've ever gotten digits from a dad.

Rick blocks the "city woman" from the paper while I dash straight out and into the SUV idling by the curb.

On the drive home, I get an email letting me know the movie was successfully submitted and accepted for use at the film festival. *Why am I not relieved?*

The next two days stretch out empty before me. I have nothing to do but worry obsessively over my schedule, what to say to the press, what to say in the Q&A after the premiere, how many calories were in that apple fritter, and whether it will show in the fit of my suit at the premiere. *And what is my life's work, anyway? Is this movie it? What if it flops? What does that say about the rest of my life?*

My mind is busy, but my heart is definitely *not* at peace.

thirteen

VALENTINE

I DON'T EVEN MAKE it past the gate without being stopped.

After identifying myself through the black security box, I cross my fingers that I'm not on some blacklist labeled "people to shame and humiliate if they show up."

But the gate opens. I drive up a winding road that dumps me out in front of a house I've only seen in pictures. The front is almost all windows, a wall of them set in a natural-wood frame. The driveway curves up behind the house to leave an unobstructed view down the side of the hill. I spot a majestic elk standing next to a brilliant aspen some 120 yards away. If I had a telephoto lens, it'd be a perfect picture.

I can't believe my parents used to own this land, and now it's mostly enjoyed by one rich, spoiled pretty boy.

I sit with Blucifer for a minute before I get out, reminding myself I'm being nice. *I'm a nice person who believes in change, damnit.*

Zack's assistant, Drew, meets me at the front door. Their

91

arms are crossed, and they raise an eyebrow at me. "Didn't expect to see you again. Must have a taste for celebrity spats."

I stand below them on the stairs, trying to decide if they're insulting me or not. "Would we call that a spat?"

"Would you prefer 'feud'?" They're still blocking the doorway.

"You flatter me, Drew. I can only aspire to be Zack Ryder's nemesis." I take another step up the front steps. "Now are you going to stop gatekeeping and let me in?"

They don't move. "What's this about? Zack's a little busy, and you didn't make an appointment."

"Is he? Because I heard he had coffee with my dad yesterday." I'd also heard my dad "had a talk" with Mark Wadson about his new intern. I didn't hear the story directly from Dad, but Dorothy at the coffee shop is now selling Dad's apple fritters with a sign that reads, "Zack Ryder's favorite pastry."

"And I brought him breakfast," I add, holding out a box of those fritters. "I hear they're his favorite."

Drew smiles a little. "He's not going to eat that. Too much sugar."

"Hmmm." I open the box. "Well, I also brought yogurt. Plain. Like his soul."

Finally, they laugh. "What does that even mean?"

I shrug. "I think we both know what it means." I have no idea what I'm talking about anymore.

They step aside. "You can come in, but only if you brought enough plain yogurt for me."

I close the box and step around them before they can change their mind. "For you, I brought granola. Lots of nuts."

"That's what she said," they reply, following me in the front door.

Drew leads me through the front room of the house, where I leave my boots, to an enormous living room with expansive views of the front yard. The elk is still there. The room looks empty at first, until my eyes catch on a pair of socked feet hanging off the end of the suede, sectional couch.

I step around the corner of the furniture and look down at Zack Ryder, hair sticking up, hands folded over his chest, staring at the ceiling. He's not wearing a shirt. His abs look like a Ken doll's.

"Good morning," I say.

His eyes zip from the exposed ceiling beams—I glance up to see them—to my face. He sits up without using his arms, just sheer core strength. I'm torn between feeding him and throwing the pastries away to preserve the chiseled art in front of me. My parents' familiar voices battle it out so loudly in my head that what comes out of my mouth is, "I thought you could use some sugar."

Cringe. Drew laughs. Zack stares at me.

I open the box so he can see that my offer is innocent and refers to real sugar. "Peace offering," I add.

He looks from the box back to my face and then stands. His forehead briefly creases, then smooths out into a neutral expression like a mask. "Really?" he finally says. "You sure you didn't come to scream at me again for, I don't know, walking around? Or existing?"

I sigh. I deserve that. *Doesn't mean I like it.* "First of all, you owe Blucifer an apology."

Zack darts a look over my shoulder at Drew.

"My car!" I snap. Obviously. These people probably don't even realize the origin of the name is deeply Coloradoan. There's a giant blue statue of a mustang by the Denver airport that I'd taken my inspiration from. It has the same name, but red eyes.

I take a deep breath. "Second of all, I'm sorry I screamed at you. That's not the proper way to teach anyone anything. Even someone clearly completely ignorant of how nature works."

He makes a face and reaches for a hoodie draped over the side of the couch. While it's covering his face as he puts it on, I give myself a second to scan his chest more thoroughly. He looks like a magazine cover I once kept taped to my closet door. He's not getting those abs walking around in nature, but when they look that good, who cares? My eyes are back on his face once his eyes are open again.

"Do you have a point, or did you come to my home just to try to win an argument?" he asks, smoothing the UCLA letters over his chest.

"I'm sorry, were you busy?" I look pointedly at the couch. But I'm getting off track. I take another deep breath. "I came to invite you on an adventure."

He pauses, mid-response to my needling, and closes his mouth. He glances at Drew again, uncertainty filling the air.

"An adventure?" Drew repeats. "As in, leaving the house?"

I turn so I can look at both of them. "Yes. In my car, this time. Without a big entourage. Just us, a phone camera, and one of the best hikes in Colorado."

Zack stares at me. "You want me. To get in your car. Alone. And drive to a second location." His gaze drops to the box in my hands. "And you're luring me with sugar."

I roll my eyes. "You have that GPS locator. Your bodyguard can track you if you're so worried. And the sugar is to help with the altitude."

"Really?" Drew sounds interested. "That's so unfair!" Like their diet has personally failed them.

I smirk at him. "Sugar and water. The water's in the car."

Drew looks at Zack. "I think you should go."

"What!" Zack stares at Drew like they've turned traitor.

"Get your mind off things," Drew continues. They take the box from me and select a plain yogurt. "There's nothing on your schedule until Saturday."

"I was going to...do a workout," Zack protests.

"Hiking is a workout," I interject.

"No kidding," Drew agrees, sitting down in a chair across from the hand-carved Beetle Kill coffee table. It has a live edge. I've never coveted a piece of furniture so much. It's gorgeous and probably cost more than a thousand dollars. Not like it would fit in Blucifer. "I thought running on a treadmill meant I was in shape and acclimatized."

"Come on," I coax Zack, wrenching my eyes away from the work-of-art table Drew is casually eating on. "I have everything we need. I brought sunscreen so you won't get burned and hydration tabs so you won't bonk."

"Sounds like she can take care of you," Drew agrees mildly, licking his spoon. I hold my breath so I won't blush. "And you did sign a contract," they add.

Zack throws up his hands. "Fine. Let me get dressed."

"Bring layers!" I call after him. "It gets colder as you go up."

"And hotter as you go down," Drew says under their breath. I don't think Zack hears them; he doesn't turn around.

"Stop being such a clichéd side character," I tell Drew, sitting down across from them on the couch Zack vacated. I help myself to one of the fritters, scattering flakes of sugar all over the couch and floor.

They grin back at me. "Hazards of living and working around the movie business, I guess."

We make small talk for a few minutes while waiting for Zack to return, and I learn they have a famous father and like their job —which they've had for two years—because they have a lot of time to read while waiting around on film sets. They're working their way through queer classics, they tell her, "like Patricia Highsmith."

Other than Gerry Roach's mountain guidebooks, I haven't

read a book since high school, so he promises to find me something "mountainy" I'd like. "Maybe Annie Proulx."

"Don't take him around crowds," Drew adds in a low voice, once there's a lull in our conversation.

I consider responding with some version of, "Isn't he a movie star? Don't crowds love him?" But Drew looks so serious that I say, "I can't guarantee the trailhead won't be busy, but once we get farther into the trail, it'll be just us and nature, I promise."

They nod. "Warn him before you get there so he's prepared."

It's an odd comment that I turn over in my mind, wrapping my head around the possibility that Zack Ryder gets social anxiety. *Is it possible that people love Zack more than he loves people?* The conversations I've had with him start to take a new shape.

"Have you been talking about me?" Zack demands when he returns, dressed like an Eddie Bauer model.

Drew and I look at each other. "No, actually," Drew says. *Mostly.*

"You're not the only topic in the world," I say, getting up. "Come on, Land's End. Let's go have an adventure."

fourteen

ZACK

WE DRIVE FOR A LONG TIME.

In the car, I can tell Valentine is making an effort. She asks if I liked the apple fritters and how coffee in Telluride compares to LA. I ask if Rick made pastries for her growing up, and she says he's only gotten into it in the last few years.

"Are you looking forward to your film premiere?" she asks, after a long pause when I suspect we're both searching the crevices of our brains for something to say.

"I'm not sure 'looking forward to' is how I'd describe it," I reply.

The roads around here, through the San Juan Mountain Range—I looked it up—are insane. I'd flown into the small Telluride airport, the type of place where you exit a private plane onto the runway, and I hadn't experienced the combination of high speed driving and flying around a sheer cliff that I'm experiencing now. There are a lot of twists and turns, and I keep my eyes on the horizon—when there is one farther away from the side of the road—trying to keep my stomach from rebelling.

The topic doesn't help settle my stomach. I should really be sitting at home near my computer and a Wi-Fi signal, in case something goes wrong and I'm needed.

"Come on, haven't you been working on this movie for a long time? This should be a celebration of your accomplishment."

I glance at her, feel dizzy, and put my eyes back out the window. "It's not finished yet."

"The movie?"

"The accomplishment."

"Really?" she sounds puzzled. "Wait, what does success mean to you? For this, I mean. Obviously you're very successful at what you do."

"Thank you," I say automatically, then feel like a fool. "What do you mean?"

"I mean, you're famous and make a lot of money, which I thought was what most people wanted when they got into the movie business. So what more would success look like? If you accomplish what you want with your movie."

I open my mouth, and it gets stuck. The answers that come to mind, I can't say to her: *More money? More fame? Every person on Earth telling me they love me?*

There's something seriously wrong with me. If people knew, I'd be shunned. No one would put my face on magazines or scream when I walked into a huge auditorium.

I would be good enough. That's the real answer.

I definitely cannot say that out loud.

"Umm," I say. "I guess it would open wide. Or get a streaming distribution deal."

"What if only a few people love your movie, but they love it a lot? You know, like a cult favorite. You wouldn't be happy with that?"

I swallow. *Are we going up? Is the air getting harder to breathe?*

She keeps her eyes on the road and both hands on the wheel,

thankfully. She's not looking at me at all. Every time another car passes us on the narrow road, I have to remind myself to breathe again.

"That's not...um. That's not my brand," I say finally.

"Your brand?" she laughs a little. Fair. It *is* ridiculous.

"Can you change your brand, if you want?"

"I don't know," I reply, my voice harder. "Can you change who you are?"

She's quiet for a moment. "Is it the same thing?"

I don't know. I just know I don't want to be having this conversation. And I want her to slow down.

"Well, your brand is-"

"I know, I know. Granola, hippie, unwashed, opinionated..."

"I was just going to say Mountain Girl."

She laughs. "That could mean anything, depending on who says it." She turns onto a gravel road. It's more like a trail for cars. She drives on it faster than I think she should. "Like, when you say it, I think you mean all of those other things. But if I said it, I'd just mean small town, hikes a lot, sleeps outdoors whenever possible. A brand is just an illusion, I guess. It is whatever you want it to mean."

"I think you have to have a consensus," I argue. "A lot of people have to agree, at least generally, on what your brand is."

"Maybe a lot of people have to agree on what *your* brand is," she replies. "I guess that's what being famous means. When you're a nobody like me, it only matters if I care what people think."

We go over a hole in the ground, and I barely notice. *It only matters if I care what people think.* The words knock around in my head, not finding anywhere to fit. After a moment, I discard the concept. It's a cliché. Something easy to say. After all, like she said, she's not famous. She doesn't have a face that was once recognized at 3 a.m. in a Tesco shop in Greenwich.

"That must be nice," I finally answer. The words come out more wistful than I meant them to. More wistful than I feel. After all, I've gotten a lot from being famous. I'm not going around complaining about it.

Especially to her.

She goes on, "The people who think they know me have known me since I was born. I grew up in front of them. You, people only know a tiny slice of who you are."

Before I have time to contemplate that, we come around a final bend, and there are cars crammed into what seems to be a small gravel lot surrounded by trees. A full-size SUV is parked precariously close to the entrance, and we have to squeeze between it and a sedan that's leaving.

"We'll take their spot!" she exclaims, far more excited than I expect to hear about a parking spot.

I can't believe how crowded the trailhead is. "There are so many people," I say as she pulls into the one open spot in the lot. A car that pulled in behind us keeps circling the lot. Beside us, a couple are putting on backpacks and hiking boots while sitting on the tailgate of their truck.

"Oh. I was supposed to... Yeah. This trailhead is busy. But a lot of people don't go very far in. We won't be hiking with a crowd or anything. I mean...look at that guy. He's wearing flip-flops." She stops pointing at the man passing in front of our car and looks at me.

Eying each other over the gear shift, we both think about our first hiking attempt.

"Yeah," I say evenly. "What an idiot."

She smiles, and instead of laughing at me she's laughing with me. "He won't make it to the view."

Between the messy braid over her shoulder and the well-worn smile lines on her face, I'd never guess this woman was capable of yelling at me. I need to remember it can happen at any moment. She's not to be trusted just because she looks like she's straight out of a Western.

"Come on," she says, opening the driver's side door. "We've come a long way since then. Let's do this."

I pull the brim of my ball cap down over my sunglasses before I open my door. My first real hike, where it'll be more than a few steps from the car. And from Wi-Fi. I have to carry water on my back.

I can't deny a small thrill of excitement. Or maybe that's terror.

The line between the two has grown very blurry over the last few months.

I check my phone one more time. No service.

I'm either going to have a life-changing experience or get murdered out here.

"Come on, City Boy," Valentine calls to me through the open hatchback trunk. "Let's check your gear."

I'm not sure which way I'd bet on this going.

fifteen

VALENTINE

IT'S like hiking with a toddler.

Zack steps to the side and looks away every time we pass somebody on the trail. He has to stop every mile to rest, because he's not used to the altitude or his shoes. He asks, "what kind of flower is this?" and "is that one of those—what do they call them —14ers? Up ahead?"

The flower is a Columbine, and yes, that's Mt. Sneffles, I tell him. "My favorite 14er."

"Have you hiked a lot of 14,000 foot mountains?"

I shrug. "A few." *Six.*

"Are they hard?" He adds quickly, "Of course they are. Are they worth it?"

"Definitely." I pause and show him some photos of the view on my phone. "You can't get a view like this anywhere else. And it's not the same when you just drive up, like you can on Pikes Peak."

We hike a little further before he has another question, the pattern of our day so far. It's taken us an hour to do two miles. I remind myself I *wanted* to encourage his sense of wonder.

"Do you think I could do one?"

I look back at him. He's been hiking behind me, letting me take the lead without protest, which says something about his trust in me. His backpack doesn't fit quite right, his "base layer" shirt is cotton, and his jacket is more raincoat than windbreaker, but he doesn't stand out as a complete newbie on the trail. He's *trying*.

"If you trained for it," I answer. "If you didn't, you'd definitely get altitude sickness. And you have to have better layers, because the temperature drops at least 20 degrees at the top. The best of 14er season is narrow, between maybe June and early September. Otherwise, you get snow. And you have to go early so you can summit before noon. The storms move in in the afternoon and they're dangerous." I glance back at him, to see if he's still listening. He's looking off into the distance, so I can't tell. "Other than that, it's just a matter of putting one foot in front of the other for a few hours."

"Cool," he says. We walk a few more steps in silence, and I think he's dropped it. The Fireweed blooming along the path brushes my pants every so often, the purple flowers swaying in a cool breeze. It's a perfect day for a hike. It's rare for me to have company on a day like this when I'm out exploring. In the silence that falls between us now, I try to appreciate it.

"I want to do that someday," he adds, two seconds later.

I roll my eyes as we keep walking. I've met plenty of tourists who plan to climb a 14er "someday."

"Not going to happen without a plan," I mutter to myself.

"I don't know where to start," he replies. I throw a look over my shoulder. *Damn, it's too quiet out here.* Or I'm too loud—something I've heard before.

"No such thing as being too loud or taking up too much space," Mom would say.

I take a deep breath. The trail is open around us, and all I see are trees, rocks, and mountains. One of the things I love about being outside is there's so much space to take up. I don't want to gatekeep that experience. "Well, I can help with that. If you want." *If you're serious.*

"You don't actually want to help," he says.

"Of course I do! If you're serious." *Oops, it slipped out.* I'm not sure I do want to help, but this is the kind of thing I think I should be doing if *I'm* serious about helping introduce people to the joys of the outdoors.

"What makes you think I'm not serious?"

It's good that he can't see my face. And maybe it's good that I can't see his. Something about it—that smooth, neutral expression he almost always wears—makes me want to mess it up. Make him yell or glare or smile or something. I picture the bare abs and messy hair from this morning for a moment, but it's in a different context, and I'm touching his skin. *Whoa, shut that right down.*

I try to refocus on the topic at hand. "Well, you don't live here full time, for starters. It's hard to train to climb a mountain from sea level."

"I'm hoping to shoot my next film in Colorado," he says.

I snort. "Don't remind me."

"What?" he says, his voice raised a little from behind me. "At least I'm actually filming here, not inserting stock images. It's hard to film in Colorado. The incentives aren't that good. And I've been having a hard enough time getting this movie greenlit on a budget."

"Don't your movies make, like, a billion dollars?"

"Movies I'm *in* make a billion dollars."

I snort. Of course. Slap his pretty face on a movie poster, and everyone I know will see the film. Even me. Hey, the movie theater has air conditioning.

"I mean, sometimes," he goes on quickly. "But they start with a bigger budget. They're the kind of movies that studios build their whole schedule around. I don't direct movies like that."

"Why not?" I throw a look over my shoulder at him. His face isn't smooth and neutral now. He looks frustrated. He pauses, and I step off the trail with him, even though there's no one around. The crowd thinned out after about a mile. He takes his ball cap off and rubs at his sweaty hair, making it stand on end.

"I don't really know how to manage a movie that big, for one thing," he says. His internal struggle shows on his face, and then it comes pouring out: "And I'm not sure I want to. I just want to tell small stories once in a while. About people like my mom or sister. They live in a suburb, and Laura's a single mom just like our mom was, like it's a family tradition somehow. My nephew will probably grow up just like me, with no clue how a man in a family is supposed to act. Like, we think women are amazing and strong and can do it all, but we have no idea how to support that because we've always just been...taken care of. And, I don't know, I think it's interesting. Family dynamics and lifestyle stuff. That's all."

I stare at him as he puts his ball cap back on and takes a little antibacterial gel out of his backpack, using it to clean his hands. Not only does he have insightful thoughts about the world around him, he just shared them. I'm not sure what to do with that.

"Well, climbing a mountain is a very 'man' thing to do," I offer. It's a dumb thing to say. But I keep digging my own hole by continuing. "Nobody can really help you do it. You have to do it yourself."

"But I need help! You just offered!" He grimaces. "Yet again, I depend on help from a woman." He winces. "I said that like it's a bad thing. That's not what I meant."

I smile. "It's actually really great that you look to women for help. That's a good quality."

He crosses his arms and looks at me from under the brim of his hat. "You're saying I have some good qualities now?"

I turn my back on him and start walking up the trail. "I knew behind every male superstar was a whole bunch of women."

"And one non-binary assistant, usually," he agrees, his voice close behind. Somehow, without looking, I can tell we're both smiling.

We walk for a while without talking. It doesn't feel awkward anymore, like we don't have enough to say to each other, but more like we're both enjoying the walk and taking in the experience side-by-side. I start pointing out plants without Zack asking, directing him to Yarrow and Asters and telling him we've come at the perfect time to see fall colors at their peak.

This is one of the things I love about hiking. There's not much to do when you're walking for hours in the middle of nowhere, but there are pretty things to look at and tired feet to be distracted from. The bonding of experiencing it together has led to some of the best conversations I've had in my life. Something about sharing the silences and the miles usually leads to deeper conversations than I've ever had in a bar or coffee shop. Granted, I'm usually alone, and when I have company, I'm usually hiking with friends—not my worst enemy.

But maybe he's not my worst enemy anymore.

I'll reserve that spot for people who don't pick up dog poop on the trail.

Eventually, we come over a crest, and I pause so I can film him on my phone as he catches sight of the lake. I timed it perfectly, so the sunlight overhead is bouncing off the surface of the water and making it look a surreal blue. The mountain slope behind it is dramatic, still covered in patches of snow.

His whole face changes. He takes off his sunglasses and emotes, and I'm so startled I almost drop my phone because my body kind of melts, like his reaction is mine and it's the happiest moment of the past few months, maybe years.

Holy cow. Is this why he's worth millions as an actor? Because he can make people feel what he feels?

I hope I didn't shake my phone too much while having that out-of-body experience. My stomach still feels light, like I'm in one of the baskets rising high into the sky every year at the Telluride hot air balloon festival.

"This is incredible," he says, walking a few steps toward the lake and then looking back at me. "It's gorgeous! And we walked here!"

I'm watching him through the screen of my phone like it's a movie, and it's adorable. I want to squirm and poke a girlfriend because this is the moment we'll talk about later. He's grinning as though directly at me, and when I raise my eyes above the phone screen, I see he is. He's looking at me, not the camera.

"How did you know this was *here*?" he demands, like I'm a psychic.

I laugh. "It's on the map. There's an app for that. I can show you."

"I feel so alive!" he shouts.

I start giggling and can't stop.

"What?" he demands, looking back at me. But he's smiling.

"I guess we're all spoiled in Colorado. We're used to this kind of view. I can't remember the last time someone reacted like this."

He laughs. "I'm overacting, probably. Literally chewing up the scenery." He spreads his arms out like he's going to hug the view. "But I can't help it!"

"No, don't stop." I'm still filming. I have a feeling I'm going to want to remember this, even if I never let anyone else see it. "You take it in as long as you want. Scenery like this should be appreciated."

He turns back to me and smiles, standing there like a portrait of a gorgeous man in front of a gorgeous vista. My heart bonks, like I just ran out of calories and need to lie down. *Shit.* What am I even doing here, giving this man an experience he's just going to put in his pocket and forget in the face of all the others—the private jets and yachts and gold-leaf champagne and freaking White House dinners I've seen pictures of him at in magazines? I'm the only one of us who will never forget. I'm the one who will be left behind when he helicopters out of this valley I'm trapped in.

I lower the phone and try not to let it show on my face that my heart has started racing. "I'm glad you like it."

Trapped. Trapped. Trapped. My heart is thumping the word. I'm not, though. I *love* it here. It's my home. I'm not sure why I'm suddenly panicking.

He walks down the hill toward the lake in front of me, and I stumble after him. It's fine. Look at the view. Look at the mountain and lake. It's beautiful. Breathe. In. Out. You're getting plenty of air. Smell how fresh it is.

But the voice in my head is nearly drowned out by another: *You're wasting your time. You are the least important person in this whole valley. He could replace you with anybody and still get this view.*

Legs collapsing beneath me, I take a seat on a rock and watch him move on without me.

sixteen

ZACK

I DON'T IMMEDIATELY NOTICE that Valentine isn't with me—which is weird, because normally I'm hyper-aware of the difference between being alone and with people.

This lake is unreal. It's like a movie, except it's real life and there's no post-production magic going on. I don't have to fake my reaction next to a green screen. There's no director telling me I'm overacting or underacting, either. Just Valentine, who prefers my natural responses.

I open my mouth to ask her if I can swim in the lake, which is when I realize there's no one around. I'm completely alone at this lake in the middle of nowhere. Did she dump me here? Is this some practical joke she's been planning? Maybe she plans to put this on her video feed and make the whole world laugh at me.

I finally pick her out of the wide-screen scenery, hunched over with her elbows on her knees as she sits on a rock back by the trail. She's not holding her phone. She's not laughing. Something's wrong. My stomach lurches, and I spring into action before I can think about how distrustful I'd been a moment before.

I run back to her. "Are you OK?"

She raises her head, face startled. "You're so fast," she says.

"I have to sprint a lot in my movies," I reply. "Tom Cruise made it a requirement to look good running."

She frowns. "Well, I didn't actually see you run. Go do it again."

I laugh, but I know what she's doing. I've done it plenty of times myself. "OK, stop deflecting. What's wrong?"

She puts her sunglasses back on, but I see her eyes harden first. "Nothing."

I hesitate, but what can I say? "Open up to me"? We're not friends. I don't really trust her; why should she trust me? *Maybe if I go first.* "I thought you'd left me. For a minute. Only thing I can think of that would be worse than being left alone in a crowd is being left alone in nature." *I'd be lost out here without you,* I think but don't say.

For a minute, I think this has backfired and she's judging me. She says nothing, hiding behind her dark sunglasses and looking at me as she sits on the rock. "Why?" she says finally. "Why is that so bad?" Her voice is quiet. Not accusing.

I shift my weight back and forth between my legs. I'm sweaty under my shirt and jacket, but the wind is cool, and the sun is hiding behind clouds that have rapidly rolled in after the blue-sky morning. *Vulnerability sucks.* "Um," I say slowly, uncertain whether I'm going to be honest even as I open my mouth. "Well, when there are a lot of people, it feels overwhelming. But when there aren't, it feels like nobody cares."

"Oh," she says. "I didn't..." She stops.

"What?" Give me something here.

"I didn't know you could feel like that," she finishes.

"What, because I'm famous and successful, or whatever?" I

cross my arms. Why am I opening up my soul to this girl? *She thinks I'm some kind of caricature.* I'm just giving her ammunition against me. Something about this place, this shock to the system we're standing in with no one else around to overhear, is making me want to tell someone my secrets. She just happens to be here.

"No," she says. In the pause between us, I hear the kind of bird she called a Mountain Chickadee trill. "Because I thought I was alone in that," she says. "Feeling like nobody cares."

We both freeze, staring at each other. A game of chicken where we both expect the other to laugh, brush off the honesty, and get on with keeping the other at a distance.

"I feel that way all the time," I say. I almost whisper it, letting the quiet around us decide whether to carry it to her on the wind. Leaving it up to nature whether she hears me. Even the birds have fallen silent, letting us have this moment I would have never predicted.

She takes her sunglasses off again. The sun is still behind the clouds, and her eyes are wet. "I felt like that just now. It's why I... needed to sit down for a minute."

I nod. "I get that." The number of movie sets where I've needed to retreat to my trailer, just for a minute, includes...well, all of them that I've ever worked on.

"Thanks," she says. She stands up and brushes off her pants. The sun peeks out at us. The moment passes like it never happened. But we both know it did. "So, should we take some video?"

I clap my hands, ready to move on from that weirdness. A director would *definitely* tell me I'm over-acting, now. "Can I swim in it?"

She smirks at me, which is fair, because I'm acting like a child. "You can," she says. "But I don't recommend drinking it and it's going to be icy cold. And I'm going to video you getting back out in a wet t-shirt."

I laugh. "Not my first time," I say, peeling off my backpack and jacket and leaving them there by the trail. I run back toward the lake.

"Take off your shoes and socks!" she calls after me. "You're not going to want to walk two miles back in those wet."

I follow her advice, but reluctantly, because the rocks are sharp wading into the water. The temperature takes my breath away, it's so cold, but I wade in to chest-height just to prove I can. Just to feel alive in this moment, having an experience that isn't mediated or created *just* for movie magic. The water is so clear, and the jagged mountains behind it are so stark. I can see the reflection on the surface if I stand very still, only my shivering disturbing the picture.

I'm freezing when I wade back out of the lake. The clouds have completely covered the sun. She captures my slog back out, and I gamely keep my eyes on the camera, my teeth clenched from the cold.

"OK," she says, lowering her phone.

"I hope you don't want me to do it again," I say, my voice a little shaky. I wriggle my limbs to try to warm them up.

"No," she says. I glance up at her to see why she's been short with me again. Her eyes are on my chest. My nipples are rock-hard through my wet shirt. She catches me looking and kneels down to look through her backpack. "I might have a towel in here."

"I wish I had that emergency blanket right now," I say, giving in to the shivering. I sit down and start rubbing my bare feet, wanting them to dry off so I can put my socks back on.

She pulls out a washcloth-sized towel and offers it to me. I look at it. She shrugs. "Sorry, it's all we have."

I take it and use it to rub my feet briskly.

"Oh, shit," she says. I look up. She's looking at her watch, the arm it's on held up at an angle and her other hand poking at it.

"The barometric pressure has plummeted. We've got to get back to the car. There's a storm moving in."

We both look up at the now-cloudy sky. Has it gotten colder? I can't tell; I'm so cold inside now. My *bones* are shivering.

She's frowning as she hurriedly repacks her bag and then starts on mine. "Come on," she says. "Do you have any more layers in here?"

"No," I admit. "I just have the jacket." I'm holding my shirt away from my body, wishing it wasn't so wet.

She pulls a knit hat with a pink pom-pom on the top of it out of her own bag and offers it to me. I'm too cold to be proud; I take it and put it on gratefully. The wisest choice, I decide, is to just take the wet shirt off and wear the dry zip-up jacket, so I do, even though it's physically painful to expose more bare skin for the few minutes it takes to change. I sense her eyes on me, waiting impatiently to start walking back to the car. I suck in my stomach and hope she likes what she sees.

Once I've got my wet shirt strapped to my bag and my shoes on, we get back on the trail. She sets a fast pace, with no talking. I appreciate it because it generates some heat to walk quickly. I'm still freezing. My pants are wet, my underwear is wet, and this jacket is too thin. If only the sun would come back out. The whole walk here, I enjoyed the perfect weather. It was a little breezy, but nothing like this. Now it feels like winter has rolled in a few months early.

We're halfway back to the car when I see white flakes floating in the air. I stop still and protest, "It's September!"

She throws a look back at me. Her face is concerned. "We're at nearly 11,000 feet."

After that, I follow her in silence, my arms crossed over my chest so I can warm my cold, naked fingers in my armpits. We make it back to her blue SUV at the now-empty trailhead, and I climb into the passenger side gratefully. The snow is really coming down now. My jacket is starting to feel wet.

"You should take your pants off," she calls to me from the back of the car, where she's loading her backpack into the trunk. She brings me a blanket when she gets in the driver's side. "Use this. I don't want you to get hypothermia."

I'm not so sure I want to Donald Duck it in her car, but my dick is so cold I'm not sure it's still there, so I spread out the blanket over my lower half and proceed to slither out of both pants and underwear. It's a slow process, because the wet clothes cling and we're bumping down the gravel road back toward the highway in a near white-out.

"You don't have any shorts or something that would fit me, do you?" The car is starting to warm up. *Thank you, god.* But I'm distracted from appreciating the warmth or the barrier between us and the snowstorm outside. The tense atmosphere in the car has me thinking I should be ready to leap into action. But my dick is hanging out.

She shrugs. "I don't know. You can look through that bag behind your seat."

I carefully wrap myself in the towel before I get up on my knees and reach awkwardly over the seat. A brush of cold air tickles my bare butt anyway before I can manage to turn back around with the bag.

I glance at her. "Sorry if I flashed you."

She doesn't look at me, concentrating on the road. "I'm driving here." But I think I see a small smile at the corner of her mouth.

The bag is stuffed with girl clothes, and not just a few. It appears to be everything Valentine owns, from dressy stuff to athletic wear to a swimsuit and sweats. Now that I'm looking, the back of the car is filled with things like a pillow, a folded chair, and a cooler, too. *Has she been living in this car?*

I glance at her as we finally hit pavement again and turn onto the highway leading back around the mountain to Telluride. I really know very little about her. Maybe she has good reason to think nobody cares. But I've met her parents, and they seem like caring people, so surely she's not all alone and homeless. I assumed she lived at their home. Now I'm not so sure.

The only thing I can find in the bag that will fit me is a stretchy skirt, so I put that on. It's something. It prevents me from feeling quite so naked.

"Date night will never be the same again after seeing you in that skirt," she says as I put the bag back behind the seat.

"Don't worry, I'm sure in a 'who wore it better,' I would come up last." I sit back down, put my seatbelt on, and put the blanket back over my lap. I can feel the warm air in the car, but I'm still freezing.

She's watching me out of the side of her eye. "I'm not so sure," she says. "But I never plan to find out. You can keep that now."

I laugh. "You sure? You could probably sell it on eBay."

She snorts, but as she opens her mouth to respond, we see a line of red brake lights up ahead, and she carefully slows down well before we get to the last car. She doesn't just stop at the end of the line; she puts the car into park. "This is probably going to take a while," she says.

"What? Why?" I really want to get back to my flannel pants and sweatshirts and weighted blanket. I can't get warm. It's like the cold is *inside* me.

I reach down to put my socks and boots back on. I'm wearing a real *look* now. Drew, who's been known to put on a skirt with black fingernail polish and eyeliner for a night out, would be proud.

"They might be closing the highway," she says. "People drive stupid in unexpected weather like this and slide off the road."

"But how will we get home?" I'm probably being dense, but I can't think of any alternative to being home in my cozy bed now. I must bury myself under multiple blankets as soon as possible. I can get Drew or somebody to light a fire in that giant fireplace.

Maybe we even have a heating pad somewhere in the house.

She's looking at me, but sympathetically, not like I'm an idiot. "We'd have to find somewhere else to stay."

"But...where?" I imagine walking into a hotel lobby looking like this. People taking pictures that go viral on social media. Having to laugh and make jokes about it in every red carpet interview for the next six months. "That's how Colorado people assume LA people dress all the time," I'll say. "Gotta live up to my reputation."

She's checking her phone. "I still don't have a signal, but you know what...maybe we should just get off the highway now before everyone else turns around. I know a place we can stay. No one will recognize you there."

I look ahead at the sea of white and red. "But maybe it will open?"

She frowns. "Maybe," she agrees. Her voice speaks doubt loudly. "But we'll probably sit here for a few hours."

"Hours?" My voice squeaks a little. I can't imagine being trapped in a stopped car on a highway in a blizzard for hours. *Wouldn't we get stuck?* The snow would pile up on top of the car and freeze us in. I look at my phone. No signal. It's like we've driven into a different country.

I sit back in my chair and close my eyes for a moment. "Let's just...wait for a bit," I suggest. "Find out what's going on."

"OK," she agrees. It's probably not what she would do without me here, but she doesn't argue. "Get comfortable, then. Are you warm enough?"

"No." I pull the blanket up to my chin, then realize I'm hogging it. "Do you want some blanket?"

"Sure, just give me a little," she says. I extend it across both of our laps, covering the gear shift. That means I'm only partly covered. I try to keep my shivers to a minimum, but it's difficult.

"You're still really cold, huh?" She turns the heat up.

"The hat helps," I say. *Pathetic.* I'm hunched in on myself as much as I can, trying to huddle in my own body heat. The snow is still coming down outside, settling on our windshield now that the wipers are off. "What if...we get stuck here?" I ask.

"I have a candle and a shovel," she says. I look at her blankly, so she explains. "The candle will keep it from getting below freezing inside the car. You light it in a can, and it becomes a heater. Not enough to stay warm, but warm enough not to freeze. And the shovel can dig us out."

She says this like she doesn't sound like a contestant on one of those survival reality shows. She's wearing three layers, but I'm suddenly picturing her as Lara Croft. Valentine will save me from this shitshow. Of course, Valentine's also the one who got me into this mess.

"Wow," I say. "Has that ever happened to you?"

"Not where I was actually snowed into my car, no," she says absently. Some of the cars ahead of us are turning around, pulling six-point turns to get out of the line of vehicles.

Maybe I should be listening to the survivalist here. "If you think we should turn around, we can," I say.

"Let's give it a little longer," she says.

I nod and adjust so my hands are also under the blanket. I'm so cold. I need a distraction. "So," I say, "have you lived here your whole life?"

"Yep." She sighs, watching the snow rather than looking at me. "Barely left Colorado. I've only ever been to the states around us. Utah. New Mexico for school trips and a bachelorette party once. My parents took us to the Grand Canyon when I was a kid." She glances at me. "It must seem very small to you. A small life."

It does, a little, but I shake my head. "I don't know what it's like to live in a small town. It must be nice to know everybody. I grew up in a suburb that didn't really have a sense of community."

She shrugs. "I definitely know everybody. And they know me. A little like being famous, maybe. Except they're less stunned to see me walking on the street and more nosy about what I'm doing with my day."

I smile because I know she's joking, but I say, "Being famous would be a lot more comfortable if I knew everyone who knew my face."

She hums. It's so quiet outside the car, nothing moving but the snow. We both look out the windows for a minute.

"I guess I don't want to be famous," she says suddenly. She's still looking out the window, but I can see from her profile that she's not relaxed. She's focused inside the car. "But I do want more people to see my content."

"It seems like it means a lot to you," I say. I've only seen that one video. But I've been yelled at enough by her that I understand a little bit about what she's trying to say on her platform. Suddenly, I want to watch her video feed and see if she names the flowers and birds and trees she pointed out to me today — and does it with a smile on her face. I'd watch that kind of content all day.

"It's not exactly the same." She throws a quick glance at me. "I suppose you think you make art, and content is a dirty word."

I snort, thinking of the green screen acting and having to film a running scene 10 times to make sure my abs look good in it. "Hardly. I mean, I don't know. Maybe it's the same thing."

"Is your new movie art? The one that's coming out at the film festival."

The question makes my stomach tighten. "Maybe. I guess we'll see what people say."

"Why does that matter?"

I hesitate. I pull one hand out from under the blanket and hold it up to the hot air coming out of the dashboard vent. "I guess I feel like...it isn't really art until you put it out there for people to judge it."

"But is it the act of letting people see it or what they think of it that matters?"

I look at her. She's looking back at me.

"Honest question," she adds. "I think it matters for what I do. Because if people don't understand what I'm saying, I'm doing a bad job educating them. It's communication, not expression. But for what you make...at least, the stuff you make yourself. Maybe you're the only one who has to understand?"

I frown. "I don't think that's quite it." I'm quiet for a long time because I'm struggling to put into words what it is. "At least, that's not quite what I want. I just made the movie because I want to feel like I'm being true to who I am. I guess that sounds stupid when I'm so successful being...whatever my brand is."

"It's not stupid," she says immediately. The way she says it, so sure, it makes something loosen inside me. Maybe it's not my art I want people to see; it's me. And in that case, maybe starting small is OK.

"If it doesn't feel like it fits, you have to find something that does, or you'll go crazy eventually." She taps on the steering wheel, her fingers restless. "I want that feeling too. That I'm being who I want to be and not just what other people *think* I am or should be. I grew up here, and everyone thinks I'm still that little girl who liked horses and black-and-white cookies at the cafe. I'm more than what people have decided to see."

"Yeah?" I'm watching her, the way she's like a live wire under her skin.

"Yeah." She looks back at me, and our eyes meet.

I don't need everyone to see me. Just a few people. It's not fair—because doesn't she hate me?—but in that moment, I think Valentine Arnaud understands me better than I understand myself.

I break the moment by shivering.

"OK," she says, and shifts the blanket back onto my lap, off the manual gearshift, so she can put the car into gear. "We're turning around. I know what will get you warm."

seventeen

VALENTINE

I DIDN'T REALIZE I could be *into* a man wearing my clothes, but wow, I really, *really* am. There's something about the vulnerability that requires confidence that gets to me.

Zack follows me into the lobby of the hot springs resort wearing my slinky skirt, unlaced boots with socks that go high up his ankles, a thin fleece showing part of his chest, and my blanket as a sort of cape. I know he's miserable but he looks so adorable I wish I could take a picture without it seeming like blackmail material.

But it absolutely would. I could probably sell this picture—Snowbound, Cross-Dressing Zack Ryder—for thousands of dollars.

Daisy at the front desk, of course, doesn't blink an eye. "Hey, Valentine. Need a guest pass?"

"Do you have any available rooms?" I can't really afford a room, but I'm not going to tell Zack that. Maybe Daisy will put it on my tab.

"Uh oh, you get caught in that storm?" Daisy stands to pick

up a handwritten ledger on the desk behind her. "Or...is it some-thing else?" Her eyes dart between them. I hope, for his sake, that Zack also gets the wave of heat I feel. He's still shivering.

But his head is turned, taking in the rest of the lobby: The mismatched old furniture, the man asleep on the couch. The smell of sulfur is impossible to get out.

"*Rooms*, Daisy," I stress. Daisy reads too many romance novels.

"Well, I only have one," she says, looking up from the ledger. "It's a King sized bed, though, if that helps."

I swallow. Zack has wandered off toward the hallway leading to the hot springs. "That's fine. We'll do that," I say quickly. Maybe I can sleep in Blucifer, despite the cold. "Can we pay when we leave?"

"Sure," Daisy replies, and hands her the key. "Free passes to the hot springs with the room. And you get robes," she adds, wiggling her eyebrows at me.

I've always sort of wanted a robe at the hot spring. It seems so luxurious. I'd have to pay extra for one with a day pass, so normally I just wrap myself in my towel. "Thanks." I go to collect Zack, who's peering in at the community kitchen. "Do you want some hot chocolate?"

His eyes light up. "Can I?"

I smile a little. "It's just powdered," I warn him. He's prob-ably used to some kind of hand-shaved chocolate. "But I think there are marshmallows."

He looks around cautiously as he follows me into the kitchen. "Are we allowed in here?"

"Oh, yeah," I reply. "I'm here all the time."

"What is this place? Why does it..." He hesitates.

"Smell like that?" I smile. "I'll show you in a little bit."

He seems to follow me around in a fog, gripping his paper cup of hot chocolate in both hands, not commenting on the one-room situation and changing into a robe without a word. The cold really went to his head. He only balks when I want to take him back outside.

"I promise it will warm you up from the inside out," I cajole, opening the door to show him the steam wafting out of the pools, captured eerily in the few lantern-like lights scattered around the grounds and almost all visible from the door to the inn. Daisy always jokes it's less a resort, more a hot springs motel. The privacy fence makes the whole area seem like someone's backyard.

"Are those hot tubs?" He eyes the rock walls of the pools skeptically as he follows me down the path to my favorite one. It has a Valentine-shaped nook in one corner.

"Hot springs," I reply. "It's sulfur you're smelling."

I hesitate a moment—my mom would be ashamed—before I drop my robe. I don't look at Zack, but I can tell he's gone still beside me. I put the robe on a chair and slide into the hot water, hurrying not because of the cold but because he's seeing me naked. I'm *not* ashamed. He's probably seen a thousand beautiful women undressed, between his professional and personal lives. I know I'm no model, but I'm happy with my capable, strong body. Still, I haven't spent much time finding my best angles, and I'd rather not stand around posing for a man who's probably slept with women on People's Most Beautiful list.

Once I'm covered by the water in the dark pool, I look back up at him standing there, still robed. "Come on! There's no one here."

It's true. With the snow still floating in the air, the pool area is empty. There might be one or two people lurking in their own pools, but the one I picked nearest the door to the rooms is empty.

"There are no cell phones allowed," I add, because he looks so uncertain. I remind myself he's a celebrity and probably worried about telescope lenses. Sure enough, he glances at the wooden fence that surrounds the pool area.

Finally, he takes a deep breath, coughs from the cold hitting his windpipe, and drops his robe by mine. I look away as he slithers into the pool, but it's hard — *heh, heh, hard* — not to think about how naked we both are in the water. Inches away from each other in this suddenly-small-seeming pool.

He hisses from the heat. "Good, right?" I tease him.

"Good," he agrees. "Can't get hot enough." He sits on a rock ledge a few feet from me, immersed up to his chin. "So...is everyone naked here?"

"It's clothing-optional." I shrug. "I usually am. I've been coming here since I was a child."

He nods. Even though nothing's visible between the dark water and the dark night, we mutually seem to try not to stare at each other. I tilt my head back and look up at the stars, mostly hidden by clouds tonight. Snow lands in my eye and I blink rapidly, looking back at the ground nearby. It's so quiet in the yard, the snow muting everything and the golden glow of lights partially obscured by the trees. Every once in a while, one of us moves and the water ripples across the space between us. He shifts and it laps against my breast like a tongue.

I can't stop thinking about it. "Are you still cold?" For some reason, I whisper. He moves toward me slightly, like he can't hear.

"I feel better," he says, just as quietly. I shift to hear. And suddenly we're sharing a rock ledge, sitting side by side. So close I might accidentally touch his fingers, our hands side-by-side bracing against the water sucking us away from our seats. "This is nice," he adds, staring out across the empty pool. Not looking at me. But eying me, I can tell, out of the corner of his eye.

"Yeah. I love it here. Sometimes I just come here and read."

"Naked?" I see his throat bob out of the corner of my vision. "When people are here?"

"Yeah," I repeat. "You should try it." *Omigod, what am I saying?* "You know, somewhere private. At a more exclusive hot spring. Where you don't have to worry about someone recognizing you."

"I'm not worried about it right now," he says softly. We look around at the silence and darkness. We might as well be the last two people in the world. Something about it feels dangerous. Reckless. Like nothing's stopping me from moving my hand. I could touch him now, on purpose, for maybe the first time since I've known him.

In the golden light, out of the corner of my eye, the sharp lines of his face are achingly beautiful. Like a movie poster that would be warm to the touch.

But I hate him. *Right? I hate him.*

"It's clean, right?" he asks suddenly. Clearly not thinking about me at all the way I am thinking about him. *Of course not.* It's hardly the first time he's been near a naked woman for non-sexual reasons. I saw his last movie. Reluctantly.

"Sulfur is antimicrobial," I say. *I think.* I clear my throat and lean away from him a little. Maybe I can subtly move back to the other ledge. I don't want to get carried away in the moment, the drunken feeling of this luxurious warmth and the first time I've brought someone outside my family to my special place.

"So...did you talk to Drew?" I ask. Zack had picked up his phone the minute we found Wi-Fi.

He rests his head on the rock behind him and closes his eyes. "Yes. He told me to enjoy being not-dead. Which I really am." He smiles, his eyes still closed. "I'm almost *hot* now. It's glorious."

I turn my head to look at him fully while his eyes are shut. Glorious. *He is. He really is.*

Shit. The sulfur smell is really going to my head. Zack Ryder is the enemy of everything I believe in. His very lifestyle makes a mockery of my own.

Or points out what I'm missing. Makes me think of wanting more.

"I cannot wait to climb into that big bed," he continues. "I am so tired."

"Um," I say, forcing the words out to get them out of the way. "Are you OK with sharing it?" I really, really don't want to sleep outside tonight.

His eyes pop open but he doesn't lift his head. "Of course," he says. "It's fine. We're both adults." He smiles and closes his eyes again. "I think I can manage to keep my hands off you, despite the circumstances."

Of course you can. God, I'm pathetic. Just another girl lusting after a movie star. Imagining if he just saw me for *who I am*, he'd want me back.

"It might be difficult," he continues. Eyes still closed. "Considering how I'm imagining you naked on all fours on those rock steps over there. But it won't be the first strict denial I've ever handled. You should have seen the diet I was on for my last movie."

I'm having an out-of-body experience. I'm having aural hallucinations. *Is this really happening? Did we die back on that trail?*

He's still talking about the diet he was on—chicken and rice, no alcohol, and he couldn't even put cow milk in his coffee—and I can't stop imagining him on top of me. With the cold snow melting against our hot bodies.

I stand abruptly, and I'm not sure all the wetness dripping down my legs is the spring water. "Let's go in," I say. "Don't want to faint from the heat."

I feel him watching me as I climb out of the pool and deliberately slow down my movements as I walk, naked, to pick up my robe. It's freezing, but everywhere his eyes brush over my skin, I'm on fire. *Touch me.* I think it fiercely at him. I have never, ever had this thought while at my hot spring. I've never been here with someone like Zack.

When I turn around, the robe still loose around me, he's right there. I look before I can stop myself and even his dick belongs on a movie poster. It's slightly hard. Maybe my thoughts aren't alone.

"Granola bars for dinner?" he asks, reaching around me for his own robe.

My hands feel numb as I try to tie the belt of my robe. I drop the ends twice before he reaches out and grabs them from me. His robe still hanging open, he wraps the fabric around me and yanks so I have to step into him. He ties it tightly around my waist.

"Fuck," I say. It just slips out. He's so close to me. My legs want to part for him. I can barely stand. *Take me right here.*

He looks down at me, eyes shadowed in the dark yard. "That can be arranged," he says.

eighteen

ZACK

I MAY HAVE OVER-PROMISED.

I haven't had sex without an NDA, a box of condoms, and a shower in at least four years. All of that requires advance notice, not spontaneity. And the women who would agree to those stipulations usually had some of their own. They didn't get surprised by going to bed with the character I played in a movie and waking up with Zack Ryder, average germaphobe.

It was the real—well, the *other*—reason I only slept with other people in the industry. Reason one is I only meet other people in the industry anymore.

But in this hippie commune Valentine has brought me to, we don't even have our own shower. The bathrooms are down the hall and shared.

Maybe if we'd turned around when Valentine first suggested it, we could have found a better room. All the hotels are probably packed with people stuck on the highway. But I don't regret ending up with only one bed.

Out in the dark, with nothing but water and the falling snow between us, nothing diluted my need. In this room, I can't stop wondering how clean the comforter is.

We sit cross-legged, wearing our robes, on the bed, as we unwrap a granola bar each for dinner. I'm actually starving, but that and the baggie of trail mix with nuts and chocolate in it are all we had in our backpacks from the hike. There's nothing nearby. The nearest restaurant is back in town. Valentine had apologized, like it was her fault.

"I might have some beef jerky in the car," she offers. But I heroically shake my head, despite my hunger, not wanting any future kissing to taste like dried meat.

And I want there to be more kisses. I'm just nervous about what comes after that, because my brain *won't stop*. It's running multiple tracks of fear over performance, fear of possible regret, fear she doesn't really want me, fear this room isn't that clean.

We each got another cup of hot chocolate from the community kitchen on our way back to the room. It's watery but tastes delicious. A luxury with our meager meal.

I get the feeling she's waiting for me to decide how this is going to go. This ongoing tension between us has become more expectant than the anger that has separated us in the past.

But I'm torn on how I want this to go. I'd washed my hands before eating, but the smell of sulfur lingers on our skin. The bedding in this room is scratchy and the bed is board-stiff.

Not my ideal seduction scenario. And usually, I need all the help I can get. I'm supposed to be a superstar. It's a lot to live up to.

She's waiting, silently, sitting across from me on the bed, nibbling at her snack dinner. I'm not cold anymore. I'm actually sweating in this rough terry cloth robe.

"So," I begin. "What do you think you'll do with all the footage you got on this trip?"

She smiles slightly, not quite looking at me. "I guess I'll cut it together into a bunch of little reels. Maybe do a supercut or something. A mini-documentary."

"It's not much of a narrative arc without something big at the end," I say. "Like if I hiked that 14er. That would be real character progression for me."

"That would take a lot of work," she says. Maybe I would have taken it as criticism in the past, but this time I grin.

"What, you think I'm afraid of hard work? Have you *seen* my before and after pictures from bulking up for my last movie?"

"They were hard to avoid," she replies. I think she might be blushing.

"I've lost it," I admit. "I'm not spending as much time in the gym."

"You still look..." she pauses, looking down at her hands. "Well, it's better in real life."

I know she finds me attractive. I got that vibe out at the hot spring. But it was almost better when she hated me. It took the pressure off. Now, I'm worried she wants to sleep with me despite herself. I'm not sure she actually *likes* me.

"I wasn't fishing for compliments, I swear," I force a laugh.

She hops off the bed, holding the robe closed as she does, and says, "wait a second" as she runs out of the room. While she's gone, I take stock of the situation and come to the conclusion I cannot have sex in this room. I'm not sure how sanitary it is, and I don't have any protection. I don't have my bespoke shampoo; my hair might smell bad. The lust won't last and we might get lice or something. It's too distracting to keep a hard-on.

I swallow hard as the realization sinks in. I'm going to disappoint her. *Again.*

She comes back with a dog-eared and well-used book with the title "Colorado Fourteeners."

"We can make a plan," she says, jumping back on the bed.

God, what is wrong with me. The way Valentine's robe gaps

open at the top, I can see the curve of her breast. Outside, I'd seen everything—everything possible in that poor lighting, anyway—and she'd been fearless about letting me look. She's soft and curvy in ways I haven't seen in awhile. And she's un-self-conscious in a way I don't remember ever being. The movie business has ruined me for regular people.

Not that Valentine is regular.

Sex is supposed to be *easy*, damnit. But I'm looking at this gorgeous woman, who has never pretended to be anything but who she is, and I can't stop hearing: *She doesn't know who you really are. She'll see the zit on your shoulder. She'll tell people if you fart in bed.*

"I'd like that," I say instead of voicing my thoughts. "Do you really think I can do it?"

"Of course," she replies easily, like she has no doubt. She ruins the little surge of confidence by continuing, "The main thing is to prepare and not be an idiot. You can do that, right?"

I shrug. "Remains to be seen."

She smiles at me. "Well, I'll tell you if you're being one, don't worry."

"Oh, I'm not worried about that." Valentine would probably call me an idiot now if she knew the fears running around in my head.

"What are you worried about?" she asks, pausing, the book held open between us to something called *Mosquito Range*. Yikes.

"Mosquitos?" I offer, looking down at the pages. I haven't seen a single one in Colorado, but who knows?

She snaps the book closed. "No, really. Don't brush me off like that. I think at this point I deserve some honesty. Haven't I earned that at least?"

I freeze. "Oh, um, of course. I mean. I wasn't trying to hide anything." My mouth keeps moving without my volition, confessing, "I worry about a lot of things."

She nods, giving me some relief from her intensity by looking down and fanning through the pages of the book. "I get that." She looks up. "Like I worry that I'll never leave Telluride."

I'm stunned that she just opened up to me. Again. What if I was one of those people who would tell her to *appreciate what you have* or *cheer up*? I'm not. But I *could* be. "I worry that I'll get old and people will stop putting me in movies because I'm only known for being a pretty face, not having real talent."

Still looking down at the book between us, she chimes in, "I worry that any talent I have is the equivalent of a child finger-painting because I have no training or education."

"I have that one too!" I shift closer to her on the bed. "I never went to college or acting school or anything."

"Really?" Her eyes are bright, assessing me. "I didn't either. Go to college."

I bite my lip to keep from reassuring her and add, "I worry that everyone will make fun of me for trying something. That the first time I tried may not be as good as it could be."

"Trying something new is hard," she agrees.

"I'm bad at being bad at things," I admit.

She nods again. She picks at the ragged corner of the book. I'm worried it's going to just give up and fall apart at the spine, so I take it from her and open it to the table of contents.

"I worry that you're not going to kiss me," she says. I look up at her. She's biting her lower lip, the fullness of it dented by her teeth.

I forget the book. It drops somewhere between us as I reach across and haul her toward me by the shoulders. She tastes like snow and chocolate. She fits on my lap like we choreographed it. My hand is inside her robe without me realizing I moved it there. She moans against my lips. Her long hair tickles my cheek.

I come back into my own body when I realize my dick is hard

and perilously close to entering her. "Um, I can't...we don't have..." I flail.

She slides her hand up my chest, through the opening in my robe. "What are you worried about?" she murmurs.

I pause, meeting her eyes. She's really asking. The question unlocks something in me, allowing me to reveal the secrets I didn't know how to say. I rest my forehead against hers and take a deep breath. In and out. "I'm worried I can't be in this moment now. I'm worried we don't have protection or showers. I'm worried I won't...be enough."

Her hand soothes me and lights my skin on fire at the same time. "We don't have to do anything else," she says. "Lie here with me and tell me why you want to climb a mountain."

We curl up, her on her left side and me wrapped around her from behind. Still in our robes, I rest my hand over her breast. She strokes my hand, linking her pinkie with mine. I put my nose in her hair and speak through the warm scent of her neck as I explain how it felt to look out over an empty vista and know I'd walked there on my own two feet.

And slowly, my hand grows bold without me. "Is this OK?" I whisper, sliding that hand down her breast so the tie on her robe opens further. "Just this?"

She turns her head back over her shoulder so our faces almost touch. "I'm OK," she says. "You're OK?"

Nodding, I keep moving my hand. I'm not worried about anything right now, with the feel of her skin under mine so natural, and my insides warmer than an inferno. I kiss her again, finally, reaching over her shoulder to do it, and my body screams, *what took you so long?* Her lips are chapped, and that keeps me grounded. Valentine is so new and different from anyone I've been with since I moved to Hollywood. She's more like the girls I used to date back home in Ohio, but the fire inside of her burns so brightly I can't really compare her to anyone else.

I want to stay in this moment with her. The way her long hair tickles my ear. How her skin jumps when I flick her peaked nipple. She's spreading her hips for me, letting the robe fall open further for me to explore. I'm hard and I'd like to sink into her, but I stick with what I'm ready for and slide into her core with my fingers.

Fuck, looking down at Valentine like this, her eyes closed, speared on my fingers, it's hard to remember how much I disliked her a few days ago. I imagine her opening her eyes and yelling at me again, and whether that could cure my intense need. "Valentine," I whisper. "Tell me if I'm doing it right."

She takes my hand and shows me the geography of her body, where to touch and where not to. She does it without yelling, without calling me a fool. And I listen. I learn. I trace the shape of her body with my tongue. I consider going into amateur adult film so I can preserve the way her ribs curve into her waist and her strong thighs into the center of her body. She's responsive, giving soft little moans and gasps as I work my way from top to bottom and back up again. I take her hand off my dick once, unable to handle it. I dip my head and touch my tongue to her core and wish I could go back in time and tell myself I'm an idiot for forgetting her name. I determine to make her forget it now.

And it feels like climbing a mountain, the view at the end of Valentine gasping and arching her back, her nails digging into my forearm. She makes a small sound that I want to hold in my memory forever.

"You sure?" she whispers, when I curl up around her again, my hand over her heart on naked skin. I nod. She nuzzles her head under my chin and falls asleep. And it's enough. More than enough for a lonely movie star whose dates never want to sleep over. I smell her hair and fall into a deep sleep.

nineteen

VALENTINE

THIS MOFO BETTER PAY ME.

I woke up grumpy. I woke up cold on my side of the bed because Zack stole all the covers and marooned me alone, like maybe he didn't want to touch me anymore. I woke up smelling of sulfur, because I didn't shower the night before. I woke up hungry, because our dinner of snacks hadn't touched my post-hike hunger. And I woke up poorer, because it turned out Zack didn't have enough money on him to pay for the room.

Oblivious to my thoughts, he comments on the pristine snow on the drive back to his house. "What a reboot! It's gorgeous out here."

Grunting in reply, I hold my tongue. We'd packed up and left before 8—I hadn't even said goodbye to Daisy, just left a note to put the room on my tab—because the closest restaurant was either back home or the opposite direction from the one we wanted to go.

And Zack had rolled over that morning and said, before

anything else, "How soon can we get back?" I'd known then, for sure, that our night together was nothing but a night.

The road had reopened overnight and the sun was out, so at least the driving conditions don't match my mood.

I didn't sleep well. I woke up part way through the night, no longer in Zack's arms—he'd gotten up to go to the bathroom, but in the haze between awake and dreaming, it felt like he'd disappeared—wondering why the *fuck* I'd let the rich asshole I've been feuding with touch me just because he whispered a few flimsy secrets in my ear. Of course the famous movie star would fuck around with the town girl when he was trapped in a room with me and had no other way home. He gave me just enough to keep me from asking too many questions, didn't he? But I'd been the most vulnerable one. This is a man who couldn't be bothered to remember my name a few days ago.

So I haven't been *held* the way he did before we fell asleep in...well. *Has anyone ever held me like that?* I remember my mother wrapped around me in bed once when I was 16 and my stupid date didn't show up. Then my mother, in true Valkyrie fashion, rained down holy hell on that boy via his own mother. The story got around town and his mom burst into tears the next time we ran into her in the grocery store. His family moved away before the end of the year.

I need to channel my mother more often. Then I wouldn't end up in situations like last night, laying stiff as a board next to the hottest man I've ever seen naked as he snored through the night, comfortable in the knowledge his *millions of dollars* are safe and far away.

Cuddles are not a form of payment. I should charge him for mileage, too.

Our conversation about climbing 14ers was meaningless. My mind was full of ideas for getting him acclimatized, getting up before sunrise to hike, showing him my favorite places. My heart was full of ideas, too. *I'm an idiot.* He probably has a whole system for disposable one-night-stands. I'm about to be let down easy. As soon as he doesn't need me any more for a ride.

As we're nearing the gate to his property, it opens for us before I can stop at the little talking box. Blucifer hauls us up the long drive and when we stop at the door on the side of the house, he takes off his seatbelt and says, "Come in?"

I don't even have his direct number, so of course I'm coming in. I'm going to get some money out of this misadventure.

So I pat Blucifer on the dash and follow him inside the giant house. We don't see anyone as we walk in, I suppose because it's early.

Zack is tapping at his cell phone. "Drew says there's leftover quiche in the fridge and apparently we still have some apple fritters."

I want to say no, get my money, and leave quickly. But my stomach growls, so I follow him into the kitchen and devour one of my dad's pastries in two bites. Zack is barely finished washing his hands by the time I grab another one.

"My trainer would kill me," he laughs, as he takes a tiny bite of his own pastry. I watch him, the way he uses a napkin to clean the sticky icing off instead of licking his fingers. There's something *delicate* about him. I'm not sure why I ever thought he could throw me on the rocky ground and take me, even with a blatant invitation.

Last night, his tongue spread me out and made a meal of me. This morning, I suspect his empty stomach went to his head.

I need to get out of here. "So," I begin, at the same time he says: "Do you want a shower?"

Thrown, I hesitate. He probably has like five bathrooms in this place, right? *This doesn't mean anything.*

I don't know why I'm still looking for secret *meanings* in what he says. He's probably hoping I forget everything about last night, as well as the money he owes me. He's probably the kind of guy who tips less than 20% if the waitress didn't keep his water glass filled, even though he can afford to buy the restaurant.

"Are you mad at me?" he asks, and I realize I've been glaring at him in silence for half a minute. "It's up to you, but I just need to get out of these clothes."

And he pulls his half-zip off over his head. He drops it on the floor and folds in half to undo his laces.

The bite of apple fritter still left drops out of my hand to the floor.

I look at it as he toes off his boots and socks and then drops the slinky skirt that he'd put back on this morning. He's not wearing underwear.

He's standing in the kitchen wearing nothing and I'm frozen in front of him. I open my mouth but have no idea what to say so I close it again. I'd been absolutely certain in my anger a moment ago. I miss having thoughts in my head.

The golden morning night coming in the wall-sized windows overlooking the private yard burnish his skin. He looks like he'd be warm to the touch, and delicious, like one of these pastries.

I realize I'm holding my empty hand up like it's still holding the pastry, reaching half-way toward Zack, and drop it.

He raises one eyebrow at me. "I'm taking a shower. Come if you want." And he turns and walks back into the house. His butt is incredible. It's not a regular-person butt at all. It's high and tight and has muscles I've never seen on a real person. He glances back over his shoulder at me once. "And I do mean come," he adds.

I'm following him without realizing I decided to move. *What am I doing?* My mind is freaking out independent of my body. *He's fucking with you!* The angry warning is loud enough to almost drown out the small, insecure question hiding in the back of my mind: *Why does he want me?*

The bathroom he leads me to is enormous. He walks directly into a gold-framed standing shower and turns on at least four shower heads at once. "You coming in like that?" he teases me, standing there with the water flowing over his naked body.

My eyes follow the water over the planes of his chest and the cut lines of his stomach. I hadn't gotten a chance to study him last night. I'd been selfish, making it all about chasing my orgasm. I'd regretted it in the middle of the night, wondering about his body. I'd touched his cock once and felt the shape of it. I wanted more but my insecurities got in the way.

I don't want him to think I'm uninterested, so I toe off my shoes. The floor I'm standing on is warm and starts to heat the bottoms of my feet. It's inviting, and so is the steam starting to fill the shower. *In or out, Valentine. Make a decision.*

He runs a hand down his front. The boldness with which he stripped down and is now lathering himself with soap in front of me tells a story of a man who has honed his body for other people's eyes. It's not like last night, when he hid in his robe and let me be the one exposed. This morning, he's ready.

I remember some of the worries he'd shared and realize I might not be the only one with insecurities.

"OK," I say. I start tearing my clothes off in a hurry, so I don't start arguing again with my smarter side. "But only because I'm so dirty."

"Yeah, you are," he smirks at me as I hurry toward him. Once I'm enveloped in the cloud of steam, he closes the glass door behind me.

"Can I touch you?" he asks, holding out a hand gloved in some kind of loofah and covered in suds.

I nod. I'm holding both arms over my breasts like some kind of prude and force myself to drop them. I'm not embarrassed of my body. I've never stepped foot in a gym, but I hike a lot and have my mother's genes. And Zack has seen most of it already. But in these lush surroundings, I feel awkward, like I'm meant to be a picture — someone *extra* — and I'm just...Valentine.

"I've been tested recently," he tells me quietly. "You?"

I'm still on my parents' health insurance, and I take advantage of it. I nod.

The heat from the shower and his nearness makes my blood boil as he soaps me up, running the scratchy glove up and down my skin: each leg, both arms, my butt. It tingles when he runs it gently over my breasts, even getting the skin underneath the mounds. Then he braces the gloved hand on my hip and runs his bare hand over my slightly-rounded stomach and lower.

I widen my stance, more because I'm afraid I'm going to fall over than to give him access, but I still have to grab his shoulder when he touches me down there.

I'm wet, and so are his fingers, so they slide into me easily. He uses his thumb to rub circles around my clit and gently thrust in and out with his hand. He really was listening last night, when I showed him how I like to be touched. I'd given him so much power over me without realizing what I was doing. Now he's using it to bring me almost to release in under a minute.

His face is so close to mine and his hard cock is resting against my hip. I grip his shoulder so tightly I'm leaving white marks with my fingers. My nipples are pointing at his face and he takes one into his mouth and moans around it. "Fuck," I ramble, my mouth opening without permission. "I hate you. What are you doing to me?"

He laughs a little around my nipple and I gasp before he lets it go and steps back. "Whyyyy?" I protest, again hearing myself speak before realizing I'd opened my mouth.

Still grinning, he gently pushes me to step back, and I find myself sitting on a ledge staring at his dick. *What? Does he expect me to take him in my mouth?* I try to stand up again and nearly butt him in the face with my head. He probably has some kind of one-blow-job-a-day minimum standard, but I'm not going to be one of those girls who's grateful for celebrity dick in the face.

"Just wait," he urges me. He gently pushes on my shoulders until I sit down again, his face serious. When our eyes meet, my thighs part a little more. *Fuck.* I cannot resist this man. Does that make me just like all the other girls?

"I hate that I want you," I say. But I do. I want his tongue to lick the droplets of water all over my body. I want him inside me *badly*.

Still leaning over me, blocking the water from hitting me in the face, he smiles. "Why?"

"Everyone wants you," I whisper. The way his arms are braced around me, it's like we're in a quiet bubble in the corner of the shower. The steam is so thick I can't see outside the glass and his body blocks out the sound of the rushing water.

"But not everyone can have me," he replies. The way his eyes are locked on mine makes me want to do anything he asks. I arch my back and lift my feet up to brace them against the ledge, on display for him.

"Can I touch you?" I whisper, my hand half-way to his body. He nods and I take his cock in my fist and pump it twice. This cock is meant to be inside me. I can tell it'd be the perfect fit, full and hot. Maybe I will take him into my mouth, after all. I want to mix his cum with the last bits of sugar on my lips.

"Fuck," he says and falls to his knees in the shower. I get a face full of water that distracts me until his mouth is buried between my legs and his tongue is diving inside me.

I gasp, spit out the water I almost inhale, and clench around him. He sucks hard on my clit and my leg slips, almost kicking him in the face. He throws it over his shoulder. I scramble to find a handhold on the smooth shower wall as he goes down on me, licking and sucking. I'm completely at his mercy for balance, half braced against the ledge and half against his body, unable to move and quivering from the sensation of his mouth.

Just when my fear of drowning in the unending spray of water starts to overwhelm how good it feels, he carefully props me back up in the corner and stands up. He flexes his calves a few times before he says, "Just one second." He gets out of the shower and I sit there, on the knife edge of orgasm, staring at the foggy corner of the shower. *How did I get here? I should go. I should definitely leave right now.*

I don't think I move before he returns, tearing open a condom and rolling it on.

He pulls me to my feet and I fall into his mouth, tongues clashing for space. His dick is so hard it almost enters me unaided. I curl a leg around his hip to help it and then he's inside me and we both gasp, mouths breaking free. It fits like I knew it would. Like a piece that has been missing.

He meets my eyes again and holds my gaze as we rock against each other like that for a minute, unable to get much leverage. When he releases me and turns me around, I miss the look in his eyes. It was like we were in each other's heads, mentally holding hands. *In this together.*

He props one of my legs on the ledge and re-enters me from behind. He has one hand on my hip, guiding me as he thrusts, and with the other he reaches around and touches my clit, rubbing gently in circles until I start to "hmm" when the pressure builds and releases with a wave of pleasure that leaves me gasping against the shower wall, trying to hold my weight up as he finishes inside me. He rests his cheek on my back for a moment, holding me to his chest with his arms around my waist. When that becomes uncomfortable for both of us, he pulls me to my feet, arms still wrapped around me, and slips out of me. He holds me like that under the shower spray, letting us both cool down and wash off, his head lolling against my shoulder. As I come down from the adrenaline and endorphins, I start to feel sleepy, like I could doze off standing there in his arms.

But he finally turns off the water and wraps us both in a towel the size of a sheet. Still holding me from behind, he marches us into a bedroom three times the size of the huge bathroom and falls into the enormous bed.

I laugh, trying to unwind myself from the folds of towel and blanket over my face without slipping out of his reassuring embrace. He laughs with me, but we finally have to give up and let go of one another. I clench my hand and watch him as he sorts out the situation, face turned away, wondering if our moment is over. Wondering if I've fallen, yet again, into the same situation I'd woken up fearing this morning.

When I get back from a quick run to the bathroom to use the toilet, he's under the bedding and holds the comforter open for me. I slide back in and under his arm. It feels familiar, now, like his scent and his warmth are embedded in my skin. He meets my eyes and keeps them open as we kiss, gently this time, just lips catching against lips.

Perhaps I should say something. "What does this mean?" or "can we do this again?" Instead I say, "Are you really going to climb that mountain?"

His lips curve. "Only with your help," he says. His breath brushes against my cheek.

"Promise?" I whisper. It feels silly after I say it, much too serious for whatever this is, but he doesn't bat an eye.

"Promise," he agrees.

We fall asleep like that, my head tucked under his chin, naked limbs on top of limbs and hair still damp from the shower.

When we wake up later, I take my messy hair out of its braid and he combs it with his fingers, spreading it out on the sheets as he takes me again, from the front this time, eyes open and looking at my face as I come.

twenty

ZACK

WOMEN USUALLY LEAVE before they go to sleep post-coital, in my experience. It's not that I kick them out, it's that there's a sort of realistic expectation—probably set by all the negotiations beforehand—we're not going to actually sleep together.

Once I even asked a woman to stay and she said no. Tessa. We'd never spoken again.

If anyone actually needed to be *kicked out*, Drew would do it. But nicely. They always put the women in a car that will take them wherever they need to go—even Sacramento for that one woman who abruptly decided she didn't want to be an actress, after all, and evacuated Hollywood to stay with family. Amanda. I wish I didn't still think about her. I'm not sure if I'm worried or jealous. But her Instagram suggests she's living a happy, fulfilled life up north. Not cursing Zack Ryder for changing the course of her destiny.

One night with me and women start to think about what they're missing. Whether it's their own, empty bed or a life outside of Hollywood, I seem to be the deciding factor that settles the question of "stay or go?"

But Valentine is still there when I open my eyes a couple of hours later. Her hair, out of the braid, is fanned out across the pillow between us. It's tickling my face, which woke me up, but I don't move.

The house is silent. I'd asked Drew to clear the staff for the day. Most of the crew doesn't get in until tomorrow morning, and I wanted—*what?*—one more day to not think about the film festival, or my career, or how many calories are in those amazing apple fritters. Vacation. That's what being with Valentine feels like.

I reach over and grab my phone. "Enjoy playing hooky," Drew has written back.

The rest of my messages are unimportant or can wait. I scan them and then put the phone face-down on "do not disturb."

But when I turn back to her, her eyes are open, and she's frowning at me. She sits straight up in bed. "What time is it?"

"It's eleven," I reply, sitting up with her. She doesn't bother to pull up the sheets to cover her naked breasts, which are really one of the nicest pairs I've seen. Heavier than I expected—the deception made sense after seeing her pull off a sports bra earlier, the compression leaving marks—and round.

"I should go." She slides out of bed.

Of course she wants to go. My stomach hollows out. "Do you have to?" The words come out before I can stop them. We've established oversharing at this point. We say whatever we think to one another.

I hate you, she'd said in the shower. But it sounded like something else.

She looks at me strangely. She's standing there naked, not hiding herself. Unashamed of her body, like she'd been at the hot spring. She's a revelation compared to the women I've been with recently, women who constantly doubt their perfect bodies. "You don't want me to?"

"Well, no. I thought..." I don't know what I thought. "My day is free," I say.

"Oh." Now she crosses her arms over her chest and bites her lip. I'm not sure what I said that made her feel less comfortable. Then she drops her arms and her face clears. "Sorry. I'm just... hangry."

"*Oh!*" This I understand. When I was doing two hours in the gym every day and eating nothing but chicken, rice, and vegetables on a strict schedule, I snapped at everybody.

I hop out of bed and grab a pair of boxer briefs. "There's a robe on the back of the bathroom door if you want it. I'll be in the kitchen making food!"

Well, I'll be heating up food. The only thing I know how to make is cereal, or the very fancy chocolate flan I learned for *The Today Show*. I'm useless for anything in between.

I dig around in the cupboards and find pancake mix and granola. There are eggs in the fridge, and cheese and yogurt. I put the ingredients all on the counter and am considering my options when Valentine comes into the kitchen. She's wearing my robe. The flannel one with the fuzzy lining that my mother got me, not the silk one I got in an Oscars gift bag last year. Even though they were hanging side by side on the door.

It makes me smile. Of course Valentine chose warm and cozy over luxurious and pretentious. That's one of the things I like about her.

"Do you want any of these?" I ask her, gesturing at the uncooked building blocks of breakfast. "Because the only one I can guarantee won't taste terrible is the one where I dump things in a bowl."

She looks from me to the ingredients and then smiles. "Sit down. I'll make us pancakes and eggs."

I grimace. "This isn't one of those times where you have to take on additional labor because I'm incompetent, is it?"

"I mean, yes." She shoves me playfully so I sit on one of the stools at the kitchen island. "But I also want to eat something edible for breakfast. So I'll do it."

"Show me?" I suggest. "Then I can do it next time."

I see the moment we both realize what I said—*next time*—and her smile flickers a little but doesn't fall. She tells me to get out a mixing bowl, and I open every cabinet before I find them.

"Do you have people to do *everything* for you?" she asks.

"It's one of those snowball situations where somebody tells you you need a trainer and an assistant, and then those people tell you you need a bodyguard and a nutritionist, and then it just keeps going until I have no idea who does what for me anymore and don't remember how I used to function when I just had half an apartment in Pasadena and worked three jobs that barely covered my rent. Also, my mom never taught me to cook."

"Well, I learned from my dad," she says.

I hesitate and then admit I never had a dad, but she nods instead of giving me the sympathetic head-tilt I often get from people, and the conversation moves on.

She shows me how to "eyeball" the pancake mix to make sure it's the right consistency, which I have no confidence I can repeat. She wraps around me from behind to show me how to whip the eggs into a froth, a lesson I will never forget now. I didn't get that kind of hands-on lesson from *The Today Show*. And she takes the knife from me when I try to chop up some cheese, saying, "I am not going to be responsible for Zack Ryder cutting off his fingers with that technique."

I watch her use the knife in "what is known as the safe way," but I don't really get the difference. It can't be more dangerous than the stunt I did on a motorcycle attached to a cable being dragged by a film truck, right? But I don't argue. I'm not insured against cheese injury.

It doesn't take her long to whip up a breakfast that looks like something my mom used to cook. "You can do it all," I tell her after searching all the cupboards to find maple syrup. I finally find it in the fridge.

"Well, I have to," she replies with a shrug. I get that it's a dig at my surplus of assistants, but it also makes me curious.

"Do you live with your parents?"

She scoffs. "No. I mean, I sleep there sometimes. Or shower. Do my laundry." She makes a face. "I guess I basically live there. That's where my mail goes."

I nod, although I don't completely understand. But it doesn't seem that weird to me. "Somebody else gets my mail, too."

She laughs. "So we're the same?"

Grinning, I stuff another bite of syrup-soaked pancake in my mouth. I'm on vacation from my diet for the day. "We have more in common than I expected, that's all."

She ducks her head back to her breakfast, but she's smiling. "Me too."

twenty-one

VALENTINE

ZACK IS ENTHRALLED with the photos I took on the top of Colorado 14ers.

"You can see the tops of *other* mountains!" he says.

We're cuddled up on the giant couch in the living room. I'd had to wrestle my way out from under Zack's weighted blanket, his limbs across my lap already making me too hot. He'd laughed at my flailing, and I'd shot back, "You could train for backpacking by carrying this thing around."

So he tried it, wrapping the heavy blanket around his shoulders and marching around the room. "Am I ready yet?" he demanded, as I giggled on the couch.

"Maybe this could be your audition for a comedy," I suggest, even though I have misgivings about bringing up Zack's work. He seems so much more relaxed now than he has when discussing his upcoming movie.

But he smiles at this. "Or a superhero role." He holds the edges of the blanket around his neck like a cape and stretches his other arm in front of him like he can take off and fly around the room. "Anxiety Man."

"I like it."

"Drawing on lived experience," he grins, and flops back down on the couch with me. He throws his arm around my shoulders, like it's natural. Like we've always sat together this way. "Show me more of your adventures."

So I show him the video I made last time I climbed Mt. Sneffels, taking the Southwest Ridge route. I captured the steep crags and serrated ridges of the mountain myself, as well as the journey up — from spotting bighorn sheep to collapsing toward the end.

He asks me the kind of questions no one asks about my videos: how I got a certain shot, why I chose an angle. My answer to most of his questions is "necessity," which is embarrassing, except he says he did the same thing with his new movie. "Most of the money went to the cast."

"Do you ever think about your next idea in the shower? Or, you know, when you're outside just trying to enjoy the mountain air, are you distracted thinking about a shot?"

"Yes!" I turn to him, so our faces are close together. "Even though I like making these videos, I don't like how they're constantly on my mind. Even when I just want to be in the moment."

He nods, playing with the end of my braid, flicking it through his fingers. "That's how I was with this movie. I thought once it was finished, I'd go back to normal, but no. I still think about how I could have done a shot better. Edited it differently. How I want to try again."

"Did you think about it all the time before you made it?" Sometimes, I can exorcize an idea once I bring it to life. Sometimes I can't quite execute it, and it lives with me for weeks.

"Yeah. That's why I made it. I couldn't get the ideas, the

pictures out of my head." He rests his head on my shoulder. "My mom says I'm an artist."

"You are," I say instantly. Based on the way he talks, I have no doubt about this. Even though — it stops me to realize — I never would have considered it of the man I knew only from magazines and movie posters.

"Then so are you," he replies. "But you knew that already."

I hesitate. Sure, I like to think of myself that way, but I only make 6- to 60-second videos for the internet. That I give away free. Zack has a movie people are dissecting online in forums. His work could become a meme I use in a future video. But I say, "Yeah. That's how my parents raised me."

"What was it like growing up with a dad?" Zack sits up. "Sorry. That's a dumb question."

"It's not dumb." I lower his head to my shoulder again and tell him about my dad taking me on my first overnight back-packing trip. It was just the two of us. I was eight and had been so proud of my heavy pack, even though Dad carried most of the gear. He'd let me put up the tent all by myself, only staking it down for me so I didn't hammer my fingers or toes.

"I have no idea how to put up a tent," Zack admits. "That sounds hard. Is it hard?"

So I jump up and run outside to get my tent from Blucifer and show him. He looks skeptical when I empty the metal tubes and fabric out onto the living room floor. But he picks up the trick to snapping the supports together immediately.

"It's not hard at all!" Zack shouts, once we put both ends of the frame into the body of the tent and lift so the fabric instantly becomes tent-like. "We did it!"

I laugh at his joy.

"We should try making a fire next!" he suggests, getting carried away with how competent he feels.

"It's a little warm out," I say skeptically. "And you won't be making a fire much camping in Colorado," I add, stomping all over his vision. "But, sure, we can," I add, seeing his face fall.

"No, no, let's enjoy what we have. Gotta live in the moment," he decides. Worrying about reality interfering with our dreaming is going to bring him down, so I don't blame him for instinctively rejecting going down that path.

We crawl into the tent together, bringing the weighted blanket with us.

"You've done so many cool things," he tells me, as we lay looking up at the roof of the tent from inside. The light filters in from the big windows in front of us.

"Right back at you," I reply. And for once, I don't compare our things in a way that makes me feel smaller. I just enjoy resting in the crook of his arm, taking up space.

twenty-two

ZACK

BY MID-AFTERNOON, my living room is covered with printed maps and notes, like we're filming some detective show. But, instead, we're planning my mountain climbing adventure. Valentine spent an hour debating the merits of every 14er in the state with herself, trying to pick my target. I've been set on Mt. Sneffels since she showed me her video, even though she warned it's a "class 3 in some places," whatever that means.

I already got my trainer to send me a quick draft of a plan to acclimatize and prepare for climbing that many steps.

Valentine wrote an outline of a script for a documentary about Zack Ryder learning to climb a mountain that we both giggled over for an hour. We'd gotten into the alcohol that the festival sent as a gift celebrating his premiere. It was labeled "breakfast wine" and Valentine had mocked it before noticing it was made from Colorado grapes and suggesting we try it.

It's syrupy, but we keep drinking it.

When I kiss her, she tastes like grapes and sugar, too—like a break from all my rules and something else to think about besides my fast-approaching debut. We laze on the big sofa in the main room, me needling Valentine with the idea of taking the wine with us on the hike. "Sugar, carbs; it's basically electrolytes," I insist, laughing at her appalled reaction. She's holding the hydration pack she brought in from the car close to her chest, like I might ruin it with just the thought.

"The Talent needs to take this seriously!" she yells, teasing me. She'd admitted that's how she thought of me in her head for some time.

"*The Talent*," I laugh. "Can put whatever stipulations he wants in the contract."

"OK," she says, suddenly jumping up and running out of the room just when I was thinking a nap sounds nice.

"Good idea," I say, following her to the bedroom. "It's been hours since we had sex."

She's holding her phone, which she'd left on the bedside table. "Ugh! No one can take my shift tonight. Julie can take half of it but..." She looks up at me, biting her lower lip. "I have to go."

I stand stock still in the doorway, startled, having never considered the possibility she'd have to leave. My toes on the bare floor are cold. She's going to walk out my front door and leave me in an empty house with nothing but worry to fill it. As the thoughts about tomorrow start to creep in from the mental box I've kept them in all day, I say, "I'll go with you!"

"What? Really?" She studies me, a look on her face like she's not sure I'm real.

"Yes! I'll just hang out at the bar. We can practically walk there from here. Do you have what you need?"

"I have to run to my parents' house. I left my work shoes there."

"I'll come with you!" I volunteer again. At the puzzled face she's still giving me, I hesitate. "That's OK, isn't it? And then...we can come back here?" I can't be alone tonight.

Her face clears, and suddenly she's smiling at me. "OK," she agrees. "It's OK. We only have to be there a couple hours. And then we can...come back."

"Great!" I only realize right then that I'm not giving her the movie poster smile—I'm wearing my real one. The one I can't really picture in my head because I never practice it in the mirror or let it be photographed.

"We have some time," she adds. "Do you want to drive to town and then take the gondola up?"

"The gondola goes to...your work?"

"Yes," she says, eyeing me like I've lost my mind. "Haven't you seen it running up the mountain? The station is right in town."

"I thought that was for skiers and cyclists to get up the mountain."

"No, it's public transportation. The only kind like it in the country. You've never taken the gondola? But that's a Telluride experience!"

I grimace, because the fact that I haven't really "experienced" Telluride is the source of most of our previous friction. "You know me," I say weakly. "This ridiculously oversized house is really just a hideout. People make me nervous, and I don't know if I even remember how to drive."

Self-deprecation seems to have worked on Valentine, smoothing over her memory of how annoying she used to find me. She smiles. "Well, you're with me now. I'll keep you safe from the mob. And nobody drives Blucifer but me."

You're with me now. I know she's teasing, but the words hit like seeing my name linked to a co-star in a tabloid. *Is that true?* I almost wonder, for a split second, if I fell into a relationship without realizing it. But this time is different. This time I'm writing the headline in my own mind: *Finally, Zack Ryder Finds His Match!* It's too much, too fast. I try to wipe the words from my brain as though she'll see them written there in bold type font.

"I'm willing to try, as long as you protect me." I give her the movie star smile and reach for my sunglasses. *I'm cool. This is just a casual outing with my casual lover.* I'll tuck some antibacterial gel in my pocket and be fine.

I hold Valentine's hand on our way to her parents' house, until the twisting roads get too challenging. My fear of dying overrules my sentimentality. We walk from the empty house to downtown, where the gondola station sits. She's right—I should have noticed this before. It's a big building with huge cables running out of it and up the hill. Big, enclosed gondolas run at regular intervals along the cables, reminding me of a ferris wheel.

I pull my cap down further over my forehead as we approach the busy building. Two long lines are queued up in front of it, moving steadily into the building. "Are you sure..." I begin to ask if this is a good idea, but she grabs my hand and pulls me up to the woman standing behind a booth at the front of the lines.

"Hey, Darla."

Darla looks up from an iPad. "Hey, Valentine! We don't see you here very often."

"Yeah, I usually drive. But I have a guest." Valentine gestures at me briefly. Darla's eyes widen slightly when they land on me, and of course I notice, because I'm hyper-aware of the people in the crowd watching us, too.

"Do you think we could have our own..."

"Of course!" Darla answers before Valentine even finishes the sentence. She turns and looks over her shoulder inside the building. The gondolas coming downhill sweep through the building slowly, allowing people to hop on and off before they complete their half-circle and head back up the hill. "Go ahead," she says, waving us in.

As I follow Valentine into the building, Darla adds in an undertone, her head ducked, "I love your movies."

I never know how to respond to shy fans. Should I push an autograph or a photo on them, as though that must be what they truly desire? In the end, I flash her a high-watt smile, letting my relief show. "You're a lifesaver, Darla."

I follow Valentine into the building, which buzzes with the sound of moving machinery. Valentine steps into an empty gondola as it moves slowly past us. I follow her in, swallowing my fears about the lack of a secondary exit if anyone follows us in.

Sure enough, Darla has screwed up her courage and is standing at the open door as I sit down. She's holding her phone. "I shouldn't ask, but...would you mind?" She's walking beside the gondola as we move along.

I slide to the edge of the bench seat near the door so I can grin over her shoulder as she holds up the phone for a selfie.

"Omigod, thank you so much!" Darla stops just before walking into the "Don't go beyond this line" sign and waves at us enthusiastically as our gondola moves past it. The door automatically slides closed, and we're locked in as the gondola leaves the floor of the building behind, jolts slightly, and starts moving quickly up the hill.

I swallow. It's not that I'm claustrophobic, but fame has turned enclosed spaces into traps in the past. I look beyond Valentine, out the windows that surround us at the other gondolas on the cable ahead of us and to our left. I look over my shoulder at the ones behind us. There are three people staring back at me from the gondola following ours. They wave, and I wave back weakly before turning back around. I try to smile at her and not worry about being mobbed at the top of the mountain.

"See? It's quiet in here," she observes. And she's right. The scenery — trees beside us, trails below us, and a mountain vista with the town nestled in the valley behind us — goes by slowly enough to enjoy it. There's a breeze from the open windows at the top of the mostly-clear gondola.

I take a deep breath and nod. "How long is the ride up to Mountain Village?"

"It's about 12 minutes unless we stop."

I lick my lips. "Does that happen often?"

"Every once in a while. People bring bikes up, and they have to be attached to the gondolas. Things like that slow it down." Valentine looks beautiful, sitting across from me framed against the backdrop of the green and brown behind her. The breeze lifts the tendrils of hair around her face that are escaping the braid resting on her shoulder. And she's smiling at me, happy in my company. I don't want to take that for granted.

"So, why don't you take this to work every day?"

She makes a face. "It's mostly for tourists."

"Hey! You told me it was a Telluride experience."

"It is! You know how it is when you live somewhere full-time, though. You take things for granted."

"Not you," I deny. "You're so passionate about the mountains and trails around here."

She shrugs a little, like I'm making her uncomfortable. "I guess."

"You guess? No, you are. And you know everything about them."

"They're all I've ever known. And I still don't know everything. I have to look up flowers and birds sometimes."

I scoff, but before I can reply, I notice we're approaching

another building. I tense, but Valentine doesn't reach for her backpack.

"We don't get out here," she says. "It's the next stop. We'll just pass through."

The door on the gondola's right side slides open when we reach the building, and Valentine slides to the edge and waves at a worker — clearly someone else she knows. I pull my cap further down. The gondola keeps moving through the mostly-empty building.

When the gondola behind us reaches the building, there's a commotion with the people inside it. One of them hops out and, as though in slow motion, I watch them start to run toward me, only to be stopped by the worker.

I slump on the bench seat.

"It's OK," Valentine says. The door slides closed again, and we're through, heading out the other side of the building. "This happens to you a lot, huh?"

I shrug. "Not as often here."

Abruptly, the gondola slows and then comes to a halt, swaying slightly in mid-air. I look around. The gondola behind us is empty now. But the people in the nearest gondola heading downhill are waving. I can't help imagining someone clawing open one of these doors to try to reach me and plummeting to their death. Nightmare. Meanwhile, the people who just vacated the gondola behind us could be calling all their friends to swarm me at the top of the hill.

Valentine turns to look when I wave back. "I think they're just being friendly," she offers. She gestures at me. "Come over here."

I switch to her side, but carefully, as though the weight will make the gondola fall. It only shifts slightly, the massive hardware it's hanging from unaffected.

She takes my hand. I smile down at the gesture, still not used to it. "If this box wasn't made of glass, I'd go down on you to distract you."

My eyes widen and my cock jumps in my pants. "That's OK," I manage. "The idea is just about distracting enough."

She hasn't done that yet. I didn't think she wanted to, and I was OK with that. But the idea of my dick in her mouth — the mouth that, until recently, mostly scolded me — makes me wish for more privacy. *Immediately.*

"But I think we could make out a little," she suggests. That mouth is smirking a little at me, a small twist letting me know she's into this idea. Then she puts her hand, hidden behind the back of the bench seat, onto my crotch. And cups her fingers.

I take a breath and smell fresh air and Valentine, which are basically the same thing for me. She always smells like evergreen and the flowers that line the trails. And the mountain air, as we hang above it, brings out the wildness in her. In us. In what we're doing.

It feels like it does when my best ideas strike me, like a spark lit under my skin. A concept combined with the belief I can make it reality.

She touches her lips to mine, and I take her tongue into my mouth and forget who I am, where I am, what I'm worried about. Not quite enough to touch her face with my germy hands, which I leave at my sides, letting her have control of guiding the tilt of our heads. But enough that I don't care if long-lens photographs are being taken of us through this gondola's windows. Unlikely, but always possible.

For her, I'll risk it. There's not much I wouldn't risk, I realize, as the gondola starts to move again. Already, my heart is more involved than it has been in a life-long series of former relationships.

Already, I'm planning for the next time we're alone, and the intimacy I imagine doesn't just involve us naked. Sure, I want to know whether she's ever had sex on top of a mountain — and whether she'd try it with me. But, even more, I want to know what she dreams about, the next idea she has for short-form video content, and where she wants to hike next.

Dangling in mid-air in this gondola, I'm not sure where we're going to end up, but I'm eager to get there with her.

twenty-three

VALENTINE

"WILL you keep those suspenders on later?" Zack's teasing me as we walk into The Bivy. He's wearing a ball cap and loose clothes, more high schooler than movie star. He'd said it was a balancing act between wearing something that wouldn't get him recognized and not looking like crap if he did. I just like knowing that I get to take the disguise off him when we get back to the house later.

Maybe I *will* get down on my knees for him, this time. The idea of Zack's cock in my mouth is gaining some appeal. I want him to thrash around the way I did for him. I want to know that my tongue has tasted every part of him.

Earlier, in the gondola, I put my tongue in his left ear, and discovered it's a sensitive spot. I love that I know this now.

My good mood as we walk into work takes a nosedive, though, when I see Tyler's there with some mutual high school friends.

I settle Zack at the counter of the bar and clock in before getting him a drink. Tyler hasn't noticed me yet, but his buddy

Mark, who moved away to Grand Junction years ago, is waving me over. I accept the inevitable and walk toward the group of four at a high-top.

"Hey guys, what's up?" We do a round of awkward side-hugs and then a round of teasing about my outfit after I confirm I work here. Hunter and Davis still live in town. Hunter works at the adventure center and Davis works at the garage that repaired Blucifer, but until the other day, I hadn't seen Tyler or Mark since they moved away.

"New boyfriend?" Davis asks, eying Zack's back. My favorite movie star is dutifully hunched over his drink, putting out leave-me-alone vibes, but he keeps darting looks our way.

"Looks like an out-of-towner," Mark says. "Valentine's not going to date somebody who's not going to stick around."

Mark and Davis laugh.

Hunter, who's heard all about Zack already from his girl-friend Mollie, raises his eyebrows at me. I wonder what he's doing hanging out with these guys. He'd usually rather pick up an extra tour than sign up for a social activity.

Tyler cranes his neck to get a better look at Zack. "Out-of-towner, huh?" He gives me a hard look. He knows. "Did you amend that contract?"

I glare at him. "It has nothing to do with that contract."

"If money's exchanged hands and there's an NDA involved, it does," he replies, taking another swig of his beer. "Tell him he's welcome to join us if he wants."

"Yeah, we've got to vet the new beau. Can't let just anybody date the prettiest girl in town," Mark adds.

Still thrown by Tyler's comment, I try to smile good-naturedly back. "What would you know, Mark? You haven't been back in over a year. The pool around town has changed since then."

He tips his beer at me in a mini toast. "I know enough, Valentine. I'm looking at you, aren't I?"

The other two men nudge Mark from either side. "Wow, dude, those the kind of moves they teach you in Grand Junction?" Hunter teases, but the edge to his voice says he'll step in if I need him to.

"He's always had those moves, Hunter," I reply, smiling at them as I excuse myself and move back behind the bar, where I'm supposed to be. The last thing I want is trouble tonight.

"Friends?" Zack asks when I stop by his seat.

I shrug. "Well, they're people from town. We all went to high school together. Hunter's a good guy but...there should be a name for people you know really well but don't hang out with."

Tyler's always been a jerk. I can't let him get in my head.

The Bivy is getting busy. Tourists are flooding into town for the festival that starts tomorrow. I can tell from the way Zack stays hunched over, his back to the bar, that he's worried he'll be recognized. I try to keep an eye on him as I rush through my half-shift, but the next time I glance over, Tyler is sitting next to Zack at the bar.

Nightmare alert! I look around for Julie, who is supposed to be taking over my shift any minute. But it's so busy, I can't get down the bar to Zack and Tyler for an agonizing amount of time, no matter how fast I refill beers or stab the POS screen to place orders.

"So the scope has to be very specific, or they're unenforceable," Tyler is saying when I finally reach them, breathless because I've barely breathed in the last five minutes. Tyler looks up at me. "Hey! Just telling Zack here about this semester of law school."

"I'm sure he finds that very interesting," I reply through gritted teeth. *Does Zack's face look a little pale, or is that the lighting in here?*

"I'm sorry I'm late," Julie says behind me. She's tying on her short apron and tucking her notebook into one of the pockets.

"I'll be right back," I tell Zack, and rush to clock out. *Hang in there*, is what I mean.

"Hush money, for example, is only illegal if you fail to disclose payment when it's legally required," Tyler is saying when I hurry back to them, this time on the other side of the bar. "Even when money exchanges hands for some other purpose, circumstances can dictate disclosure requirements."

"Ready to go?" I interrupt.

Zack stands up. "Speaking of money…"

"Don't worry," I reply, although I'm really running up my tab for him. "It's comped. Thanks so much, Julie!" I throw over my shoulder as I grab Zack and head for the door.

"Hope to see you both around town this weekend," Tyler calls after us. "I'm sure I will."

"I'm so sorry," I tell Zack once we're outside. "Tyler likes to stick his nose into everything. He's always been like that."

Zack takes his ball cap off the minute we step away from the lights in front of the bar. He runs a hand through his hair. "He was talking about nondisclosure agreements."

"Yeah…I figured," I say. "I showed him the contract I made with your people. It was a mistake. I was…anyway. Yeah."

We walk toward the SUV down the street. Zack's driver is waiting for us.

"The nondisclosure agreement in that contract doesn't really cover sleeping with me," he says. I'm not sure how to read into that. Is he regretting that he didn't make me sign something before we slept together?

"I wasn't planning on telling people about that," I say neutrally.

"No, of course," he replies. "But usually I have one."

I stop and turn to him. "You have women sign an NDA before you sleep with them?"

He turns toward me but looks at his feet. "It's not the sleeping together so much as...the details. But," he rushes to add, looking at me, "I trust you."

I hesitate and cross my arms. "I'd sign one if you wanted me to." I probably shouldn't promise this without consulting a lawyer. That's what Tyler would tell me. But I'm confused by this conversation, how serious it is, when I only want to hold his hand and go back to the bubble we were in all day. How many women has he had this talk with?

"No...it's fine." He shakes his head. "Sorry. Just a weird moment back there."

He reaches out his hand and I uncross my arms to take it.

"Let's go home," he says, and the idea sounds so nice I forget what else I was going to say.

* * *

When I wake up the next morning, it's to a new house. I can hear people rustling around outside the room. Zack is missing from the bed.

I get dressed—even putting on a bra—and follow the sounds of multiple people to the kitchen. Zack is holding a coffee mug and looking at a tablet with Drew at the counter. Two young women who look like hungry lions, all bones and wild hair, are sitting at the table going over a thick stack of folders with highlighters and pens.

A man with an actual chef's hat on hands me a cup of coffee. "Take this," he says. "You'll need it."

Zack and Drew look up. "Valentine!"

Drew waves, and Zack hops to his feet and comes over to me. "I was hoping to come back before you woke up, but I got pulled into about a million things. We're trying to make sure I'm ready for the screening today."

"I understand," I say quickly. I know how important this screening is to him, even if I can't imagine hundreds of people showing up for anything I'd made. That alone seems like success. Sometimes, Zack seems ungrateful. I try to remind myself that his circumstances are different and fame is a whole other beast, but that just makes me realize how far apart we are as people.

"Can I make you something for breakfast?" asks a woman who appears at my elbow. "Eggs? Grapefruit? We have keto pancakes or regular. I can also make a breakfast salad that complies with Whole 30."

I look to Zack, but he's been pulled like a magnet back to the tablet Drew's holding.

"Um, can I just have...something for my coffee?"

"Oat, almond, soy, coconut, or cow? I can also do a keto version if you like." The woman seems to have endless patience for all these options.

I usually use whatever carton doesn't need to be refrigerated. "Cow, I guess?"

The woman comes back with a list of fat content options. I'm starting to wish I hadn't gotten out of bed.

"Does Zack take something in his coffee? Just give me whatever he has," I say. Anything to make it stop.

Zack, as it turns out, drinks ghee in his coffee, which has got to be the most Hollywood thing I've learned about him so far. *What would he do with a cup of coffee made over a fire that still had grounds in it?*

I can't even picture him there, compared to this kitchen full of people on his payroll.

He'd warned me last night that he had interviews starting at 1 p.m., but I'd thought we could squeeze every last minute together out of the morning. Maybe I should have known it wouldn't be like that...but I didn't.

I sit down at the counter and play a game with myself trying to guess the jobs of all the people in Zack's kitchen. The chef seems obvious, except he seems to be taking orders from the woman who offered me coffee, and *she's* not wearing a hat at all.

Mindy, who I've met before, shows up a few minutes later and gives me an assessing look but seems distracted by the two young women and their stack of folders. PR team, I decide.

None of them are locals.

Just as I think I've mostly matched jobs with people, another man in a bright tie-dyed shirt walks in and says, "Zack, I've got a few options for you to wear."

"Valentine, will you help me pick?" Zack asks as he gets up. As we leave the kitchen, Mindy approaches Drew, and the two of them seem to be watching me as I follow Zack. Trying to decide what to do with me, probably.

The outfits Zack has to decide between are casual. They all seem about the same to me. Jeans with one, trousers with another. A jacket with one; another without.

Zack looks gorgeous in everything he tries on.

But Tie-Dye Shirt fusses over him, commenting on whether "that sheen will play on camera" or "this looks too stripe-y."

He doesn't seem to appreciate it when I joke that Zack should wear his new hiking gear.

But Zack, at least, grins and says, "I'll never wear that t-shirt again without feeling like I'm freezing."

When we go back to the kitchen, Drew sidles up next to me, and I brace myself. But they say, "If you want to stick around today, you can, but you'll have to hang with me."

I look at them, puzzled. "For...what?"

"We try to avoid any distracting elements while we shuttle the press through, and even the hint of Zack having a date would end up being the lead of every story. We want them to talk about his movie."

"Oh." I try to force myself to offer to leave. But...I don't want to. I don't have to work today, and it's my turn to see Zack's daily life. "No problem, I can follow you around if that's OK. I'll pretend to be your assistant."

"Body man," Drew replies. "We prefer body man."

"Really?" I pester them about this gendered term until the media starts trickling in. They park everybody in the living room and offer them a buffet of snacks and packaged drinks.

"We usually do this at hotels to avoid them getting into Zack's personal things," Drew explains to me in an undertone. "I'm mostly here to make sure nobody tucks a souvenir into a briefcase."

I try to mimic their *I'm-bored* expression and *don't-talk-to-me* body language, but it's difficult because everything is so fascinating. The media that eventually fills the living room range from wearing all-black to TV-ready plastered-on makeup. Some of them have big cameras and others have a notebook clutched to their chest. Most of them look like Zack, with his jaded gaze, but a few of the younger ones' eyes dart all over, taking in the inside of probably their first movie star's home.

One-by-one or two-by-two, they disappear inside the room where Zack is camped out with Mindy and the other two skinny women.

"Want to see an interview?" Drew asks halfway through the afternoon, after a lunch in which my "a sandwich is fine" response turned into another marathon of options. We're hovering in the living room with a few waiting reporters.

Drew whispers to Fred that we'll be back and to "watch the old dude," and then leads me into the other room, following a crew with a camera.

Mindy blocks our way almost immediately. "You're going to

distract him," she hisses. She's so far ignored me all day, like we've never met before.

"He'll be fine, he's a professional," Drew replies coolly, unflinching before her glare. "We'll stand in the back." They wave her off like she's a fly.

"Don't worry about it," they tell me, once we're standing well behind the man setting up the big camera and Mindy has moved on to some other irritant. "Just don't say anything, or you'll get me in trouble with someone who is actually scary."

Zack, who has been making small talk with the woman sitting across from him in the bright pool of light, glances away from her and meets my eyes for a moment.

I sense he smiles behind his eyes at me, even though he doesn't acknowledge me by waving or nodding his head. That makes sense. Like Drew said, he's a professional, and I'm a distraction right now.

When the camera starts rolling, the woman asks Zack what it "felt like" to direct his own movie, "how does it feel" to be opening at the Telluride Film Festival, and "what feeling do you expect to have when the screening starts tonight at the Palm?"

"What is this, therapy?" I whisper to Drew, getting very close to their ear to say it quietly.

They give me a little side smile and write on the pad they'd tucked under one arm, holding it so I can see it: "Celebrity feelings sell."

At the end of the interview, after Mindy tells her she has one question left, the woman asks Zack, "You were recently linked to your co-star Marisol Williams. Are the two of you still dating?"

Zack's smile doesn't falter, and he doesn't look over at me. "Mar and I never dated."

"Are you dating anyone right now?" the woman persists, even though Mindy steps into the light and says, "We need to wrap this up." I feel bad for her, being blown off by everyone in the room. I wonder if Mindy secretly hates her job.

"I'm a free agent at the moment," Zack replies. I press down hard on my lower lip because I want to contradict him. *He's not free; he's mine.*

Who the hell do I think I am? I watch the camera man start packing up his gear as the interviewer thanks Zack and he shakes her hand and takes a drink out of his water bottle.

We had one day together. It doesn't mean anything.

I'm as much an outsider to Zack's life as I am now, standing outside the pool of people gathered around him in the center of the room. He stands in the light, and I'm loitering around in the dark.

twenty-four

ZACK

I HAVE no way of knowing how tickets are selling for the screening. The film festival won't tell me. I've asked them, Drew's asked them, and they give away nothing.

But I know the only reason we were given one of the bigger venues tonight is because of my name. People want to see my movie so they can either mock it or love it. There's no in-between.

We're headed to town after a long press day, but Valentine wanted to drive Blucifer, so she's not in the SUV. She'd been weirdly worried about not having a ticket to my screening and offered to wait in line for one of the last-minute tickets the festival gives away free if not all the seats are filled at showtime. "You're with me, don't worry about it," I'd said, but for some reason, she still looked uncertain when she left.

Drew is warning me about holding hands in public. "You don't want a new relationship to take over the narrative."

Mindy, sitting on the edge of her seat without a seatbelt, is nodding with her lips pursed. Drew probably warned her to stay quiet. They know I'm more likely to listen to Drew than to one of my PR handlers.

"It's fine if she's with us in a group, but you shouldn't be seen too much together without others around you, or people will start asking questions." Drew continues. They're being unusually earnest about this.

I'm watching out the tinted windows as we pull into town. "You called Diane, didn't you?"

Drew glances at Mindy. "One of us did," they acknowledge coolly.

Mindy's face goes white, like she's pressing her lips so hard no blood can escape. "Only in your best interests," she says meekly. Mindy is interchangeable with a lot of the other "PR girls" I get assigned by a studio or someone on my team like Diane. They can't make decisions themselves, so they're more worried about covering their asses than loyalty to the client. Instructions over strategy.

But I have to trust the strategy is sound. Or I'll go crazy second-guessing how my team manages my life.

"OK," I say. "We'll keep some distance." Even though I want to drape myself over Valentine and lean on her like a crutch to reassure myself I can win over someone.

There's no red carpet or big spotlights when we arrive in town, but a few people on the sidewalks stop to watch me get out of the SUV. I hear the ripple go through the crowd as I lift my eyes to focus on the horizon. *Don't get sick.*

It's just one screening. But the buzz from this film festival will follow my movie into the world and change its prospects for distribution. It will affect my ability to make any more. And I want to make another movie. I want to get better at making movies, even if this one isn't the best. I need more than one chance to prove myself.

I wave at the people hovering. There suddenly seem to be

more of them. Fred and I walk over, and I start shaking hands, taking selfies, and signing festival programs.

Out of the corner of my eye, I see Valentine. She's talking to the young woman who works for the town paper, the one who accosted me in the coffee shop. The one her dad said was "from the city."

What the hell? I can't tell if Valentine needs rescuing. The two seem to be chatting. They both have their phones out.

I try to keep an eye on them while also paying attention to the people I'm talking to, spelling names right on autographs and turning on my Hollywood smile for pictures.

Drew is standing behind me. "Check on Valentine," I urge them when I get a moment.

They walk over to her but are back within a minute. "She says she's fine," they tell me, stepping up behind me to speak quietly. *Is she? What is she telling that aggressive reporter?* I'm frustrated by how trapped I feel, unable to talk to Valentine myself and warn her. But I have to give the people what they want, or it will come back to bite me later.

Finally, I can give Fred the signal and step away from the growing crowd. I wave at them one more time and walk toward the Palm, bypassing a line of people waiting for the doors to open. The building looks like a school, and I feel like I'm about to get my posted grades.

I avoid looking Valentine's way through sheer force of will, trusting Drew to make sure she gets scooped up and ushered inside with the group. I have to talk to the organizers about appearing on stage after the movie. I want to make it a pre-show appearance instead. What if everyone hates the movie and I walk up afterward in deathly silence?

I might throw up. But I just keep smiling, waving at the people inside the theater and taking pictures with the ones who ask, as I try to find the person in charge. I assume a lot of volunteers from the local community run the show, but I don't really know. Valentine probably knows all of them by name.

I remind myself not to touch my face after interacting with so many people, touching hands and other people's pens. My hands feel like foreign objects, dangling off my arms and held carefully away from my body. I need to find an organizer and then find a bathroom.

Every second that passes takes me closer to judgment time. *God, why didn't I let my mom and sister come to the premiere like they'd offered?* It'd be nice to have a couple more allies at my side. Familiar faces who will love me whether I'm fingerpainting or making a million-dollar film.

At the same time, I turned them down because I knew what it would feel like, having them sitting beside me as the lights go down in the theater, forming their own opinions in the dark as my movie plays. *Why did I think bringing Valentine was a good idea?*

Throwing in the towel on finding someone to change the schedule, I instead spend some quality time alone in the bathroom, contemplating how my life brought me here as I wash my hands over and over. I can hear when they start letting people into the theater.

I wish for a quiet moment alone with Valentine, when she might take my hands and say something my mom would say, like "you're already a success." But if I asked Drew to bring her to the bathroom, I can imagine their face. I have to handle this alone.

It's no longer my movie, it's the audience's. And there's nothing I can do about that.

I just wish I didn't have to face them all in person now.

twenty-five

VALENTINE

LAYING in bed in Zack's big bedroom alone is like trying to sleep in a church. The ceilings are vaulted, and I can't hear anything but my own thoughts.

I know there are other people in the house because I left Zack on a conference call with his entire team in the kitchen. But he turned on his sound machine before kissing me and telling me he'd come to bed "soon." The white noise drowns out anything in the other room.

The King-sized bed feels huge.

What am I doing here?

"I liked it," I'd rushed to tell Zack when I saw him after his movie screening. But some of the images in it confused me. Like when the reflecting pool in front of the Lincoln Memorial turned into the Pacific Ocean. Or when the Washington Monument turned into the red rock Independence Monument that's up near Grand Junction. What was he trying to say? That everywhere was the same?

I've never been anywhere, so how would I know? I probably

missed the point. The movie made me feel stupid, but I didn't say that to him.

He'd gotten a standing ovation when he climbed on stage after the credits. But he'd said it "doesn't mean much" when I pointed this out.

"Most of the screening was my friends, people I asked to come," he said. "It was for me, not the movie."

He introduced me to a few of them after, people I've seen on screen or in magazines. They were full of references to their private jet waiting to fly back to LA or the chef they flew down with them who "for some reason" brought a pasta maker. People with lives so far removed from mine, I mostly stayed mute in their presence.

Drew told me Zack wanted me to come back to the house— we'd driven separately—but I wasn't so sure. He seemed morose when I got there.

Eventually, I stopped trying to say things to make it better because everything I said seemed ignorant about his business. I know a little about creating something and not knowing how people will take it. But what do I know about fame and living up to expectations? What do I know about expectations set so high, they're almost impossible to fulfill?

My parents' expectations for me were more about *not* doing things—mainly, selling out.

When I look at Zack, I don't see someone who's selling out. At least, not anymore. He's putting his work out there, being vulnerable, being creative. And finding success.

I grab my phone from the bedside table and search for hashtags about the festival, but I can't find anything. Not that surprising; it's an elite festival—they even make the press pay to attend, according to the intern who works with Mark—in a hard-to-reach town. There will be think pieces about the festival once it's over, but maybe not live coverage.

My own notifications have mostly tapered off. I've been ignoring them and their demands to "post more Zack content."

Maybe I'm not supposed to make *any* unapproved content, according to my contract, but that seems to have become more like "loose guidance," anyway, considering what's going on with me and Zack. So I start editing together a short video using the footage I took of the line waiting for the screening last night, a crowd of 600 people standing in front of a breathtaking mountain vista no one was looking at. I got a very brief, surreptitious video of Zack on stage after the movie and edit that together with some earlier video of the night sky I took while camping, using the caption, "The real stars come out at night."

That seems neutral enough. It could even be fan content.

The way the theater erupted with applause when Zack's name was announced and he stepped on stage startled me. Even though I knew he was famous, that people loved him for nothing more than his face on a movie poster, I'd never encountered that kind of mass reaction in real life. He's a person, but people seemed to be clapping more for his brand. Or for having someone that famous among them. Mark's intern told me Zack is the most famous celebrity in town for this year's event.

The young woman, Jenn, had watched my video feed— "Mark couldn't figure out the app," she said—and asked me a lot of questions about my editing technique and idea generation. It'd been nice. Almost like having some real talent to share with someone. My own little press event. Standing on the fringes of Zack's celebrity made me feel small in a way I haven't since I got Blucifer back. A reminder that I haven't been anywhere or done anything and no one will remember my name.

I post the video. Maybe a few of my new followers will be satisfied, and it doesn't technically break any rules. *I don't think, anyway.*

I'm still awake when Zack finally comes to bed after 1 in the morning. He slides his arms around me and murmurs, "Sorry."

I pat his arm. "Everything OK?"

He sighs. "We'll see in the morning, I guess. When the reviews come out."

"Ah." I don't know what to say to that, so I turn toward him and put my leg over his hip. I can tell he's too stressed for anything else, so I just hold him like that, breathing the same air, until we both fall asleep.

twenty-six

ZACK

REALITY HIT SLOWLY, not like a wave but a trickle.

My movie is a flop. "Doesn't appear to be anywhere close to Ryder's lived experience and therefore is hard to take seriously," was in one particularly scathing review.

The last straw is when organizers politely inform me the film won't be part of the "TBAs," or repeat screenings added for the festival's most popular films.

I spend a slow hour staring at the ceiling after Drew takes my computer away so I can't keep reading bad reviews. Valentine is gone, working.

I want to talk to someone—someone who has been through this before. But my position is so rare in Hollywood. To be already famous but try to say something no one wants to hear. To let down 100 people on my payroll depending on me staying beloved with what...a vanity project?

So I call my mom.

She's taking care of my nephew, like she usually is, and she's surprised to hear from me. Her face on my screen, makeup-free and lined, is a relief. "Aren't you busy with that festival this weekend?" She carries the phone around straight-armed, like I need to see her whole body and not just her face. I must've gotten my "stiff and inexperienced" cinematic style from her.

"I am, but…" I'm not sure what the "but" is. But I want to rewind to before I was discovered and had a simpler life? But I called to whine about how privileged I really am? I finally conclude, "But it's not going well."

"Oh no!" She pauses to dissuade young Caleb from playing with something on the floor. "Are people misunderstanding your movie?"

That's a generous interpretation. "Maybe *I* misunderstood my movie," I sigh.

The screenwriter had been at the screening. It was her first film and she'd looked thrilled when it was over. I'd pulled her up on stage and her hand had been shaking.

I hate to think how crushed she must be today, reading the responses.

But the script *had* been good. It was my fault. Something about my choices. I'm so green I don't even know *what* I got wrong. The critiques are so focused on the differences between my brand and this movie that I can't pull any real understanding from them. There's no constructive lesson here. Just ice cold failure.

"Oh, honey, it was only your first try. You can learn and try again, yes you can, just keep on trying, that's right," she says, her voice trailing into baby talk as she shows me Caleb, scooting along the floor on his belly.

"At this rate, I'll never get to try again," I sigh, not distracted by the cuteness of a baby. "No studio's going to fund another movie I direct."

She turns the phone back toward her face. "I'm sure that's not true. Look at you! You're already so successful. Don't forget that. I was in the store the other day and there was your face, on not one but three of the magazines at the check-out. I bought them all." She smiles, like it's a secret. "Don't tell my son."

I smile a little and shake my head. "Just remember they make a lot of things up, Mom."

"They said you're dating your co-star! Is that true?"

I grimace. "It's not true. She got spotted at my house once and it became a whole thing."

"Are you dating anyone else? Don't make me hear about it in a magazine."

I hesitate. I don't really know what to call me and Valentine. I'm going back to LA next week and she...well, maybe she could come with me? What would she really leave behind here? A crappy waitressing job? And I have a house here; we can come back whenever we want.

The idea unfurls in my mind with a pop, like champagne. A silver lining to this mess.

"Maybe," I tell my mother. "I met somebody but I'm not ready to talk about it yet."

She's distracted by Caleb again but laughs. "Well, I won't start hiding in the bushes with a camera to get the story out of you."

"Thank God."

She looks at me again, direct through the phone. "Just remember how much you've done, Zack. Appreciate what you have and don't fixate on what you don't."

I nod, chastened. "Right. OK, Mom."

"I know you and how you beat yourself up. You're doing fine!" She shakes a finger at me on the other side of the screen.

By the time we hang up, I'm smiling. Not a lot, but it's more than I have in two days.

twenty-seven

VALENTINE

I WANTED TO COME, but I'm regretting being here.

It was sheer stubbornness—when I suggested one of the free movies in the park to Zack, he didn't want to be out in the crowd. I decided to go by myself to make some kind of point about my independence. He's been ignoring me in favor of moping about his movie, anyway.

Now I'm here alone, wondering what he's up to without me.

At least Mark's intern, Jenn, spotted me in the crowd and spread her blanket out beside mine.

The movie isn't very good. It's neither as obscure as Zack's directorial debut nor as appealing as his more popular blockbusters.

But it's nice to be outside, with the mountains overlooking the screen and a light breeze lifting my hair. It's not too cold nor too hot this evening. Zack would have liked it. If he'd come.

He shows up half an hour into the movie, wearing a ball cap and sneaking onto my blanket like he's going to steal my purse. Seeing him gives me a small thrill up my spine. We haven't had sex since his movie premiered. He touches me a lot—a hand on my back or butt when we're at the house, whether or not his staff is around—but he's seemed too distracted for anything else, even last night when I slept over after my shift at the bar.

He kisses me hello, but his face changes when he sees Jenn. "Hi?" he says.

Someone trying to watch the movie "shh"s us nearby.

Jenn moves in a little closer to respond, and Zack leans away from her. It's subtle, but I can feel him shift toward me, like Jenn is going to attack him right here in the middle of a friendly event of mainly people who live in town.

"Sorry I came on a little, um, strong? Last time we met?" Jenn whispers.

"Right," he says, giving her nothing.

"How's your weekend going?" Jenn continues, ducking her head a little so her quiet voice floats to our ears.

"Is this on the record?" Zack snaps back. Someone else "shh" s us.

I put my hand on his arm. *OK, so he's having a rough weekend. He doesn't have to take it out on Jenn.*

The younger woman bites her lip. "I mean, it would be great to get a comment. Nobody's giving us access, and we can't even afford to go to most screenings, so I haven't seen your film." Her shoulders are slumped. "It's been hard for me to do my job."

I study Zack's profile. His jaw is set. But after a moment, he says, "I'll give you a quote."

I relax a little. Jenn lights up and pulls a notepad out of her purse.

"Telluride is a welcoming place for artistic experiments, and I was thrilled to debut mine here," Zack says, speaking slowly as Jenn writes. "Next, I'll return my focus to films like White House Rising 2, which comes out next summer."

I frown. It sounds like Zack is putting his art firmly in the rearview mirror. I open my mouth, but Jenn beats me to it, asking: "Will you be taking anything from Telluride with you?"

Her eyes dart to me. Zack's face gets even frostier. "No comment," he says.

"OK, thanks!" Jenn starts gathering up her stuff. "I've gotta go to work! Great to see you again, Valentine! Thanks, Zack!"

She jumps up and winds her way through the annoyed people around us to exit the park. I try to ignore the glares we're getting. Mrs. Strecker, from the library, is giving us pursed lips. I'll be hearing about this later. Possibly via my mother.

"What was that?" I whisper to Zack.

"What was what?" He pretends he has no idea what I'm talking about, staring stubbornly at the screen.

I swallow, uncertain I should confront him here. My throat is full of something that feels a lot like tears. I want to be around Zack, but I want it to be like it was when we were in his house together, alone. I turn back toward the screen, but it's impossible to follow the movie. I don't want to be here anymore. "I'm going to go," I whisper, and gather up my things quickly.

He follows me out of the park to the street, where we can talk with normal voices again. "Do you want to come back to my place?"

Part of me does. But will we actually talk there? Or will he want to pretend nothing has changed, despite the pit in my stomach that says it has. I don't actually know him. I don't know what it's like to fight with him and still want to be together after.

So I shake my head. "No, I want…" Some space? That's not really what I want; it's just what I need right now. "I haven't had a night outside in a while."

Briefly, I wonder if he'll offer to share my tent. Perhaps, in neutral territory and looking up at the stars together, we could talk. I could admit I still struggle to name the stars, despite my many nights outdoors, and he'd tease me about not being the superstar nature guide he thought.

But he doesn't offer.

"OK," he says. "Do we have your phone number?"

How little we know each other. We haven't even texted. I've had more casual contact with a Hinge date.

"Your people do," I say numbly.

"OK, because I don't have my phone on me," he says, as if that's normal. "Tomorrow, I have to do more press. But maybe we could do dinner?"

I shift my weight between my feet. Is he going to give more interviews like this one, where he talks about his blockbuster movies and acts like he didn't just pour his blood out on screen? "I'm working tomorrow night," I say.

His face doesn't fall, but I can tell he's disappointed. "Ah, OK. Well, maybe I can stop by again." Something about the way he says it lets me know he won't. He hated it last time he came to the bar—and no wonder, with Tyler throwing his weight around.

I just nod, even knowing he's slipping away. "I can try to find someone to cover my shift." I really shouldn't, though. I need the money for this month's car payment.

"No, don't worry about it. I don't want you to rearrange your life for me." He smiles, and it's the brilliant, movie star smile he gives everyone else. "We'll catch up soon."

He leans over and kisses me on the cheek, across my folded arms. By the time I drop them, he's already turning away.

"I'll see you tomorrow," I say, manifesting more than anything. "We'll make it happen."

He nods and waves as he walks down the street. His SUV with the darkened windows is probably waiting for him, a driver reading in the front seat.

I turn the opposite direction. At least I have Blucifer to keep me company. That's more what I'm used to, anyway.

twenty-eight

ZACK

DIANE IS in my kitchen when I come out for breakfast.

I skid a little on my sock-clad feet as I stop under the archway. "Oh no," I say.

"I get that a lot," Diane says, standing framed by two of her skinny minions. "It's appropriate."

Drew is sitting at the kitchen counter, looking at a computer, and makes a face when I turn to them for support. They get up and start pouring a cup of coffee. The rest of the staff seem to have cleared out, likely at the sight of Diane.

"Is it that bad?" I ask, not because of the coffee but because she's here at all.

"It needs to be addressed before it is," Diane replies crisply. She waits as Drew hands me the coffee, and I take a sip, gripping it tightly between both hands. It's not my usual order, but I'm not complaining.

"First item," she says, and I'm scared because she seems to have a list. "We were able to obtain an early copy of a draft being shopped around." She gestures to the open computer on the counter.

I step over to it and have to sit down when I see the headline: "Is Zack Ryder's New Girlfriend a Telluride Local Who Criticized Him?"

The name on the story is Jenn Hollis. "I knew it!" I say. "That intern who works for the town paper. Are they printing this trash?"

"She's pitching it to a few of my magazine contacts."

I'm scanning the pitch. It's in the form of a brief email with bullet points. "She says she has quotes from both of us."

I look up at Diane and Drew, and they're both looking at me patiently.

"OK, I gave her a quote, but about the movie—not about dating anyone."

Diane sighs and looks disappointed in me.

"She looks about 19 years old, OK? I didn't know she was cutthroat." I cross my arms and then uncross them to keep drinking my coffee. I'm going to need it. "I don't know what Valentine said to her."

"But she did talk to her?" Diane says sharply.

I nod miserably. "I saw them together."

Diane and Drew exchange looks. The oat milk in my stomach starts to curdle. I've been in denial that Valentine wouldn't hurt me, haven't I?

"That leads me to the second item," Diane says. She reaches over me to the computer. The sharp smell of citrus that envelops me does nothing for my stomach.

She opens a page of videos, and I immediately know it's Valentine's feed. Diane points at the top two videos. "These were posted in violation of our contract."

I put my coffee down. "Drew, can you get me something to eat?" I ask before I watch the videos. My stomach feels like acid.

The first one uses footage of me on stage at the screening. It's painful to watch the way I'm grinning at the applause. But I'd been so grateful to receive the response, even if I knew it didn't mean much.

The second short video mocks the celebrities flying into Telluride just for the film festival, knowing nothing about the history or culture or people of the valley, not contributing to the local economy but flying in their own special food and even staff. She doesn't name me, but she might as well have. I know I'm culpable. *So this is what she really thinks.*

I shrug, trying to be flippant. "So? This is her brand. We knew that." I stand to wash my hands after touching Diane's computer.

Turning with me, Diane's forehead doesn't move, but she frowns at me with her eyes. "The combination of these two things means that soon we'll be dealing with managers and studio executives who want to know why their multimillion-dollar star is criticizing them in public. People won't want to work with the person whose girlfriend is mocking their lifestyle, Zack."

I take the chia pudding Drew offers me and hunch over the counter to eat it, hoping it will make the cavern of my insides feel less like it's caving in. The last thing I need is another reason for people to hesitate over working with me. Have I achieved success only to tear it down? For what—a stupid dream about being a director? About climbing a mountain?

"I can talk to her," I say. But I don't know if it will matter. I didn't vet Valentine. I don't know if she has a cat named Floof or a secret hobby of playing D&D. Maybe she's exactly what she seems to be: someone who tears other people down for influence. Maybe she and that intern have been in it together the whole time. Maybe...the time we spent together meant nothing.

But we'd giggled together on the couch and shared our

worries. We had more in common than I'd ever imagined. My instincts say I know her and who she is.

Still, my instincts have been all wrong lately.

"I can kill this story," Diane says, gesturing at the computer. "But only if you cut ties. And immediately. You need to come back to LA with me so we can set up some in-person meetings. Smooth things over."

I meet Drew's eyes. They look sympathetic, but they shrug. It makes sense. There's really no way to know another person's motives unless they're on your payroll.

Still, I should at least talk to her, right? See if what I thought was there...really isn't?

I look at Diane. She looks so certain, and I hired her because I trust her. I take a breath and nod. "OK, let's get a flight set and pack." There's nothing keeping me here. Not really.

twenty-nine

VALENTINE

MAYBE I SHOULD HAVE PICKED a neutral location. We could have met on a mountain top, amid the fresh air. The sounds of nature might cushion the blow I'm sure is coming—the inevitable goodbye I don't want to say.

But when I got a text—"Hi, it's Drew"—asking me to come to Zack's house, I said, "Why not mine?"

So we end up at my parents' place.

Zack's black SUV is already in front of the house when I get there. I went for a hike to clear my head, hoping the fresh air and signs of wildlife would keep me grounded. Instead, I spent an hour picking up other people's dog shit along the side of the trail, grumbling to myself about humans ruining nature. I'm in a bad mood when I arrive, in other words.

Mom meets me in front of the garage, wearing leather gloves with safety glasses pushed up on top of her messy hair. "Your dad seems to see something in that boy," she says. "I don't know what." She eyes me like it might be contagious. "You, too, I think."

I shrug. "I don't know, Mom. I thought I hated him, too, and now I want him to…" I glance at the kitchen window, which overlooks the driveway and front of the house. No one's there. But I can only gesture that direction, helpless to define what I want other than "stay." I know he can't stay. He doesn't belong here. And I do.

"Hate is a big word, just like love," Mom says. "It is not necessary to put this kind of label on it."

"I know. It's early." *I've known him, what, a week?*

"Not just that. Your father and I, we don't use these words. You've never noticed? We use, 'I respect you,' 'thank you for doing the dishes,' 'I made this for you.'"

I bite my lip. I have noticed. I just hadn't applied my parents' relationship to mine. "But," I say slowly. "You and Dad…there's no risk there."

"Hm! There is always risk in relationships. But especially in the beginning. The key is to not take risk alone. Take it together." Mom shakes her head and grabs her glasses before they almost fall off her head. "It is not wise if the risk is only on one side."

I nod, taking this in. Instead of hugging me, she gives my shoulder a hard squeeze and aims me at the front door of the house. "Now go, don't put it off," she says. "Who knows what your father has him talking about." She pats my butt as she goes back into the garage.

Zack and Dad are in the kitchen, of course, talking quietly about something when I come in. Dad, who is standing at the stove, immediately offers me a cookie. They're on cooling racks taking up the entire counter and kitchen table. "Peanut butter and chocolate chunk. Did you know Zack here prefers dark chocolate?"

I hadn't known. There are so many things I don't know about him. But I know at night, if I get out of bed to go to the bathroom, when I get back in he will rub my back. I know when we reach a scenic point in a trail, his face lights up like a child at Christmas.

Zack's face is not lit up now. He's leaning against the counter by the stove and doesn't move toward me for a hug or kiss. "I came by to let you know I have to go back to LA today," he says, as if he needs to just get it out of the way.

I nod. Dad glances back at me, asking with his eyes if he should leave the room, but then the oven timer beeps, and I move farther into the kitchen so he can open the oven door and take out another sheet of cookies. The heat washes over me as I avoid getting too close to Zack in the small space.

"What about..." I swallow. *What about me? What about us? What about climbing that mountain?* The mountain is *this* conversation, right now. I lean back against the counter and look out the front window, trying to imagine I'm outside with the sun on my back and freedom in front of me. Zack leaving me behind doesn't mean anything to a woman with a world of paths to choose from. "The videos?" I say finally.

He looks down at his feet. "My team is pretty upset that you've been posting unapproved ones. The one with me in it broke the terms. I wish you had just...showed it to me, before, or something."

He wants me to be smaller. To stay in my small corner of the world and make small art. I cross my arms. "Why should I have to show you before I'm ready?"

Zack gives me a look, like I'm being unreasonable. And maybe I am, but I don't know what my art is until I make it. I have to flow with the muse where it takes me. He must understand that. But does he?

"Well, anyway, they canceled the contract," he says. "You should have an email."

For lack of anything else to do, I open the app on my phone, and there it is, a "Contract Termination" email, along with 100 others because I never check my inbox.

The email before the one about the contract is from Mark Wadson. "I'm sorry to say..." it begins, in the line visible in the preview. I glance up at Dad and Zack.

Dad frowns. "What is it?"

I open it. It reads: "I'm sorry to say my intern showed poor judgment, or perhaps I did in choosing her, by writing and submitting a story I would never run in the town paper. I am attaching a copy for your reference, and because I thought I should warn you that she made you a part of it. My plan is to end her internship, effectively sending her home since the paper pays her in housing, but wanted to ask if you prefer that I continue working with her in an effort to teach her a different form of journalism—an ethical one. I have no idea if this will be effective, but perhaps we owe it to her and to Telluride and to journalism to try."

I start reading it aloud halfway through what turns out to be a very long email.

"That sounds like Mark," Dad says. "Maybe he can help her understand. People are more than sources."

Zack crosses his arms. "She shopped that piece around to magazines after Mark turned her down, so I'm not sure she can be helped."

Dad gives Zack the same shoulder-clasp Mom gave me a minute ago. "Perhaps Mark sees something in her," he says, echoing what Mom just told me about Zack himself.

Dad smiles gently at me as he leaves us alone in the kitchen with the slowly-cooling oven and racks of sweet-smelling cookies surrounding us.

Zack moves over to the table and sits down in a chair. He looks up at me, like he's waiting for me to speak first. But I can't, so instead I walk over and sit in the chair across from him. A gesture, instead of words. A detente between us. He came to me, after all, rather than making me come to him. Perhaps he *is* risking something.

"Come with me," he says, so softly Dad won't be able to hear it in the next room. "To LA. We can find you something to do. Whatever you want. And you can stay with me as long as you're comfortable."

I jump to my feet and pace back and forth across the tiny kitchen. An invitation to LA, all expenses paid, is tempting. Of course it is. I've never been anywhere, and now he wants me to go somewhere with him. But what would I actually do there, while he is out and about being a movie star? Work at some fancy restaurant, serving his friends? *It is not wise if the risk is only on one side.*

"What, as your servant?" I snap at him. If I don't yell, I might cry. "Maybe I can wait on you, just hanging out at the house until you have time in your busy schedule."

Offense crosses Zack's face, but he looks down at his hands held loosely between his legs, and when he looks up again, it's gone. "Do you want me to stay here?" he asks, his voice still much quieter than mine. "We don't have to stay at my place. Maybe your parents would let me crash here for a while."

I look at him sitting in my parents' tiny kitchen, a shining star among the chipped counters and cracked stovetop. He doesn't belong here. My world is cairns and wide-open spaces, climbing over car seats and the back of the bar. His world is fancy hotels and entourages, people who fold your napkin for you and gifts worth thousands of dollars. My family never locks their doors, and he has a security system that talks back.

"No," I say quietly. "It wouldn't work."

He looks at me silently for a beat.

"You must see that," I whisper.

He nods, slowly. Reluctantly. "I see it," he says.

We look at each other for another moment, the smell of chocolate swirling in the air around us.

Zack stands. He tugs his shirt sleeves down and brushes off the front of his pants. "The terms of the contract breach allow you to do what you want with the footage you took. I asked them to put that in. So...yeah. Make whatever videos you want now." He nods again.

I'm not sure what to say. Thank you? I'm not going to thank him; my heart is broken. I just nod back.

"OK," he says. "See you." He has to carefully squeeze by me to leave. When he's across from me, our hips almost brushing, he hesitates for just a millisecond. And I think, *maybe?*

But then he's gone. There was never a maybe for us. There was only a weekend.

Part Three

The View is Worth the Climb

Zack Ryder Learned a Lesson at 8,750'

By Vanity Monthly

Zack Ryder sits across from me looking like a Gucci ad. He's wearing sunglasses and an open linen shirt, and his smile — straight off a movie poster — could blind a less jaded reporter. He's also drinking a beer and telling me about bearproofing.

"Bears have an incredible sense of smell. If they smell something in your trash they want, they'll come from hundreds of miles away. And then they remember where they found it and they'll come again and again."

"Sounds like my in-laws," I joke.

"Except it's so much worse for the bears," Zack insists. He's earnest about his topic, like a spy using his cover to distract. In this case, he's avoiding talking about his directorial debut, "Zeitgeist," a movie that flopped so spectacularly at its first film festival this past summer, he hasn't talked about it publicly since.

Zack learned about bears in his second home, Telluride, Colorado, a small mountain town in the southwestern part of the state. Movie stars go there to ski and attend the Telluride Film Festival. It's a remote location free of most paparazzi. But, apparently, it's full of bears.

He never actually saw a bear while he was living there, Zack admits. "But that's because I learned to take bearproofing seriously!"

When I gently broach the subject of what else Zack learned in Telluride — elevation 8,750' above sea level — his answer is revealing yet cryptic. "Dreams are worth having but need to be grounded in reality."

Instead of asking Zack about "Zeitgeist" or the rumors he

dated a local woman while on holiday from the madness of L.A., I ask about what comes next. "What is your dream now?"

His smile is small, nothing like the billboards plastering this town for his upcoming release "White House Rising 2." The hotly anticipated popcorn flick opens May 16, starring Ryder as the vice president and Marisol Williams as the first lady. The two stars have appeared on the cover of other magazines in various states of undress, fanning the flames of rumors they're romantically involved.

"I'm looking forward to talking about this movie on the publicity tour," he says, the first lie Zack's told me. Then he adds a truth: "I'm excited to be talking about something people are excited about."

Unlike bearproofing, I guess.

thirty

VALENTINE

"SHE'S JUST GETTING OLDER, that's all," Davis says, as if this isn't the cruelest possible thing to say in front of Blucifer, who is doing her best after all these years. "I wouldn't drive her on these roads this winter. Just asking for an accident."

I try not to let the chasm opening in my stomach show on my face. "Not even to get to work?"

He looks at me seriously. The smell of the garage and the impact of his words make my stomach rock. "You shouldn't be driving her at all until you get that axle replaced and the suspension fixed. And that might be a money pit, uncover more issues. You can't replace her?"

I can't even respond to that. Even if I had the money, I wouldn't talk about it here, in front of my beloved car.

"Come on, Valentine, you can take the gondola to work," he tells me, as if that solves everything. "Live with your parents a few months and save up for the repairs or something new. I'll even go with you if you want to drive up to Montrose next summer and look at used lots."

My legs might not hold me up much longer. I just nod. "Can you…" I swallow. "Can I take her home?"

"To your parents'? I guess you'd be OK driving that far. But just this once, Valentine. I'm serious. I don't want to see you driving her around once the snow sets in."

I nod numbly. He hands me the key. Blucifer and I need to get out of here, away from these people who want to put her down like it's nothing.

I cry on my way to my parents', terrified at every bump in the road that Blucifer is going to simply fall apart under me. "I'm sorry, I'm so sorry," I whisper, touching the dashboard when I park at the curb in front of their house. *Is this the last time I'll ever drive her?* The idea is too horrible to contemplate for long.

The garage door is open, and Mom comes out to meet me on the driveway. My face must not hide the tears very well, because she takes off her gloves and grabs my shoulders in her rock-hard grip. "This is over the boy?"

"No!" The last thing I need is to be reminded I've lost even more in the last month. "It's Blucifer. They said at the garage I can't drive her anymore."

"Ah. This is a hard thing. Loss and the uncertainty that comes with it. Go talk to your father," Mom orders. "He will feed you his orange scones and set up your bed."

"Thanks, Mom." I endure her briskly flicking tears off my face before I go inside, where Dad does exactly what she predicted.

Halfway through my scone—orange with orange marmalade—I get a text from a number I never expected to hear from again. It's just a link to the Colorado secretary of state's website for registering a nonprofit.

Did they mean this for someone else?

Then another text: "It's not so hard. I've set one up before; I can walk you through it. You should also consider a crowd-sourcing campaign."

I stare at Drew's words on the screen for a solid minute before texting back: "Why do you want to help me?"

They send a link to one of my own videos, the one about altitude sickness and acclimatization before a hike with elevation gain. "If I'd seen this before our hike, it would have been less embarrassing."

I flick my screen back to the link they sent. The requirements look overwhelming. Can I actually do this? Could I reach more people, more regularly, by launching an educational organization?

I start typing back to Drew: "I don't know if I can do this." Delete. "I don't have any money." Delete.

Finally, I send: "I don't know how to do something like this."

They reply: "That's why you met me! My whole job is building confidence. Mostly I do it by providing info. Or hiding it, depending on the situation."

This is crazy. There's no way I, a mountain girl who has never left the state, can launch a charity that will reach and educate people nationally. My dreams are too big. They're too big for my car, and maybe too big for my heart. I reply: "I don't even know where to start."

But their response is simple: "You already have."

thirty-one

ZACK

MARISOL IS MAKING PANCAKES, of all things, filling my seldom-used kitchen with the scent of warm carbs.

"I didn't know you could cook," I say, then add, "...something with that many calories."

She throws a face at me over her shoulder, the oversized hoodie falling down over her bare shoulder. Marisol is a size 2 at most, and the hoodie is a men's large, big enough to hide the fact she's probably not wearing any shorts. "Hey, despite what the tabloids say, I know how to eat. I've been eating since I was a baby. And I'm not in training right now. Neither are you, by the way."

I sit down with my mug of ghee coffee, handed to me unobtrusively by kitchen staff who are staying out of Marisol's way. "I've been enjoying not being in training a little too much the last month, if you know what I mean."

She gives me an up-and-down scan. "Nobody could tell."

I shrug. There are so many cameras aimed my way in LA. If I gain a few pounds, if I don't look like I did 10 push-ups before getting in my car to run errands, the tabloids will say I've let myself go.

I'm just back from two months in Alberta, doing my best to play a mountain man who would pass Valentine's test for authenticity. Probably failing. But I'd stopped going to the gym and started spending my time outdoors, taking climbing lessons and guided hikes. The film brought in someone to teach me how to cut firewood for one key, shirtless scene. I'd used muscles my trainers never showed me before.

"Anyway, don't worry," Marisol adds. "I'm making three pancakes, so one each. And I made them with monkfruit and almond flour."

That's more like it. The first time I met her, on set when she was playing the First Lady, she'd been wearing a tiny American-flag bikini. She made me stand side-by-side with her and compared ab muscles, joking about whether eating grilled chicken for breakfast was really "the American way." Marisol is great. She gets this business—the pressures of working in a visual medium, running a brand, and how it's all part of making something that might not be great art but pays the bills.

She's not Valentine. She would never yell at me over breakfast.

Drew saunters in wearing just socks and joggers. Their hair is wet from the shower after what was probably a longer run than I've done in months. "Everybody showing me up today," they mumble into their coffee.

Marisol smiles at us as she plates three small pancakes. She sprinkles them with sliced almonds and agave syrup and passes one to each of us at the stainless steel counter.

We're preparing—all three of us—to hit the road for the media tour, where Marisol and I will be asked, over and over, about our supposed relationship. We'll demur repeatedly without actually quashing the rumors. The speculation is good for business: for our brands and for selling movie tickets.

The media tours are fun and exhausting. A bunch of half-grown adults crammed together, trying to concentrate on talking points but more focused on having a good time. This one will last a full month. We'll be back and forth between LA and various big cities a few times before going international. As the stars, Marisol and I have to be at more than half a dozen premieres.

Drew feeds on the energy of the tours—the new places and adoring crowds, the details they have to track, and the closeness that develops. They say the trips are like a throwback to high school trips to Sacramento for politics classes or Big Bear Mountain for snowboarding lessons. And Marisol has some kind of zen practice that seems to keep her centered. She's a goddamn professional. But for me, the tours have become the worst part of my job. I have to turn on my movie star persona for so many strangers in such tight quarters, over and over, for days. I'm away from my bed, and it's hard to fit in calls to my mom. I never have any new ideas on tour; I only have to come up with new ways to talk about work I've already done.

I'm particularly dreading this one. And so I've gathered my partners around me, my confidants, my allies. Marisol and Drew will keep me sane.

thirty-two

VALENTINE

I DON'T HEAR anything about him for a while, a cruel fulfillment of what I used to want.

And then the clips start to trickle in—the magazine covers and social media posts. The memes about #relationshipgoals with him and his co-star on the red carpet, interrupting each other's interviews or joking about making each other "vindictive pancakes," the kind of gesture that "seems sweet but is really about sabotaging my diet."

I avoid his new action movie playing at the theater in town for a weekend, and then I slip into a screening as early in the morning as possible. I grip the armrest of my seat for the entire two hours and 37 minutes. He's beautiful every second he's on screen. I hate it. It says nothing about him, who he is, or his dreams.

My parents, who haven't been to a movie in the theater since 1997, go to Zack's movie because Dad convinces Mom to go with him.

"He seems different in it," is all Dad says afterward.

Car-less and stuck at my parents' with too-easy access to Wi-Fi, late at night I find myself reading every press clipping possible for a mention of Zack's Telluride movie. He never seems to talk about it. It's like it—and that whole weekend—never happened.

The tabloids say his co-star, Marisol Williams, was seen sneaking out of his home in Hollywood Hills.

My video feed has gone back to nature. I hike a lot and post about using WAG bags and silver-infused pee cloths, not walking in trail run-offs, and best bear-proofing practices. I haven't posted any of the footage I still have of hiking with Zack. People are asking less, and my engagement has dropped off a cliff.

Drew asked me why I haven't used the Zack video during one of our video calls to talk about nonprofit plans. I didn't tell them about my side project, turning the footage into a longer video. It's still only the beginning of a narrative—the part where he discovers the mountains, not the part where he conquers them—but somewhere along the way, I started finding it soothing to work with clips of Zack. The pieces of him that feel real.

Still, Drew keeps asking. "The fundraising needs something flashy to get it started," they insist.

"It would make me uncomfortable," I finally admit. "I don't want to be the person using him."

They drop it after that. Drew's been traveling a lot—we never talk about where they're at or their traveling companions—but they makes time to chat with me every week, to talk me down from whatever I'm freaking out about, tell me how to find money in weird nooks and crannies I'd never thought of before for fundraising, scan a form with me and spot the loophole I was missing.

It's still hard to believe Drew is helping me. But they've stopped letting me thank them and started joking I had an affair with a movie star and all I got was a bi "sidekick."

"You're not a sidekick," I grouse when they make me fill out yet another form. "You're a drill sergeant."

And then, later, once it's official and I am actually the founder of a nonprofit called Nature's Valentine, I say, "I hope you consider yourself my friend."

"Darling, we don't have friends in Hollywood. We have allies," they reply, painting their nails on a Zoom call from somewhere in Europe. "Anyway, I could tell you needed a few more of them."

My nonprofit exists now—at least on paper. Now comes the hard part. The part Drew can't help me with. I need to find a way to make other people care as much about nature education as I do.

thirty-three

ZACK

THE PRESIDENT CALLS to congratulate me on a Wednesday, after the movie crosses the billion-dollar mark.

"So, when are you going to stop playing me?" asks Alex Drake, who was the vice president before he became president.

I laugh, because, weirdly, we've had this discussion before. I sit down on my suede couch, the trailer my agent sent me paused on the big screen in front of me. The studios are making trailers for scripts they want me to take now. People are literally begging me to sign onto their films. "It's hard to stop when the movies are doing this well," I say.

I've already signed on to another sequel. I'll be making almost twice as much as I did for *this* film. It's a mind-boggling amount, a fee no real person should ever be making for one job.

"Hard for the *studio* to stop," the president corrects me. "They're only looking at their bottom line. What about you? What gets you up in the morning?"

I swallow, the phone in my grip immediately sweaty. Risk-taking isn't a subject I like to explore much lately. "Well," I say, trying to come up with a polite deflection. "I made enough with this movie to buy my mom a new house. So that's...pretty great."

"That is great," President Drake agrees, his voice coming clearly from the other side of the country—from the freaking White House where he apparently screened my movie in the theater in the basement when he had a couple of hours free from leading the world. "But I bet you have enough money in the bank at this point that the mortgage isn't going to be a problem."

"No..." I laugh a little. "Sorry. This is surreal. Talking to you about this."

"I like to chat with people from all different walks of life. It's helpful, don't you think? To learn a little bit more about the world and people outside our own bubble."

I nod, even though he can't see me. I know I'm in a bubble. My bubble has gotten more solid lately, so I can see the edges of it. The walls are so firm now that sometimes I'm not sure I could walk out of them.

"But it's important to get beyond what makes people successful, what makes them come to my attention. There's always something behind the success, in my experience. Something that got them there that isn't obvious."

"What is that for you?" I blurt out. "Oh. Sorry. Mr. President." God, I'm an idiot. Mindy is on the other end of this call, listening in, and the president's people are, too. I'm probably going on a blacklist right now.

But President Drake laughs. "Well, there's my family, who pushed me into politics early. But I think the real reason I am where I am is my wife. Finding someone who shined a mirror back at my own ambition and goals and helped them make sense. I don't think it's about finding success so much as finding your enough."

Enough. That's a word that sounds foreign to me. I repeat it out loud.

"It sounds like you haven't found that yet, Zack," the president says sympathetically. "If you want some unsolicited advice from someone who is completely ignorant about your business..."

"Yes, please," I say, interrupting.

"I'd suggest you spend some time thinking about what enough is for you."

When I hang up—the president needs to talk to the leader of China or something else that doesn't sound real—I turn my phone over and over in my hands, trying to imagine what having *enough* would feel like. I'm alone in my giant house, empty because Drew is sleeping elsewhere for once. My Golden Globe is sitting silently on the mantle, cold and uninterested in how I feel about my career. My kitchen smells like Clorox and steel because no one has cooked in it since I hosted a catered party for the cast last month.

I open my contacts list and find Rick Arnaud. "In case you ever want the sunglasses back," he'd said when he gave me the number. I've never had a dad. I don't know if it's normal for them to be forgiving, to accept a text out of the blue from someone who possibly broke their daughter's heart.

I don't even know why I want to text Valentine's dad. I only know I miss the feeling I had, sitting or standing across from him, eating his handmade pastries, and feeling heard.

Does she hate me now? I want to ask. *Again.* It was only a brief interlude when I deluded her into seeing something in me that wasn't worth hatred. *Does everyone there hate me?*

The only people who see something worthwhile in me are making money off me. Or they're family. And technically, my mom and Laura get a lot of money from me, too. But if they knew I thought about it that way, they'd refuse to take any more. I know that without question.

Often, in Alberta, I'd wished I could bring Valentine on as an authenticity consultant. The studio had enough money to throw around; I could have floated her a fat fee. I looked up her video feed and wondered what would happen if I left a comment from @ZackRyderOfficial. I didn't, of course.

Drew is standing in the doorway to the living room, overnight duffle bag slung over their shoulder. "What kind of sad nonsense is going on in here?" They turn on a light that I had turned off for a better trailer experience.

"It isn't enough," I say morosely.

"What isn't?"

"Everything."

Drew drops his bag. He studies me. "You just came to this conclusion?"

"I bought my mom a house. The president called me." I wince, because the list of good things happening in my life definitely sounds like it should be enough. "Maybe it's me. *I'm* not enough."

"You know..." Drew pauses.

"What?" I demand.

"There's this nonprofit I'm aware of that could use some help."

thirty-four

VALENTINE

I WAKE up to $250,000 in my fledgling crowdsourcing campaign and a text from Drew that tells me to check my inbox.

It's a contract. *The use of the likeness of Zack Ryder can be used to promote Valentine Arnaud's fundraising campaign* if I agree to assist him in climbing a mountain no less than 14,000 feet above sea level (to bear no liability), for the sum of $500,000, to be paid in two installments, one immediately and one after posting the footage of the climb. *No creative control is requested...*

My eyes skip over the text, from one unbelievable clause to the next.

I text Drew back: "WHAT???"

In case they don't understand, I add: "What the hell is this? Did you make this happen?"

Drew responds: "It was his idea. I just did some steering."

Like hell they did. I've learned to appreciate Drew's subtle, backseat driving. The gentle nudges they give, the cues they lead people into, to make whatever they've decided should happen seem like someone else's idea. They don't get enough credit, and they like it that way.

They add: "He wants to feel good about a cause, and he believes in yours. Let him have this."

There they go again! Before I can protest the amount of money, Drew makes me feel like letting Zack donate is the kind thing to do.

This is insane. This means I can actually launch my nonprofit. This means I can make content that hundreds of people might actually see.

This means I can hang out with Zack again.

Holy shit. I'm not ready. I'm living with my parents, taking mostly baby hikes that my dad can accompany me on, working double shifts to pay for Blucifer, and I haven't had a haircut since I saw Zack last.

I haven't become a completely different person yet. Someone who could fit into his world.

I get out of bed and take my phone with me to the kitchen. My parents are both there, for once, my mom wrapped in my dad's big, flannel robe. I'm interrupting a private moment, one of the many I've interrupted by living here these past months, but they both turn toward me with smiles. *If anyone's going to talk me out of this...*

But they don't.

"Keep your eyes on what you get out of this," Mom advises, after putting on her glasses and reading the contract. She complains the phone screen is too small and makes me forward it to her tablet. "Not what he wants. What you want. Before it all goes away."

I make a face, and my mom warns me: "Nothing lasts!"

I gesture between my parents, their 20-year-old kitchen. "This does!"

They look at each other.

"She has a point, Val," Dad says with a smile. He's taking quiche out of the oven.

Mom waves off the point. "This is choice every day. You think I wake up and think, 'oh, my life will stay the same today'? No. You think I ask, 'what does Rick want today?' No. I ask myself, 'what do you want today to be?' And then I go out and make that happen." She gesticulates at Dad. "He just comes along if he feels like it. And same for when he wakes up and asks himself what he wants to do with the day."

"But...but..." This sounds too simple. "What about the money? He's...buying me?" My voice goes up at the end because that's not quite what the contract feels like. But I think I've found a criticism my parents can't resist, and I'm feeling masochistic.

Instead, Mom scoffs. "Half a million dollars. This is nothing to him."

"But it is to me!"

"I think what your mother means to say is, and I don't mean to put words in your mouth, Val, but let's just be clear." Dad puts pieces of steaming quiche in front of each of us. "The money is not the point. We have money. We can give you this money if you want it. But we don't, because what you really want from us is a roof and a washing machine and a car to borrow. What you want from Zack is different."

Hoo boy, is it. We all let the simmering sexual tension I have with Zack sit there for a moment, unacknowledged.

"Yes, this is it," Mom says. She might be talking about her bite of quiche—a recipe Dad's been trying to perfect for a week —but she's pointing her fork at me. "He supports your dreams, you support his, you keep your eyes on that. Money," she says, holding her right hand as if weighing it there. "Keeping him from dying on the side of a mountain," she continues, holding her left hand as if weighing that. She lifts the imaginary scales up and down and then shrugs and goes back to her quiche. "You both get what you want."

What I want. Because maybe Zack and I actually want the same thing. Just right now. I shut down thoughts of anything beyond that, the idea that maybe we'll reach the top of that mountain and look out into a shared future.

"I'd still drive that contract up to Grand Junction and run it by a lawyer this time," Dad adds.

Mom nods vigorously and gestures between him and me with her fork. "Yes. Don't be stupid again."

I laugh. But I follow their advice.

The contract is signed by the end of the week. I warn Zack, through his attorneys, that we have to make the climb before October to avoid the risk of winter storms. It's April now, with most trails still snow packed. I have time to breathe before I see him again.

"But he should come out here before then to acclimatize," I add. "After all, he has somewhere to stay."

The message is partly to remind myself how different we still are. He is the movie star with the mansion on a hilltop. I am the underemployed waitress with a video feed who lives with her parents.

But at least, after nearly six months, I finally have the funds to get Blucifer out of car jail. I've got my eyes on what I want.

thirty-five

ZACK

MY TRAINER THINKS I'm crazy. My agent thinks I'm crazy. Leaving LA for a month to climb a mountain isn't part of the business plan. I need to capitalize on my momentum.

"Think about their motives," Drew reminds me. "They're all making money off you."

"So are you." Marisol throws popcorn at them. We're sitting down to watch the first half of the footage Valentine released leading up to my apparently crazy mountain adventure.

"Hey, I make money whether he works or not. I'm the smart one," Drew replies smugly, tipping an imaginary cap at me.

"Don't remind me how pathetic it is that I have to pay someone to hang out with me."

"You're not paying me!" Marisol protests, sitting down between the two of us on the couch. She pokes me in the arm, and I grin.

"OK, you are my one true friend, then."

"I would hang out with you if you weren't paying me," Drew

grumbles as the platform loads on the internet TV. "Probably. Sometimes I stick around on my day off."

I laugh. "Don't hurt yourself."

"My therapist would tell you to reframe it," Marisol says serenely, spreading a blanket over her lap. "You're not paying people to hang out with you; you're sharing your good fortune with the people around you and making everyone's lives better."

"Is that what you tell yourself?" Drew teases her.

"It is! Shut up!"

"Shh," I say as the video starts. It opens with a contrast between the sweeping vistas in that part of Colorado and...me. My fame, my face on movie posters, the line of people at the film festival waiting to see me. Drew must have sent her this shaky cell-phone footage of me about to step onto a red carpet, taking a deep breath to prepare for facing the barrage of cameras when it was my turn.

Then it cuts to me getting out of the car dressed like an idiot to go hiking. Drew and Marisol laugh, so the comedic timing is good, even if it's embarrassing for me.

Valentine has a little footage of me talking about wanting to climb a mountain because it's "a real accomplishment, something solid," and then she even interviewed someone who's climbed every 14er in the state.

"It changes you," the man says. "Standing up there above treeline, the whole world laid out before you. You start to see the world a little different, even once you climb down."

It keeps going with footage taken from other hikes and attempts at hikes. Breath-taking views are scattered throughout as reminders of why this is a goal for some people.

The movie closes on a slow-mo shot of me in that freezing lake, my shirt clinging, my pants a little tighter than I remember. I walk toward the camera grinning, and it fades to: "To Be Continued" and a short link to the Kickstarter.

"Oh my god, take all my money," Marisol bursts out.

"She has a good eye for it," Drew comments. They both stand and head for the kitchen with the empty popcorn bowl, talking about the way the movie ended as they go, leaving me sitting there, staring at the screen.

Seeing myself star in something as myself—not the movie star, but the real me—takes me aback. The entire concept of the movie, the idea that I can find myself by climbing a mountain, is silly if I look at it too closely. But it doesn't feel silly. It feels real.

Who I am through Valentine's lens is the real me. The Zack who curls up on a couch with his two best friends. The Zack who makes an arthouse movie just to see if he can. The Zack who spent half an hour trying to get his nephew to say his name on a video call yesterday.

The movie has already been viewed a million times. The crowdsourcing campaign is doing extremely well. I wonder if Valentine will even be approached by some of the distributors I'd hoped to hear from on my own movie. The idea delights me, rather than making me jealous.

I've gotten a little obsessed with her backlog of short videos, in particular the ones about how many workers in Telluride live in their cars. The people who work at the ski resort and in the service industry are a community of the "working homeless," as she calls it.

Drew has been warned already that I want to hire local staff when we move back to Telluride to train for the mountain. It will take more time to train them, but "it's worth the investment," I told them. I hate to think of people working for me who can't afford a roof. This is a start, at least.

This trip is all about training, anyway. Training to be the kind of person I want to be moving forward, one who isn't battered around by what other people tell me to do all the time. Training to let people see the real me, flaws and all, even if it means being a little less beloved.

thirty-six

VALENTINE

HE'S BACK IN TOWN.

The buzz starts early, when he begins hiring people from town to staff his big house. "He's offering room and board," Julie tells me when she cuts back on hours at The Bivy to take a job with him.

The contractors he hires to transform his mansion into half-dorm are local, too.

Drew texts me that I should come get footage of Zack training at his home gym, and the plan eats a hole in my stomach all through my shift at The Bivy.

I know he's nearby. I think I'd know even if Drew hadn't texted. But so would everyone—the town is lit up with his projects: the 14er goal, the hiring local.

The news about Zack is all good. I just don't know if it's good *for me.*

"I heard he talked to the ski resort about making his place affordable worker housing during the season," Davis told me when I picked up Blucifer this morning. She's sitting, freshly bathed, right outside where I can peek at her every once in a while out the window. Davis tried to tell me it was "only a matter of time before she has another problem."

"It's worth it to me," I insisted. I'll keep fixing Blucifer until I'm dead.

I'm ignoring the emails inviting me to "meetings" in LA and "phoners" with agents. Now that I have the opportunity to leave the valley, it doesn't seem real. I don't know what to do with it. I'm terrified.

"Listen to your heart," was my parents' sound legal advice.

"Don't overcommit just because you can," Drew said.

But I'm the idiot who wants to hear what Zack would say.

I sleep with Blucifer on public land that night, for the first time in months. As I look up at the sky, I understand that I can't drive up to Zack's mansion to see him for the first time in months. There are too many memories there, too many associations. It feels too big. I need space around me when I see him again.

So I text Drew: "Ask Zack how he feels about a practice mountain."

* * *

The same giant, can't-see-into-it, black SUV rolls up to the trailhead, the gravel kicked up by the wheels marring the otherwise spotless exterior.

I let out my breath when I realize I'm holding it, waiting for Zack to get out of the car.

When he does, he scrambles out. "Sorry we're late!" he calls, grabbing his backpack and hurrying over to me. Then he stops short, as if he was about to hug me and thought better of it. We don't do that anymore. He stands in front of me, holding his bag and staring.

I stare back. He looks good, of course. He hasn't gotten less movie-star-like since I saw him last. Behind his sunglasses, I can't see his eyes, and mine are similarly hidden. But somehow, I know our eyes connect.

"Go ahead, let me have it," he says, breaking the silence. "What's wrong with my outfit this time?"

I smile, because his voice is teasing. Self-deprecating. He has a new backpack, one that might actually fit, and he's wearing layers. But I can't tell him he looks "perfect," at least not out loud. So I say, "You're fine. Practical, for once."

"That's the movie poster quote." He nods and slings his bag onto his back. I turn away to get my bag out of my trunk so he won't see that I can't stop smiling.

"How's Blucifer doing?" He comes toward me and puts his hand on Blucifer's back bumper. I watch the gentle way he touches my car out of the corner of my eye as I buckle straps.

"Had a rough winter, but she's fine now."

"Yeah?" He strokes Blucifer's frame, and it makes something in me ache. "Glad she's doing OK."

"You ready?" I ask instead of responding. "Is Fred going to wait for you here, or is he coming back to pick you up?"

"He'll come back. He's tracking my GPS."

I nod, because as much as I want to offer Zack a ride home, I can't. I can't have him that close to me, in Blucifer, chatting like we're friends. We're not friends. This is a business partnership.

We're too different for anything more.

Even though Zack is wearing a hat again, I notice some people at the trailhead eying us. "Shit, have you become trail famous?" I whisper, guiding him away from the group standing by the map board.

"You did kind of associate me with hiking around Telluride in your viral movie," he replies drily. "People are on the lookout now. Hope it's good for tourism."

I realize he's wearing a watch similar to mine when we both turn our wrists up to start the activity at the same time. He sees me look and gestures at it defensively. "It seemed like a good idea."

I nod but can't speak. It *is* a good idea. Something about this —setting out on a hike with someone else who is well-equipped —sets my stomach bouncing. It certainly isn't happening because of the trail. It's popular because it's little more than an uphill walk.

"Can we get a picture?" Our avoidance tactics aren't enough. Zack is approached no less than four times on our way up the hill. Since the trail is also a 4-wheel road, at one point, a jeep stops, blocking the narrow road with its steep drop-off, and the woman inside asks for his autograph.

"Sorry," I grumble. "This isn't what I pictured." I've been getting footage of the celebrity scrum, but I have no idea how I'll use it. It's not exactly the idyllic getting-back-to-nature narrative I've been promoting as Zack's arc.

He brushes off the attention. "Hopefully it won't be like this on the real hike."

I shake my head. "I don't think so. This is pretty touristy. I could have picked a different trail, I guess." I picked this one to see the early wildflowers blooming, the brilliant red Indian Paintbrush and pale blue Wild Irises.

"Don't worry about it." He's not huffing or puffing, at least not any more than I am, on our way up the slope. He brought plenty of water and his boots are broken in. I'm actually pretty impressed with his preparation for this.

Once we reach the waterfall, we stand side by side taking it in, the brim of his cap pulled down over his eyes, hoping to remain unnoticed for a few minutes.

As we're standing there, his pinky finger brushes mine. It seems like an accident until I shift away but it happens again.

I look at him. "Are you trying to hold my hand?"

"It seemed like a good idea," he shrugs.

"We're not—" I cross my arms and look away from him. "We're just working on this project together. It's good for both of us. Drew said it was helping your, like, Hollywood stock rise or something. Which is gross, by the way."

"It is helping my brand," Zack agrees calmly. "That doesn't mean it's all it is."

"But it is. All it is." My words tumble over each other in my rush to get them out. To make this simple and black and white. Like my parents always taught me. Messy, unethical sell-outs versus pure-hearted, passionate, peaceful people.

Except Zack doesn't seem that unethical anymore, and I don't feel like a sell-out when I'm around him.

"We don't believe in the same things," I say, knowing it's a weak argument. "I have...mountain values. And you...live in LA."

He gives me some side-eye. "So...you don't think you can have 'mountain values' in LA?"

"Do you even know what mountain values are?" I snap back.

He turns to me and smiles. It's his real smile, not the one from movie posters. "Do you even know what we're talking about right now?"

"Aren't you..." I hesitate, hating myself for bringing up something from a tabloid. "Dating Marisol Williams?"

He shakes his head. "No. She's just a friend."

I swallow and nod, trying to accept a world where rumors about dating a Hollywood celebrity are common.

"Hi...sorry to bother you but..." A woman with two pre-teen girls hovering behind her interrupts us. She's holding her cell phone.

And I lose him again to his fans for a few minutes, long enough to wonder what we had been talking about, exactly. And whether my objections were any more real than Zack's affection.

* * *

I see the picture of the cat first—a white, long-haired puffball with a grumpy look on its face. The picture is open on the phone lying on the bartop as I approach a new customer with a glass of water and a menu.

Then I look up at the woman's face and see Zack's...whatever she is? The person who bosses everyone around. Diane.

"I led with Floof because I suspect you're a little like Zack and need to see the human side of people before you do business with them," Diane says. She doesn't even glance at the menu. "I'll take a gin martini as long as you can make it very cold and very dirty. And I'd like you to take your break with me, if you can."

The Bivy is quiet, for a summer weekday. But I didn't get up this morning hoping for a nice chat with one of the most intimidating women I've ever met.

"I'm not going to stop making the movie about Zack," I say. I have so many confusing and conflicting offers about the second half of the movie; the one thing I know for sure is I'm definitely making it. Whether he makes it to the top of the mountain or not. After that, who knows.

"Like I told Zack, I'm not here to tell him what to do. I'm here to make what he wants to do look better to the public. I can do the same for you." Diane puts the phone away as she talks, even though I could have used that icebreaker a little longer.

"Let me get you that drink." And maybe one for me.

I return with a beer, Diane's martini, and my apron wrapped around my order book. I set it on the table beside my drink and take a long swallow before raising my eyes to Diane, waiting for her to begin whatever spiel she brought today.

The other woman smiles. She taps her martini glass with one finger. "This is good. You made it?"

I nod.

"A woman of many talents."

I shrug. I've made plenty of bad drinks in the years leading up to being competent, most of them at restaurants that cared less than The Bivy. "Necessity."

Diane shakes her head. "Lesson one, if I may offer it unsolicited. Don't downplay your accomplishments."

"Making a martini is an accomplishment?"

Diane takes another sip. "Everything can be an accomplishment." She flicks her free hand to capture the scene around us. "Growing up in one of the most beautiful parts of the country. Waiting tables for a living. Sleeping in your car. Hiking a mountain. It's all part of the overnight success narrative. The backstory."

Uncertain what narrative we're talking about, I gulp my beer. "Who's the overnight success in this scenario?"

Diane taps her glass again. "You are."

I laugh and gesture around us, much less elegantly than Diane had. "My life is not exactly successful. You said it—I sleep in my car. I didn't go to college, I make less than minimum wage, and I have no benefits."

"Let me guess," Diane says. "You have an inbox full of offers and your phone is full of unknown calls. But you're just trying to 'focus on the work' and ignore the noise at the moment because that's what you know best."

I sit back on the barstool and swing my legs. I purse my lips and sigh. Of course, Diane is accurate. But I didn't realize I was a stereotype.

"It's normal," Diane says. "I can't tell you how many people I work with who nearly overlook a life-changing opportunity because they got overwhelmed. It's my job to lighten that load and make things a little more clear."

"Are you..." I frown. I can feel my forehead wrinkling and am more conscious of it because Diane's forehead never seems to move. It's as smooth as a baby's. "I don't know, trying to sign me or something?" The last thing I need is another offer to add to the pile.

"I think we can help each other. I'm a fixer," Diane says. "But I am trying to start my own one-stop-shop where agents and publicity work together in-house. You would be one of my early clients."

I sigh. "I don't know what I'm doing. I don't really even know what I want to do, but I don't want to sign onto a whole thing…"

Diane raises her hand. It's a gracious movement, but it effectively cuts off my protest. "Let me get you a deal for the second half of your mountain movie with Zack. I'll do it without a long-term contract. If you're happy with the results, then we'll talk about the future."

"Why would you help me?"

"Valentine, you're frankly a hot commodity in Hollywood right now. Or you could be, if you responded to any communication attempts." But Diane smiles slightly, like I'm in on the joke and not the butt of it. "If I make you a great deal, a flashy deal, something that gets written up, people know I'm making a play for new business and I can back it up. This is not a charity offer by any means."

I use my empty pint glass to make circles in the moisture on the bartop. "Does Zack know you're talking to me?"

"No. But you're welcome to ask him for a business reference, if you want. Zack has a very particular way of hiring people. He hires on trust. That's why I showed you the picture of Floof."

I raise my eyebrows. "Is your cat's name really Floof?"

Diane smiles, and her face is suddenly much softer. "It is. I have a lot more pictures if you want to see."

I stop swirling my glass. "Did Zack *actully* hire you because of Floof?"

She shakes her head. "He hired me because I'm good at what I do. He trusts me because of Floof. Just like he trusts you because of..." She pauses and her forehead almost crinkles a little bit. "Blucifer?"

I feel heat creep into my face. "Is that what he said?"

Diane smiles. She pokes one of the olives at the bottom of her glass with a toothpick and eats it. "He said you were a loyal person who goes out of your way to care for things that matter, and he could tell by Blucifer. Whatever that means."

I nod and keep nodding, because I have a lump in my throat. Zack sees me, after all. And I want to keep being who he sees.

Diane gestures at her own untouched water, and I pull over the glass to relieve my dry throat. "Can you help me sort through the craziness so I can still be that person on the other side of all this?" I finally ask.

Diane nods. "I can help with the first part. You are in charge of the second. But I'm here to support you. And," she adds, looking up from poking a second olive with the toothpick, "if you'll forgive a bit more unsolicited advice, it helps to have allies who've been through it all before. So lesson two: Zack is here to support you, too."

thirty-seven

ZACK

I'D THOUGHT training to play a former Marine who could sprint through fire carrying a 90-pound girl over one shoulder while firing a 20-pound machine gun with one hand was hard.

But scrambling over loose rocks for four hours at 11,000 feet above sea level with nothing between me and the blazing sun feels harder. Valentine telling me, "This is nothing! You fall here and you won't even die!" doesn't help, either.

She'd brought her friend Hunter, who worked as a tour guide at the adventure center. He was kind, other than laughing his ass off when he heard Valentine's plans for me. "You're training for a whole month? You'll be fine," he assured me when we parted ways. "I've hauled folks fresh from New York City up a mountain before and they made it. Barely."

Now, I'm collapsed on my sofa with an ice pack on one ankle and aloe on my face. Drew brought me an enormous cheeseburger, as requested, but it's so hard to reach on the coffee table. I'm gripping my ice water with both hands. Valentine hadn't been joking about bringing two liters of water on the hike. I've drunk almost all of it and still crave more.

My cell phone, resting on my chest, buzzes.

"Heard you got a workout today," says a text from "Dad Rick." I should probably change that ID before someone sees it.

"I'm so tired," I type back, slowly, with fumbling fingers.

"Good tired?" is the reply. I imagine Rick in the kitchen, waiting for something in the oven, his reading glasses on as he peers at his phone.

"Good tired," I agree in response.

"Come by for a pastry," Rick writes back. "You earned it."

"I'm not sure I can get up for a while."

"I'll ask V to bring one by."

I hesitate. Valentine hasn't been to the house since last year, when we broke up...or decided we weren't dating...or whatever that was. I sense she's been avoiding it.

"I think I'll get a second wind in a little while," I text back. "I can stop by in an hour?"

"Sure, I'll still be plugging away on these cake donuts."

If that isn't motivating, I don't know what is. I've decided I can eat whatever I want today, given that my watch tells me I burned 800 calories on our "practice" hike.

Drew just raises their eyebrows at me when I invite them to come along for donuts, so I take Fred and the SUV into town.

Rick waves at me to come in, through the open window above the sink, when I pull up to the front of the house. I leave Fred in the SUV with the windows rolled down and walk in like I live there. The kitchen smells as warm and welcoming as I'd imagined, but Valentine's mother is also there to greet me in the tiny space.

Valkyrie Arnaud is one of those people I always picture having her hands on her hips, even though at the moment her hands are filled with a donut and a glass of milk. She's standing with one hip propped against the counter, like she's only got a few minutes for her break. She has a pair of safety goggles pushed up into her mess of dark brown hair, and there are gloves on the counter beside her.

I suddenly don't know what to do with my hands. Fortunately, Rick pops a donut into one and offers me milk or coffee to drink.

"Uh, coffee, please, thank you." I'm learning to drink it without specialty additions. I'm practicing being flexible about my diet. Like a normal person who doesn't always have staff to cater to my every whim. It hasn't been that bad. Last time I visited my mom, it almost felt like I fit into a normal life again.

I take a bite of the donut and it immediately sticks to the top of my mouth, so when Valentine's mom says, "So you think you can win over my daughter," I can only swallow and roll my tongue around in my mouth trying to clear it as my eyes water.

"This batch is a little dry," Rick says apologetically. He hands me a mug. "It'll just be the home batch."

I take a drink to wash down the bite of donut. "I'm just trying to climb a mountain," I tell Valkyrie, who is still patiently boring a hole into my forehead with her eyes.

"Never bullshit a French woman," she says without any rancor in her voice. "The mountain is a symbol for you."

I take another bite to buy time and immediately have to take another sip of hot coffee. I want to sit down, but I don't want to lose my height on Valkyrie, either. I look at Rick for support, but Valentine's dad is busy using tongs to ease a raw donut into the pot of boiling oil on the stove.

"I promise I'm not trying to hurt her," I say, because that must be what Valentine's parents are really worried about.

"Hurt," Valkyrie says, waving it off like she'd say, "pshaw." "Life is hurt. You," she says, pointing at me with the middle finger of the hand holding the last bite of her donut, "just don't use her."

"I wouldn't—" I begin to protest, but Valkyrie keeps going.

"Don't climb up with her help, only to leave her up there." Belying the tone of her words, she casually dips her last bite of donut in the milk and pops it into her mouth.

I pause to try to parse her words and what she might mean by them. She finishes off her milk as I do and puts the glass in the sink. She pats me on the shoulder as she passes me to leave the kitchen.

"Just remember who you are and you'll do well," she says. "And take that man in my driveway some of these donuts!" And then she's gone, leaving me a puzzling mix of affirmed and terrified.

Rick, concentrating on his donuts, throws a smile over his shoulder at me. "She likes you."

"She does?" The donut churns in my stomach. I can't imagine what I did to earn *like* from that woman. *Am I going to disappoint these people?*

"You keep coming back," Rick replies. "Valkyrie likes people who show up. Keep trying, even when they fail."

That makes a little more sense since it implies I failed once. I slowly move out of Rick's way and sit down at the table. "What if I keep failing?" I ask.

Rick doesn't even glance up. "You will. And then you put one foot in front of another until you can try again. It's a lot like climbing a mountain."

I like these people. I wish I could introduce them to my mom and sister, because I think they'd get along. They all have the same grounding effect on me — that sense that despite every-thing, I'm still just Zack and that's a good thing.

If people like this can believe in me, not just because of my latest release or my upcoming one but because of who I am, maybe I can believe in myself.

I know I shouldn't ask it, but the words come out anyway. "Do you think Valentine will let me try again?"

Rick smiles a little as he takes a sheet pan of donuts out of the oven. He pauses to hunch over two pans set side by side, one batch fried and the other baked, and pokes at the donuts with a toothpick. He mumbles to himself about the results. I wait, finishing my coffee. As anxious as I am to reach the next step, I'm also happy to be here in this kitchen, with no urgency to perform or achieve anything at all.

"It's a tough thing," Rick finally says, and he could be talking about the donuts until he continues. "Building up trust in the beginning to allow another person to fail, over and over, and still expect them to stick with it." He shakes his head over the donut he's crumbling on a plate. "That's the tricky thing about relationships. You don't know what you're starting until you're well into the hike."

I nod. I dunked my piece of donut in the coffee one too many times and now it's bobbing around in my mug. I try to pluck it out without dipping my fingers in the hot liquid. "But maybe...if she sees me pick myself back up and keep trying?"

Rick puts his oven mitt down and turns to me, putting his full attention on me again. "Maybe so." That might be the most encouragement I'm going to get today.

The other man adds, "The thing about a life of trying is, you don't know if you'll make it until you do. The trying has to be worth it to you by itself."

He could be talking about Valentine, my career, *or* climbing a mountain. Or maybe even my tiny spark of a plan to try again at being a director.

And Rick has a point. But I know I'm going to succeed at one thing because I'll keep trying until I do. There's no other option for me but to win Valentine's heart.

thirty-eight

VALENTINE

I STILL REFUSE to visit Zack's place, so we're running intervals outside on a hill.

Zack's trainer came up with the plan we're following. It's full of words like "VO2 Max" and "drop set." I'm skeptical about the weight-lifting parts of the routine—"the best muscles are the ones you get doing the thing," I insist—so Zack does those by himself in his home gym.

But running up a hill, walking down, then running up again —that makes sense to me for training to climb a mountain. And watching a shirtless Zack doing it isn't bad, either. The wildflowers are blooming, the sky is blue but not too hot, and Zack Ryder is a compact form of fast-twitch muscles gathering and exploding with every dash. I keep getting distracted by his hamstrings, of all things.

It's annoying how good-looking he still is when he's sweaty. We never really worked up to sweaty sex while we were having it. Things between us were more...tender. Like building a foundation of trust for a relationship that never went anywhere. And never could.

Every time my brain wants to think "maybe," I imagine myself as the help in Zack's kitchen, because that's the only thing I could contribute to his lifestyle in LA.

Zack flops down on the ground, his chest heaving. "I might be training harder for this than my last movie."

"This is nothing," I maintain, even though I fell behind him a few laps ago. Apparently, his gym time is paying off. I'd consider joining him, but I can't bring myself to walk into that house. "You'll see when we're another few thousand feet above sea level."

"But we're not going to run up the mountain, are we?"

I grin, sitting down on a rock nearby that's surrounded by lupine flowers. "Would make for terrible camera footage."

There's a question I want to ask him before we try this. The weeks are passing, and we're getting closer to "go" day, but I haven't worked up the courage. We mostly keep our conversations focused on training and snacks for the journey. Zack has sent me more than one late-night text on that theme—asking whether people really bring pickle juice on hikes, or if jerky "always tastes that way."

I default to our safe topic now, offering him one of the baked protein balls my dad made with oatmeal and peanut butter.

"Protein balls?" Zack repeats as he's cleaning his hands with antibacterial gel. He grins, and I can read the joke in his head.

"Protein is serious, Zack," I say primly. "You don't want to bonk up there. What would your trainer say?"

He holds up the brown ball, examining it. "He'd probably say this is the perfect snack. A good balance of protein, carbohydrates, and fat. Rick made this with butter?"

"Of course he did." My dad told me to report back on whether they were too crumbly. And urged me to send extras home with Zack. My dad's relationship with Zack has more potential longevity than mine does. The two of them will probably be trading snacks and small gifts, like the sunglasses, for years to come.

The thought is bittersweet. Much like the protein ball.

"Zack, why are you really doing this?" The question pops out at last, as it was eventually bound to considering my internal filter is flimsy at best.

He looks up at me from where he's sitting on the ground, the shirtless movie star nibbling on a homemade snack. It occurs to me then that Zack might not eat just anything unwrapped that was handed to him. But because it came from my dad, he trusts it.

And maybe he trusts me, too.

It's morning, and the air is still cool, but the sun is rising in the sky. I blame that for the wave of heat that passes through my body.

"It's grounding," Zack says. "To be humbled by something I can't do easily. Something worth doing. It reminds me of the person I want to be. The person I am, when I'm around the right people. Like some of my friends, even Drew. Like my mom and sister. Or your dad. Or you."

I point at my chest. *Me?*

"You have such a strong sense of who you are, of what's important to you," he says. "I want to be more like that. Less about my brand. And that scares me. Just like doing this does." Then he smiles, that big movie-poster grin. "Dreams grounded in reality. That's my new thing."

"I'm not sure that can be a thing," I scoff because doing anything else would mean throwing myself in his arms. Asking to be his dream.

But that's not reality.

"My goal, then," he replies, still grinning. Unabashed by how earnest this conversation has gotten. "Don't you think we're being realistic about this one?"

"This one, yes," I agree. The dream of holding onto Zack's coattails in a place like LA—and making it last—is much less realistic than climbing a tall mountain after a whole month of training. I decide deflection is the safest course of action. "If you get up and run up that hill a few more times!"

Zack leaps up, jack-knifing from his rock-hard core like an action star, and takes off running. I'm a few steps behind, like I'll always be.

thirty-nine

VALENTINE

THE PLAN WAS ALWAYS to camp the night before the climb so we don't have to get up two hours earlier to make the drive to the trailhead.

I just didn't realize how camping with Zack would feel.

Camping is usually when I spread out, get some alone time, walk around naked—although having neighbors on public land is getting more and more common lately—but with Zack here, camping is something completely different.

It's intimate.

I find a spot that's close to the trailhead but not too close to everyone else planning to summit tomorrow, so we're alone aside from the glow of a light in someone else's tent yards away. We unpack the car and set up the camp on the most level ground, so it'll be easy to grab what we need and go tomorrow in the dark.

I have to explain how to poop outdoors—in a WAG bag, since I've stopped burying my poop as more and more people started camping in the area. He listens carefully, like he's more interested in learning than being grossed out by a natural human function. I document this conversation, like everything else, filming it on my new collapsible tripod. I don't know yet what footage I'll use. The American public might not be ready for a conversation about Zack Ryder's poop.

He sets up the tent by himself, waving me off with "I remember." He's so proud after. I discreetly check his work while he's peeing out of eyesight to make sure it won't collapse on us, but it's solid.

The plan is for Zack to sleep in the tent, and me either outside or in Blucifer. The forecast calls for scattered rain showers that will clear before sunrise.

We don't have a fire, since there's a drought, but we gather around my cookstove, and I warm up a hearty lentil soup with crusty bread from Dad. We talk quietly, as though the thick spruce trees giving our campsite some privacy shouldn't be disturbed.

"Do you think we'll make it?" he asks, for possibly the dozenth time. I get that this is a big deal for him. It is for me, too, because of the movie.

It's also my fourth time climbing Mt. Sneffels, if I count the time when I was still small enough to be carried in a big, supportive backpack and my parents took me up.

"Probably," I say now. "But you should be prepared to turn back if conditions aren't right. If we don't summit before noon, a storm could move in, and it's not safe to be that high up."

"But we'd try again if that happens, right?"

I shrug. "Yeah, if you can stick around. We kind of need to." I gesture at the camera, which is still rolling. I wanted to get some of this for the movie—a conversation about doubts builds tension.

But I have no illusions that Zack will stay another month in Telluride if it's not good ROI. This movie is good for his brand, like Diane told me. "But Zack's time is also money," she'd said. "As in, he's not making any right now and his team is putting a lot of pressure on him."

"When do you have to get back to LA?" I ask.

Zack shrugs. "I don't have any commitments for a while. I've been..." He pauses, gesturing at the camera. "Can we turn that off?"

"Say something about how committed you are to this first."

He nods, waits a beat, and then says, as though answering me, "I really want to see this through. I feel like, if I can climb this mountain, I can do anything."

I smile slightly. "A true professional," I say, as I switch my phone camera off.

"I meant it. That helps."

It's getting colder. The nightly temperature plummets in the mountains, even though it's July. I zip my jacket up and take out gloves. Zack, a true warm-blooded Californian, is already wearing a beanie *and* hoodie turned up over his head.

"What were you saying?" I ask.

"Oh, um," he says, like he forgot what we were talking about. I know he didn't. He's nervous, in a way I haven't seen since his movie premiere. "I've been working on a script. Writing it, I mean. Just noodling around."

I nod, trying not to scare him with a big reaction. But this is big news. Zack is trying to create again. "What's it about?"

"It's about...well, me. It's about a family that moves to a mountain town and doesn't know what they're doing. How different it is from the suburb in the Midwest they moved from." The pace of his voice increases, getting excited about his ideas. "It's a single mom with a kid. But a daughter, not a son. She's a teenager. It's about finding your way. I want it to be a coming-of-age story, sort of, but for both of them."

"Why make it about women?" I ask quietly.

Zack looks at me quickly. "Is that arrogant? I wanted it to be about, you know, someone who was willing to learn. I think sometimes men are macho about change, like they're born who they're going to be, and it's not manly to ever question that. But someone like my mom has to change to survive."

"I don't think it's arrogant," I reply. "I just think if it's about you, you could make it about that. About being a man who's willing to change."

I pause, hearing my own words. It's true. But it makes my cheeks burn because it speaks to exactly what I wished for, back when we were on the cusp of something. When I'd thought maybe we could be more than a late-fall fling. Silly, wish-fulfillment stuff to think that because Zack can change, that I can change into someone he would be with long-term. Someone who understands his world. Someone who won't hold him back.

"Do you want some tea to warm up?" I ask, changing the subject because I can't sit here any longer, looking at him, without wanting to touch him. Because maybe I'd hold him back long-term, but right now we have nothing better to do.

"Could we sit in Blucifer for a little bit?" he asks instead. I love the way he says Blucifer. The name had started as my joke, a reference to a statue that killed its creator, and it stuck. But when he wraps his lips around it, it sounds like a kiss. "I'm having flashbacks to that time I thought I'd never get warm again."

"Sure," I say, and lead him to the car. It seems like we're walking toward a lot more than a warm, contained space, especially when he suggests we get in the back, where the seats are folded down and I already have a pile of blankets ready for bed.

He's shivering, tucking his knees under his chin and between his arms even after he wraps himself in one of my blankets. "I can turn the car on for a while," I offer.

"Can we cuddle?" he asks, words that should be on one of his movie posters. Just his face and those words. Every woman in

America would put it on her wall and see the film 50 times — no matter what it was about.

I don't even remember saying "yes." I just turn around to back into the curve of his chest and accept that I'm the luckiest woman in the world right now. Zack wraps his arms around me from behind, bringing the blanket over my body and scooting me in closer to him. Butt to crotch. I can't breathe.

It's silent in the car. The windows are cracked just an inch for airflow, but it's warm under the blankets and in Zack's arms. The man's like a space heater. His chest moves up and down as he breathes, and after a few minutes I realize I'm matching his breaths.

"I'd like to go down on you," he says. It's so quiet the words don't register immediately. "Can I do that?"

I make a small noise, not an assent but a "is this really happening?" sound.

"Yes?" he asks, his hand slowly traveling down my belly. That's all it takes for me to be ready. For his hand, his mouth, his whatever.

"Yes," I say. The word comes out without thought, without doubts about the cramped space or getting up early tomorrow or anything beyond that.

He pops the button on my water-proof, rip-resistant hiking pants. I briefly wonder what it would be like to be a woman who wears cute, lacy underwear under her practical attire instead of the plain briefs I'm actually wearing. Just to surprise him. But the thought flees my head when he slides a hand inside, skin to skin, slowly moving down until he touches me in a spot that makes me jump and exhale.

Then he hesitates. "I haven't washed my hands," he says, apologetically.

"It's been a few hours since I showered," I warn him softly. I know how Zack feels about germs. This might be the end of our encounter. And perhaps it's for the best.

But he says, "I like your germs. They taste the best."

And then we're both laughing. I don't remember laughing like this, ever, in bed. There was Tyler, whose humor was very different from mine. The last person I was with, before Zack, was a tourist I met on a dating app. It was just a hook-up and we both knew it. There was no laughter, no variety to how good he made me feel. The ways Zack makes my skin heat are endless. He adds new ways to fill my heart every time I'm with him.

He gently moves me onto my back and makes sure my head is propped up on my pillow, a luxury I allow myself despite the space it takes up in the car.

He keeps the blanket pulled up over his shoulders as he moves down my body to my unbuttoned pants.

He kisses me there, on my lower belly where it's rarely exposed to anyone else. His nose against my stomach turns me on for some reason, because it makes it really real that we're here, alone in my car with nothing to do but each other.

I thread my hands through his hair. "Zack," I whisper. "Fuck me."

"Hm, no, this is about you tonight," he replies, and lifts my hips so he can edge my pants down my hips.

"But..." I protest, even though his fingers are parting my lower lips and I can barely think straight.

"I've gotta wait until I climb that mountain to get off. I'm superstitious," he says, and I'm not sure if he's joking.

"What about me?" I manage, even as I arch away from the seat of my car because he blows on my clit. "I don't...have to wait...?"

"You're in charge. We need you to be relaxed up there," he replies, his lips moving against my pussy in a way that makes me forget what we were talking about.

And he starts to lick. He alternates licking and blowing, thrusting his tongue deep inside me, patiently coaxing me past the point where I worry he might be getting bored of this, until I'm on the edge. And then he puts two fingers inside me and curls them as he makes circles around my clit. I come, clenched around him, curling up involuntarily over his head in the car.

I stare at the roof, at the mystery stains that I had no idea were there, as my body rides out the endorphin rush.

"We should do this more often," Zack says, laying beside me on his back, spreading the blanket back over both of us even though I'm overheated. The inside of the windows are fogged over.

"Special occasion," I say, without thinking about it. "For the mountain. Mountain fuck." I'm babbling, but it has a certain amount of logic to it. We teamed up for this one project that benefits both of us. We're in a bubble that won't last. But while we're in it, we can do anything. Everything, if he wants to.

He props himself up on one elbow and looks down at me. "What if it's more than that?"

I look back at him. He's serious. I gaze at the dome light on my ceiling again. *Blucifer help me.* "This isn't one of your movies. It's different while we're here...in my town. Away from the rest of the world. But out there, we don't work. We're so different."

"Are we though?" He says it simply, like he's found the obvious hole in my argument.

"You're...famous," I reply weakly.

"That's not who I am. That's my job. Being famous. It's like a bullet point on my resume that gets me more work. Just like your million viewers is going to get you more work after you finish this movie. Are you going to let it change who you are?"

I grimace. "I hope not."

He nods. "That's something we can help each other with."

Zack is here to support you, too, Diane had said.

"I don't know," I finally say, hoping he'll let it go. But also not wanting him to. I'm afraid to believe, because the minute I do, my world could be turned upside down.

"OK," Zack says, suddenly resolved. I'm worried I've convinced him. My logic *is* persuasive. "How about this. If I can make it to the top of this mountain, we can be together."

"What?" I try to laugh, but it sounds like I'm choking. "How does that make sense?"

"Because being together will be hard work sometimes, too. But if we just keep putting one foot in front of the other..."

We'll get there. We'll...stay together?

I swallow. Is it possible? Could we help each other remain who we are as individuals, holding on tightly enough to stay together?

He moves so his chin is in the crook of my shoulder and neck and his lips are by my ear. "Just say yes," he whispers.

The climb is going to be harder than he thinks, at least at the end. I'd consider that last stretch to be at least class 3.5. And that final 1,000 feet or so are when it feels like you can't get enough oxygen and you have to rest every few steps. Something out of our control might come up, too. We really might not make it. And maybe we *shouldn't* succeed. Zack hasn't had enough training. I'm not a real guide.

I leave it up to fate. Fate and the possibility there's more to the world than I've seen in this valley. "Yes," I agree, holding his hand and hoping reality never sets in.

forty

ZACK

THIS IS EASY! Like taking a walk. Sure, we're going steadily uphill, but if the slope stays this gradual, I'll barely feel it. We're walking through a meadow of lush wildflowers—red, blue, purple, and yellow. The sun is just beginning to rise, illuminating the top of the diamond-shaped summit ahead, and I feel well-rested. The conditions are perfect, and I'm so ready to prove to Valentine that I can do this.

The sun brightens our surroundings, and something starts to bother me. "Are we on the mountain?" I ask, holding my breath because the ground rises up in front of us toward the sky, but we don't seem to be getting any higher.

"We're still on the approach," Valentine replies. She looks back and sees the horror dawning on my face. "We're on the trail. We've started."

We drove up a bumpy road early this morning in the dark, and I thought that put us at the very base of the mountain. But it didn't. I don't ask if it gets harder—because that's obvious. I have an actual helmet hanging off my backpack, which Valentine assured me wasn't overkill.

When she told me the hike would be about six miles, I'd smiled because it sounded like so little walking compared to some of the practice hikes we'd been on. "I can get to the top of a mountain in less than two hours?" I'd scoffed.

She warned me it would take longer than six miles on flat ground. So now, an hour later, when I pause to take off a layer because the sun is starting to get warm and climbing is making me sweat, I look around and still can't tell where we're going. But at least we're on a mountain, so we must be getting somewhere.

The trail opens up to a field of loose rocks at an incline Valentine calls "scree." She traces a path with her finger pointing upward. It's not so much a trail as a dotted line. "Here we go!" she announces, and I follow her into the rocks.

She stays ahead of me, leading the way as usual. She's stripped down to a tank top, and her strong arms flex as she keeps three points of contact with the ground, the way she taught me. She's beautiful. I can't believe I'm here on this mountainside with her. A year ago, I rarely saw the outside of SUVs with tinted windows, hotel rooms, and my brand-new house in Hollywood Hills. I was trapped inside my own success, unable to find a way out.

Now here I am, in the sunshine, on a path I chose. Sure, I have no idea where it's leading—how hard it will get, or whether it will truly be worth it—but I have a companion to help me along the way, fresh air, and as cheesy as it sounds, I'm just happy to be on the journey regardless of the ending.

I'm smiling like a fool when Valentine looks back at me. She's already wearing her helmet, with her phone strapped to it and the camera running.

"Enjoy it now," she says. "It'll take your breath away soon."

"Look around!" I call back to her. "It's so cool we're doing this!" I mug for the camera, and she laughs.

We stop mid-morning for a snack of trail mix and homemade jerky. I wipe my hands and face with an antibacterial wipe first, but the dirt on my hands seems like the least of my worries up here, where the air is thin and my butt muscles burn. The shadow of the mountain makes it cold enough that I put my fleece back on.

"Still good?" Valentine asks. "Want to keep going?"

"Yes!" I say without thinking. I'm tired, and raisins and nuts have never tasted so good, but there's no way I want to stop now.

"Where is the summit?" I ask, because now that we're actually on the mountain, it's impossible to see it. We're above treeline now, and it feels like being on top of the world, but I know we're not there yet.

"Don't worry, it's still there," she says. "We'll know when we get to it."

She makes me put my helmet on when we get to the "V-notch." We've passed a few people and been passed by a few—including one guy going down from the top already—and she says the people ahead of us might knock rocks down on our heads inadvertently.

Most of the people we've encountered eye Valentine's camera setup suspiciously, but they don't bother to check me out. I haven't been recognized at all. It's nice. People are more interested in the mountain than in me.

I can see why, as I stare up at a gully of loose rock. "Is that the top?" I ask, looking at where the sky meets the rock.

"Not quite, but this is the last hard part," she says. "Just go slow."

In the helmet, I'm even less recognizable. I put all my attention on where I put my feet and hands as we climb the big rocks in the gully going almost straight up. *Three points of contact, three points of contact.* Valentine's guidance keeps echoing in my head. I can hear myself huffing and puffing. There's less oxygen up here, and my heart is working hard.

We keep stopping to catch our breath. My stomach turns over when I look back down the way we came, so I keep my eyes raised. One foot after another.

"I want to try something," Valentine says, and we switch helmets for a while so she can get some first-person footage of me climbing. I forget to be self-conscious about gasping for air after I've worn it for about two seconds. The lack of oxygen prevents me from thinking about anything but pressing ahead. That and how much I want a cheeseburger. With bacon. And fries.

"Rick's apple fritters sound so good right now," I say, the words coming out like a moan. Valentine huffs down at me.

I watch her move slowly ahead, pausing every few steps to put her hands on her hips and bend over, finding air. *We can do this.*

I say it out loud, or rather, gasp it: "We can do this."

She looks back at me and smiles, probably because I look exhausted. "It's OK if we can't, you know. It's not the end of the world."

I take a deep gulp of air and push past her, taking the lead. It's easy enough: we just need to keep going up. I'm going to prove to her that I won't give up.

She trades helmets back the next time we stop but doesn't take over. I keep going. When we come out of the notch, it's only been half a mile, according to my watch, but it's the hardest half mile I've ever walked. I just feel more determined.

She gives me a fist bump. "Almost there," she says.

I grab her arm before she can pass me. "Do you believe me now?"

She pauses, looking at me seriously. She takes her helmet off and runs her fingers through her sweaty, matted hair, so I take mine off, too. She fiddles with her camera instead of looking at me. "Maybe," she finally says.

"Then let's keep going," I say, because I'm going to show her.

It's a few more hundred feet before, suddenly, she's right—the summit appears. There's a handwritten cardboard sign that says 14,157' pinned under a rock and a dozen people up there, taking pictures or lying on the ground. Everyone is bundled up because it's freezing up here, even with the sun now overhead.

The view is breathtaking—or would be if I had any breath left. The mountains around us spread out, but nothing is as high as our perch. We're looking down at the world. Below us, I can see bright blue alpine lakes reflecting the sun back at us. It's almost blinding how gorgeous it is.

I look back at Valentine. She's holding her phone, so I spread my arms and do a circle for the sake of good footage. When I look back, she's put the camera down and walks toward me.

"Are you sure?" she asks.

I know what she's asking. "I'm sure," I say, grasping her forearms. "I want to keep trying. And probably failing, sometimes, and then trying again. With you. Because you're the only person I've ever met who makes me want to climb mountains."

"I never thought I'd be here with you," she says. "You make everything look different. I love that."

I smile again. We're not there yet, but her words tell me we're close to *I love you.* Another summit we can reach together. Climbing this mountain didn't just convince her we could make it; it convinced me I could be what she needed.

She kisses me, and it's suddenly 10 degrees warmer on this mountaintop, because we did it. We still have a ways to go, but we'll tackle it together from now on.

forty-one

VALENTINE

I'M SORE, but in a good way.

Zack talked me into sleeping at his place—convincing me hadn't been that difficult, given his bed is more comfortable than either the ground or the twin-size bed I usually sleep on at my parents'—but I left him in bed to scrutinize the new contract Diane sent, on my phone's tiny screen in the kitchen.

It's a little awkward, encountering Julie, my coworker, at Zack's house. She offers me coffee and then disappears like a professional rather than trying to make small talk, only dropping the comment that "it's a great place to work."

Rather than confuse myself trying to guess at the meaning of the legal jargon in the contract, I call Diane.

"It's a great deal," she says. "But I think it can be better if we show them some of part two. Do you have any clips ready?"

"No...but I could put something together." I'm not sure when. I've spent all my time with Zack since we got off the mountain.

"It would be really helpful if you could come to LA, take some meetings, showcase your work in person."

My stomach cramps up. *This is what you want! Opportunity!* "I can look into that," I offer weakly, as my fear and elation war it out.

"Great," Diane says. "I'd be with you the whole time and you could speak as much or as little as you like. You should ask Zack. He knows what these meetings are like."

Drew walks into the kitchen then, looking sleepy and with bare feet. They see I'm on the phone and gesture to ask if I want to be left alone. I shake my head and wave them toward the coffee machine. Maybe they'll make me another cup; I'm a little intimidated by that stainless steel beast.

"OK, I will," I tell Diane, then thank her and hang up. "Diane thinks I should come to LA," I say to Drew.

"Great! We can show you around!" They punch half a dozen buttons on the coffee machine before it whirs to life. Then they turn around. "And you know, Zack has plenty of space. I bet you wouldn't need to get a hotel."

I nod slowly, because I hadn't thought of that, but I'm not sure if staying in a strange hotel in a new city is more intimidating or sleeping in a movie star's mansion. Is he on Star Maps? Would we be chased by paparazzi every time we went out?

Drew slowly adds, "You should maybe know, though, that Marisol sleeps over sometimes."

My brain empties of all those clearly lesser worries. "What?"

"Oh no! Not like the tabloids say," they add quickly, face anxious. "I mean..." They grimace. "No one knows this, so. Don't share it, please. She sleeps in my room."

I blink. "You're the one who's sleeping with—" I pause and correct myself: "Dating Marisol Williams?"

Drew turns back to collect their mug from the coffee machine. "For a while now. Since the location shoots for the last movie."

"And you've managed to keep it quiet this whole time?"

They laugh a little. "The tabloids are much more interested in the narrative that she's sneaking around with Zack." They sit down at the kitchen counter with me and raise an eyebrow. "Which is something you might have to get used to."

I think about this. Even if I am—with Zack, the tabloids might make it sound like he's with someone else. *Can I live with that?*

"Unless you become so interesting the tabloids start putting your name on the front page," Drew adds with a grin over their coffee.

"Ha! No thanks," I grin back.

Drew shrugs. "You remember that intern's story about Zack's new girlfriend being the local who criticized him? It's a pretty juicy narrative. I'm just saying...be prepared."

I swallow. More acidic coffee isn't sounding so good all of a sudden. "But you've done it. I mean, you've been around it your whole life. Right? And you're..." I wave at them, and they raise another eyebrow, waiting for my description. "Mostly normal. You're nice."

"A ringing endorsement."

"I mean," I say, exasperated. "You're good people! You and Zack both. You don't have to go crazy living in that world. Right?"

"Right," they say, firmly. "But..."

I brace myself.

"You do have to change. Not who you are, but how you handle things. And you have to learn the difference."

"Good morning! What are we talking about this fine day?" Zack sweeps into the kitchen and bounces over to me, hugging me from behind. Clearly in a great mood. I can't help smiling, despite the serious conversation I was having with Drew.

"Diane sent me an amazing deal. And she thinks she can land me an even better one if I come to LA."

"OK, that's fantastic news," Zack says, turning me toward him on the kitchen stool. "Diane doesn't overpromise. Ever. And you can stay with me in LA!"

"It might take a while. She was talking about multiple meetings."

"That's OK!" Zack kisses me on the nose. "Stay forever."

I smile at him, because it's sweet, but I have misgivings. Should I offer to pay rent while I'm there? Would he fly me in his private plane? I can't keep up with his lifestyle.

"Stop worrying about paying me back," he orders. He steps back and goes to the coffee machine. Drew jumps up and waves him away.

"You broke it last time," Drew says. Zack raises his hands and backs away.

He sits down on Drew's vacated stool beside me. "Things aren't always going to be exactly even," he tells me. "But we're going to be stronger together if we pool our resources."

"What are my resources, though?"

"Are you kidding?" He makes a face at me, then at Drew, who is leaning against the counter with their arms folded. "You're going to make me look great in your movie, and that's going to mean I can get another deal. For my script or to direct or produce. I haven't figured out what I want to aim for yet. You can help me with that, too."

His words make me feel like I'm back on that mountaintop, with the whole world beneath our feet. Like I don't have enough oxygen, but everything is wonderful, anyway. Like all my fears are beneath my feet, unable to overwhelm me.

"I guess I'm coming to LA, then," I say. Zack grins at me. He looks back at Drew, who is grinning, too. And I realize I can't stop smiling.

Maybe everything won't turn out the way I want. But I have everything I need to figure it out right here.

forty-two

ZACK

IT'S a long drive to LA from Telluride, but of course Valentine isn't going to leave Blucifer behind.

And I'm not going to leave Valentine, so I send Drew and most of my things home on my private jet but find myself packed inside a full car with a two-day trip ahead of me.

I'd suggested—briefly—that we come back for Blucifer if she decides to stay. She flared that she didn't want the only thing that felt like *her* in LA to be her boyfriend.

All in all, I'm proud of us for negotiating without an actual argument. It bodes well for the future, and her first sight of my home behind its gated walls.

I've already dropped a few hints that I might like to move away from LA, with its expensive real estate and intense media scrutiny. I have a feeling she won't like the city, and now that I'm thinking about it, I don't really like it that much either. Now I know there are places like Telluride, where I'm not anonymous but mostly I'm not bothered, either.

I hold her hand as we cross the border into Arizona, the first tangible sign we're really leaving her state behind. "We'll be back soon," I offer. We both know what a good thing we have in that town. The people, the scenery. The homemade apple fritters and donuts. I'm not going to take it for granted.

She nods. I'm not sure what she's thinking. "Are you scared?" I ask gently.

"Of course," she says. "Aren't you?"

"I'm less scared because you're here," I reply. It's goofy, but it's how I feel. I imagine taking her to my next movie premiere. Despite the complications of her not knowing the protocol—that the photographers will want to herd me away from her for individual shots, that I've learned to stand a certain way and smile a certain way to avoid a bad picture—I'm excited to show her that part of my world. I'm excited for her to make it feel more real. I'd taken Marisol last time and we'd made fun of it the whole time, in small asides to each other, but soon I won't have to borrow someone else's girlfriend as a crutch.

"I feel that way, too," she tells me. "But I'm still kind of scared that if I'm too far away from the mountains, I won't be the girl I am there anymore."

I smile at her. "You'll always be that mountain girl to me."

She laughs. "I guess I will, huh."

"In a good way." I pause, looking out the window at the desert-y landscape. "And if we ever get caught up in the spiral, from the fame or money or work, we can come back. Even if my house is full of ski workers, we can stay with your parents."

She smirks. "If you don't mind sleeping on the floor."

I grimace. "I'll buy them a bigger mattress. I'm serious, though," I add. "Anytime. We can jump on my plane."

I see another argument cross her face and ready myself to remind her that as uncomfortable as she might be flying in my private jet, I'd be more uncomfortable getting mobbed flying commercial.

But she doesn't say it. "We'll always have the mountains?" she asks, throwing me a look. She's asking more than that, I can tell.

She doesn't know yet how confident I am in us. If geography and budgets help keep us together for now, so be it. We have plenty of time to build an even stronger bond. To blaze our own trail. It's a project we'll work on together.

"That's right," I say. "One foot in front of the other." *Forever*.

Ryder and Arnaud Accept Silver Medallions

By Jenn Hollis

Telluride Film Festival presented "White House Rising" star Zack Ryder and hometown hero and documentarian Valentine Arnaud with Silver Medallion awards on Monday in recognition of their contributions to the film industry and specifically Telluride filmmaking.

"This recognition means more than I can say," Ryder said at the ceremony. "My work is personal and its impact on others is so hard to predict. This film festival is one of my favorite events of the year and, with this award, now I know the love goes both ways."

While the award, with its distinctive silver "SHOW" logo, is nominally a lifetime achievement award, organizers said Ryder and Arnaud made impressive contributions in a short amount of time that "reshaped the future of film in Telluride." (Disclaimer: Ryder and Arnaud are investors in this newspaper as part of their Keep Telluride Local initiative.)

"I never expected to win an award at a fancy film event for making little videos on the internet," Arnaud said. "I've learned so much about this industry in the last two years and I'm so thankful to be accepted among the ranks of so many talented people."

Organizers also cited in their criteria Arnaud's educational foundation Nature's Valentine, an outgrowth of the documentary filmed in the local area that became one of the most-streamed movies of the last year, the fact that Ryder has premiered both of his directorial efforts at the festival, and that both Ryder and Arnaud are filming their next movies in the state.

(Editor's note: Keep Telluride Local's annual grant to this paper, which has made it one of the most coveted internships in the country and helps support articles like this one, was also cited by organizers as proof of Ryder's and Arnaud's commitment to the community.)

Ryder's latest film "Suburban Nice," which he wrote, directed, produced, and stars in, was an audience favorite and sold out both screenings at the festival this year. The film also stars Marisol Williams, Ryder's often-costar, who attended the festival for the first time, lending more star power to a film celebration that has long been a prestigious underdog.

"Suburban Nice" signed a distribution deal this weekend, according to Ryder, who did not provide details. One of the highest-paid actors in Hollywood, Ryder "took a step back" this year from the "White House" series that made him a star and set up his own production company. That company will produce Arnaud's next documentary, which is expected to follow a #VanLife couple's attempts to raise a family.

Arnaud, whose family is local, may be spotted camping in the area for the next few weeks as she films additional content for her educational efforts.

"I'll help until I get tired of sleeping on the ground," Ryder said in an interview.

"They don't pay him the big bucks for nothing," Arnaud said in the same interview.

While marriage rumors swirled all weekend and the two were asked directly at one Q&A, this reporter was able to secure a promise for an exclusive "when it happens." Fans will note that's not an if.

The couple has been together two years, and divide their time between LA, Telluride, and Ryder's family's home in Ohio.

"We're very happy," Ryder said. "We'll keep doing this kind of work as long as we keep learning something new. It's kind of like being on a path with a lot of twists and turns and unexpected views. We're just exploring life together."

acknowledgments

As always, this book had a lot of early readers who provided invaluable feedback. That includes Valerie Pepper, A. Boss, and Sarah Brenton. Gerry Roach's book *Colorado's Fourteeners* helped me describe the climb up Mt. Sneffels more accurately. Erik caught many final typos.

The friends who've climbed 14ers with me also deserve thanks—Halee, Mary Clare, Kate, Rebecca, and that family that gave me a ride down from the summit of Mt. Blue Sky when a storm was coming in—as do the many PR flacks I've worked with while covering the movie industry as a reporter (particularly Corby, who once coordinated a junket in Beverly Hills).

Thanks also to Melissa Doughty, who took my direction to "make a cover that looks like the *Notting Hill* poster but with backpacking" and turned it into something really special.

And finally, thank you to the readers who take a chance on reading an indie author. You're making dreams come true.

Colorado romance author Alicia Wilder writes about real people finding real love. Welcome to the Telluride Temptations, where imperfect people get happily ever afters. A bonus novella set in Telluride is exclusively available to newsletter subscribers at: https://aliciawilder.com/newsletter/

also by alicia wilder

Telluride Temptations

The Hookup Holiday: A Christmas novella

High On Love: A 4/20 novella

Aim For Love: A small town adventure romance

Leave No Trace: An enemies-to-lovers romance

Colorado Geek Series

Cosplay Cupid: A second chance, geek romance

Level Up: A gamer novella

Mountains & Monuments Series

Photograph Me: A forced proximity novella

Breadcrumbs: A fake dating novella

My Secret Vice: An escapist political romance